A RECKONING
IN THE BACK COUNTRY

ALSO BY TERRY SHAMES

A SAMUEL CRADDOCK MYSTERY

A
RECKONING
IN THE
BACK COUNTRY

TERRY SHAMES

SEVENTH STREET BOOKS®
AN IMPRINT OF PROMETHEUS BOOKS
59 JOHN GLENN DRIVE • AMHERST, NY 14228
www.seventhstreetbooks.com

Published 2018 by Seventh Street Books®, an imprint of Prometheus Books

Cover image © Shutterstock
Cover design by Nicole Sommer-Lecht
Cover design © Prometheus Books

This is a work of fiction. Characters, organizations, products, locales, and events portrayed in this novel are either products of the author's imagination or used fictitiously.

Inquiries should be addressed to
Seventh Street Books
59 John Glenn Drive
Amherst, New York 14228
VOICE: 716–691–0133 • FAX: 716–691–0137
WWW.SEVENTHSTREETBOOKS.COM

22 21 20 19 18 • 5 4 3 2 1

Library of Congress Cataloging-in-Publication Data

Names: Shames, Terry, author.
Title: A reckoning in the back country : a Samuel Craddock mystery / Terry Shames.
Description: Amherst, NY : Seventh Street Books, an imprint of Prometheus Books, 2018.
Identifiers: LCCN 2017035820 (print) | LCCN 2017040223 (ebook) |
 ISBN 9781633883680 (ebook) | ISBN 9781633883673 (paperback)
Subjects: | BISAC: FICTION / Mystery & Detective / General. | FICTION /
 Mystery & Detective / Police Procedural. | GSAFD: Mystery fiction.
Classification: LCC PS3619.H35425 (ebook) |
 LCC PS3619.H35425 R43 2018 (print) | DDC 813/.6—dc23
LC record available at https://lccn.loc.gov/2017035820

Printed in the United States of America

To Carol, Anne, Joan, and Mary Ann.
Everybody should be so lucky to have friends like you.

CHAPTER 1

Loretta doesn't bake as often since she started taking art classes at Ellen Forester's workshop, so I'm happy when I hear her call out as she walks into my kitchen, holding a familiar pan.

"Oh, that smells good," I say.

She sets it on the counter. "I'm sorry to barge in. It's cold out there and I didn't feel like standing out on the porch."

I'm still not used to Loretta's new looks. Several months back, she showed up with a stylish new haircut and a blond tint instead of her curly gray hair that I was used to. And she has started wearing slacks. She used to wear only dresses and expressed a low opinion of women who wore slacks. If she takes to wearing blue jeans, I'm going to think she has decided to become a teenager.

"Loretta, when did we ever have to stand on ceremony?"

"I don't want to be pushy."

"You can be pushy anytime you want, if you're bringing cinnamon rolls. Sit down; have a cup of coffee. When are you leaving town?" She and half the people I know are on their way out of town for Thanksgiving.

"Tomorrow. I told you that." She sits down and I hand her a mug of coffee with a big dollop of cream, the way she likes it.

"I know you did, but it's been a busy weekend and I lose track." I take a cinnamon roll out of the pan, put it on a plate for myself, and sit down. She won't eat one. She'd pick at it until it wasn't salvageable. The kitchen is the warmest place in the house, but it's still drafty. It takes cold winds like we've been having the last couple of days to remind me of the chinks in the house's armor.

2

"What's kept you so busy?" Loretta asks.

"We've had some dogs go missing."

"Dogs?" Loretta's face screws up in distaste. "Probably just ran off."

"You may not like dogs, but people get attached to them."

"I know it. Ellen brings that yappy little dog down to the art gallery every day. Not that he's as bad as some of them."

I have a soft spot for Ellen's dog, Frazier, since he saved my life a while back, going for the gun hand of somebody who had ill intentions toward me. And contrary to Loretta's prejudice, Frazier rarely yaps.

"I thought the same thing at first, that the dogs had run away. But it's happened three times now and I think someone is stealing them."

"Who would steal a dog?"

"I'm not sure, but I suspect it doesn't spell good news for the dogs."

"Anyway," she says. "Speaking of going missing. Have you heard that Lewis Wilkins is missing?"

"Lewis Wilkins?"

"Doctor Wilkins, I should say. He and his wife are lake people."

Her tone is dismissive. In the last few years we've had a flock of outsiders from cities like Houston and San Antonio build homes on the far side of the lake. The real estate is cheaper here and the lake is a popular recreation site. Most of the lake people visit only occasionally, over holidays or on summer vacation, and they don't blend in with the local community.

The one thing people appreciate is that they have brought prosperity to town. The grocery store, the general store, the marinas, and the couple of cafés have thrived.

"How did you hear about it?" I ask.

"He's a friend of Dooley Phillips, and Wilkins's wife, Margaret, comes to sewing circle sometimes with Dooley's wife, Connie. Not that Margaret does needlework. She sits and watches. She doesn't say much, but she's nice enough. Anyway, Connie said Margaret called their house this morning to ask if Dooley knew where Dr. Wilkins was. She said he didn't come home last night."

"Dooley didn't know?"

"He said he didn't." She arches an eyebrow.

"You don't believe him?"

"Men are always sticking up for each other. He's probably fooling around."

"Now, Loretta, you don't know that. Is that what Dooley's wife said?"

"Well, no, but where would he be?"

"A lot of places. He could have had a wreck, or been felled with a heart attack or a stroke."

"She told Dooley that she had called the hospital and they didn't have him."

"Well, all I know is she hasn't called me."

But that situation changes as soon as I get into work. There's a message on the phone from Margaret Wilkins. In a shaky voice she says, "I live out at the lake and I'm calling because my husband didn't come home last night. I don't quite know what to do."

I return her call and tell her I'll be right out to talk to her. It's up to me because I'm short-handed. My new deputy, Connor Loving, is off for two weeks of training, and Maria Trevino has five days off. She has been talking about her sister Lupe's wedding plans for three months.

I'm walking to the squad car, ready to head for the lake, when my phone pings with a text message from Ellen Forester, asking if I'm free for lunch. I type back that I've been called out to look into a problem and I'll see her later. She texts me right back. "Oh. Too bad. I have something important to talk to you about. Never mind."

I tamp down annoyance. Ellen is sometimes coy. Why not come out and say what's on her mind? Still, I like Ellen a lot. We have fun together. It took a while to break down the wall of defensiveness and suspicion she had erected because of her abusive ex-husband, and occasionally she still closes up on me.

The wind has let up, but there's still a bone-chilling nip in the air, and I slip into the car before I send a quick reply that I'll see her later.

The homes on the west side of the lake are isolated because there is no direct road between there and town. I have to drive ten minutes south on the highway toward Cotton Hill before I reach the county road that leads to the west side. It takes another ten minutes to reach the private road where the homes are located.

The houses line the west side of the road, on big lots. Most are modest vacation places, but some of them are grander. At the near end, they back up onto fenced pastureland, but halfway down the pastures end abruptly, giving way to back country—acres and acres of thick brush, post oak trees, and poison ivy. Although a lot of the foliage is gone by this time of year, it's still a thicket and looks even more intimidating with the brown leaves of the trees hanging against a gray sky.

Before the dam that created the lake was built, it was all bottom swampland, and it's still alive with critters, mostly snakes, opossums, raccoons, and mosquitoes. People report seeing the occasional bobcat as well. Legend has it that a panther attacked a child here back in the 1930s and dragged it away into the swamp, and the child was never seen again. I have my doubts.

Margaret Wilkins told me that her house is two doors down from a carved wooden bear. The bear is life-sized, easy to spot. As I pull up in front of the Wilkins house, I realize that I recognize it. A few years ago, it was owned by a couple who kept a lot of guns, and the man accidentally shot his wife. This was before I had taken the job as chief, but the story was on the news and in the *Houston Post*. The husband was exonerated, but shortly thereafter, he killed himself. The house went on the market at a lowball price, but it still took a long time to sell.

The house looks like a hunting lodge, giving it a grander appearance than some of its neighbors. The bottom half is made of local stone, and the top part is wood siding, painted an awful pea-soup green. It's got a screened-in porch all the way across the front, and it is furnished with massive wooden chairs facing the lake.

I park on the gravel driveway in front and get out of my squad car. I used to take my truck everywhere, but Maria claims it's unprofessional. It's also because of her that I usually wear at least a uniform shirt, even if I forego uniform khakis in favor of Levi's. It's always easier to give in to Maria's notions than to argue with her. Today, with the chill in the air, I'm wearing a zip-up jacket.

Before I mount the steps, the screen door opens and a woman steps out to meet me. In her late forties, she's tall and scrawny, dressed in jeans and a heavy gray sweater. Her limp brown hair is pulled back by a clasp at her neck. Her face has the stunned look of someone who has had bad news, and I wonder if she has heard something since she called me.

"Mrs. Wilkins?"

"Are you the chief of police?"

"Yes, I'm Samuel Craddock."

She frowns. "Oh. You're . . . different from what I thought you would be." She most likely expected a younger man.

"Have you heard from your husband yet?"

She shivers. "No. Can we talk inside? I can't seem to get warm."

Inside, she's got a fire in the fireplace, which makes the room warm and stuffy.

She walks into the kitchen, which is separated from the living room by a long, wide counter, and asks me if I'd like a cup of coffee. I decline, but she pours a cup for herself, and I see that her hand is shaking. Holding the cup in both hands to warm them, she leads me into the living room.

The room is crowded with furniture that should make it feel cozy, but there's no charm to it. There's an oversized sofa and two big, rustic chairs that match those on the porch—thick, rough-hewn pine that has been sanded and varnished, and decorated with square, hard-looking cushions. Everything is grouped around a massive, chunky wood coffee table in front of the fireplace.

I'm always interested in the art people display. Above the fireplace there's a woven wall hanging in muted colors. Another wall contains a few small, amateurish watercolors of the lake.

On the wall farthest from the fireplace there are two large, full-length oil portraits of Margaret Wilkins and her husband dressed in evening clothes. I walk over to look more closely. In the portrait Margaret is pretty in her full-length blue gown, her figure more filled out, her cheeks rosy. She's wearing expensive-looking jewelry, gold and diamonds. But despite the elegance of the picture, there's something wistful in her expression. Her husband looks at ease in his tuxedo, with a wide grin and friendly eyes. He's got a solid build, bushy eyebrows, and a thick shock of dark hair.

"That's your husband?" I nod toward the portrait.

"Yes, that's Lewis." She comes and stands next to me.

"When was it painted?"

She shrugs. "Seven or eight years ago."

"Do you have a recent photo of him?"

She goes over to a table shoved up under the windows and picks up a small photograph, a picture of her and her husband. In the photo, she's looking at him and he is looking straight at the camera, one eyebrow cocked, his expression challenging. This photo shows a remarkable change from the painting. Wilkins's formerly healthy, glowing face is sagging, his hair thinner and graying at the temples.

"Do you mind if I take this with me to make copies?"

"Of course. Whatever you need to do."

She moves to the sofa and sinks down onto it as if her strength is gone. I take a chair across from her, the large expanse of the coffee table between us.

"When did you last see your husband?"

"He left yesterday morning before I was up. He poked his head in and said he had errands to run. I was half asleep, so I didn't ask where he was going." Her voice is very quiet. I imagine she wishes she had gotten up to see him off. "But then he called yesterday afternoon and said he was going fishing and then would probably go out afterward to have a meal with a friend, and that he'd be back late."

"Have you contacted the friend he was going out with?"

She stares at me. Her eyes have turned bleak. "I don't know who it was."

"I understand he's friends with Dooley Phillips."

She frowns. "How do you know that?"

I smile. "Jarrett Creek is a small town. Not too many secrets around here. I heard it from a friend of Dooley's wife, Connie."

She nods. "I called Dooley, but he said he didn't have any idea where Lewis could be."

"But your husband did say he was having dinner with a friend. Any idea who it could be?"

She sighs. "My husband doesn't like for me to pry." I wait for more of an explanation, but that seems to be it.

"Has he ever done this before—disappear overnight?"

"He's been gone overnight, but it's not like him not to let me know if he doesn't plan to come back." She gnaws on her thumb.

"You're from San Antonio?"

"A suburb. Monte Vista."

"What brought you here to Jarrett Creek?"

She waves her hand vaguely. I notice she isn't wearing a diamond engagement ring, just a plain gold band. "Oh, you know. We wanted a vacation house."

"How long have you had this place?"

She draws a sharp breath, "Is this necessary? I don't know what it has to do with finding Lewis."

"Bear with me. I'm trying to get a general picture of your husband's normal routine."

"Okay. Sorry, I'm jumpy." She expels a breath. "We've owned this place three years in January."

"How often do you come here?"

"When we first bought it we didn't come that often. A weekend every couple of months, but in the past year we've been here a lot more. Lewis seems to like it." Her eyes dart around the room. There's a vague distaste in her expression.

"You're here for the holidays?"

"Yes. We arrived a couple of days ago. Our kids are coming tomorrow."

"You said your husband was going fishing. Does he have a boat?"

"No. I thought he fished from the bank."

"He ever catch anything?"

She grimaces. "He knows that if he brought fish home I wouldn't be happy to clean it, and he certainly wouldn't do it himself." She runs a hand back and forth over her forehead. "No. Oh, wait. I remember something he said. He said he did 'catch and release.' Whatever that is."

I would laugh if it weren't clear that Lewis Wilkins was lying to his wife. Game fish get caught and released, usually in the ocean. Or fish that are scarce, like if a river is overfished. Jarrett Creek Lake is stocked with bass, catfish, and perch. And crappie, if you want to count them, which I don't because they're full of bones. These fish are not scarce, and I can't imagine anybody catching and releasing them. The question is, where was Lewis Wilkins going when he said he was going fishing? Loretta may be right. "Fishing" may be an excuse for something else.

Margaret jumps up and strides to the window, peeking out the side of the curtain. "Where could he be?"

"Do you have any idea at all? Even if it seems far-fetched, you should tell me."

She shakes her head. "I thought maybe he had had an accident, but I called the hospitals in Bobtail and Bryan, and neither of them had him."

It's possible he took a back route and went off the road and no one has discovered him. "What kind of car does he drive?"

She tells me it's an older-model white Chevy Suburban.

I get up. "I'll call it in to the highway patrol. You know, it's likely he and his friends went fishing and maybe drank a little too much, and he's sleeping it off."

"I suppose." Her expression is skeptical.

"I'll stop by the marina and talk to Dooley. Maybe he has some ideas. Meanwhile, if you hear from your husband, let me know." I give her my card with my cell number.

CHAPTER 2

I'm getting into my car when a large SUV swings into the driveway next door. I walk over and wait while a short woman with at least twenty years and thirty pounds on Margaret Wilkins climbs out of the vehicle as if she's climbing off a ledge.

She glances at the squad car and looks me up and down with frank interest. "You the police?"

"Chief of police. Samuel Craddock."

She sticks out a tiny, but firm, hand. "I'm Gloria Hastings. Call me Glo. I'm glad to see a healthy man. You can help me carry these groceries in, if you don't mind."

I tell her I'll be glad to. Her house is the same size as the Wilkinses', and like theirs the interior is furnished with mismatched discards, but there the similarity ends. The sofa and chairs are comfortable-looking, upholstered in cheerful colors and saggy in spots. Lived-in. There's a piano up against one wall, with sheet music on the stand.

She sees me eyeing the room. "I know, it's not a palace, and Lord knows some of these cushions should be re-stuffed, but until my grandkids are out of the jumping-on-the-furniture stage, it'll have to do." That's when I notice that kids' paraphernalia is heaped in every corner and on bookshelves—games, balls and bats, books, gizmos that I suspect must be computer game–related, stuffed animals, and the like. Their artwork is plastered all over the walls.

"How many grandkids you have?"

Her brown eyes sparkle at the question. "Six. I have three kids and each of them has a pair of young 'uns." She points to some photos on the piano. "Cutest little dickens you ever saw." There are several pictures of her with the kids. The way they grin at her, you know she's special to them. She turns her attention back to me, looking with shrewd appraisal. "Now what can I do for you? I can't imagine that you stopped out here just to help me with my groceries."

"Do you know Margaret Wilkins next door?"

She frowns and cocks her head. "I do and I don't. I know her to speak to, but we've never been in one another's homes."

"You know her husband?"

She lifts an eyebrow. "Compared to him, she's downright chatty. She'll exchange the time of day with you, but . . ." She shakes her head.

"You've never had any particular problem with them, though?"

"Oh, goodness no. I don't mean to imply that. I mean they aren't involved with their neighbors. Some people are reserved like that. What's all this about?"

"Mrs. Wilkins is worried because her husband didn't come home last night."

"Oh, my goodness."

"Do you remember the last time you saw him?"

She looks at the ceiling, hands clasped in front of her. "I couldn't tell you. My husband might remember."

"Is your husband around?"

"Heck no. He leaves the house at the crack of dawn most days and fishes all day long. Thank goodness. At home he drives me crazy following me around." She moves over to the kitchen and starts taking groceries out of the bags.

"Does he have a boat?"

"If you can call it that. More like a tin can. But he loves to go on the lake in it. He either goes by himself, or he and Arlen Moseley from a few houses down go out. When Arlen's wife died last year, Frank felt sorry for him and asked him to go fishing. Now they go out all the time. I never saw such a pair." She sets the empty sack on the floor and starts on the next one.

"Dr. Wilkins told his wife he was going fishing yesterday afternoon, and he hasn't come back."

She stops and stares at me. She's holding a jar of dill pickles, which she sets down gently and then leans against the counter. "I don't know what to say. I didn't even know he fished. He doesn't seem like the type. If he did, though, it's possible Frank saw him out there . . . but it's a big lake."

"Your husband never went fishing with him?"

She snorts. "*Doctor* Wilkins? Not likely. He's too important for the likes of my husband."

I give her my card and cell number and ask her to have her husband call when he gets in.

"I'll sure do it. You want to come out and have supper with us later?"

I tell her I appreciate the offer, but that I can't. "I'll take a rain check," I say.

"You better come before my grandkids get here tomorrow, because you're not going to want to be here when those little heathens are on the loose." She laughs and I can't help smiling.

I head toward the other side of the lake, making the drive through Cotton Hill, back on the highway, and then off the frontage road that leads down to the park and the marinas.

Dooley Phillips owns the biggest of the three marinas, which has a little café and grocery store on the premises. The bored-looking teenaged boy at the cash register says Dooley is helping some people get a boat engine repaired and he should be back before long. It's past my lunchtime so I order a roast-beef sandwich with coleslaw. I'm finishing up the sandwich when Dooley clomps into the store, wiping his hands on a rag.

I only know him to speak to, but I've seen him around for years. He's a big fellow, well over six feet with a bristle of reddish-blond hair and a nut-brown face from being out in the sun all the time. His over-alls are grease-stained from the engine work he's been doing. I introduce myself.

"Why sure, I know who you are," he says. "I won't shake hands, because mine are full of grease." He excuses himself to go get cleaned up, and when he comes back he has on a clean shirt. He goes over to the refrigerator, hauls out a soft drink, and downs half of it in one swallow.

"You probably don't remember," he says, "but we met at a barbecue benefit for the rodeo a few years ago." He gets a concerned look I'm familiar with. "That's when your wife was still alive. She was a lovely person. What has it been, a year now?"

"Longer than that, but I appreciate you asking."

"What brings you over here? You going to buy a boat?"

"Not me. I like the water to bathe in, not ride on top of. I wonder if I might ask you a couple of questions."

"Questions?" He frowns.

"I understand you're friends with Lewis Wilkins?"

"I sure am. Is this about him going missing?"

"It is. Margaret Wilkins said she called you and you didn't know where he was, but I wanted to check."

Understanding dawns. "You mean in case I know something I didn't want to tell Margaret?"

"That, or if you've had any thoughts on it since she called you."

"No, on both counts. It doesn't sound like Lewis to go off like that, but I don't know where he could be. It's troubling."

"How do you know him?"

"Hold on. Before I start that story, I could use a beer. You want one?"

"No, thank you. I'm on duty."

"Right." He chuckles. "I didn't think of that."

He pulls a longneck Lone Star out of the drinks case. "Let's go sit outside. It's a little chilly, but the sun has come out and we ought to be fine."

We sit at a picnic table. "You asked how I know Lewis. Me and him go way back. We met in college, at UT Tyler. Lewis was the smart one. He went to medical school. I got a degree in wine, women, and song."

"Did Lewis meet Margaret at UT Tyler?"

If I hadn't been watching, I would have missed the flinch at the mention of her name. "Naw, they were hometown sweethearts from Seguin."

"Do you know if Lewis has other friends in the area?"

"We've played cards with a couple of fellows a time or two, but I wouldn't call them 'friends.' He and Margaret don't spend that much time here, so he hasn't settled in."

"When was the last time you saw him?"

"They got in town a few days ago, and me and him went out for barbecue Saturday."

"You know if he's ever run around on his wife?"

He throws back more of the beer and wipes his hand across his mouth. "If he has a woman on the side, he never told me." He meets my eyes. "Tell you the truth, when Margaret called to say he was missing, I guess I didn't take it seriously; but, now I think about it, I wonder where he is."

"His wife said he told her he was going fishing. You know where he fishes?"

He shakes his head slowly. "I don't recall him ever going fishing." He trains his gaze a couple hundred feet away, where two small boats are tied up. A young guy has an engine taken apart out on the dock and seems to be hoping if he looks at it long enough it will fix itself.

"So he doesn't have a boat?"

He looks startled. "What made you ask that?"

I'm surprised at his response. "I wondered if maybe he went out in a boat and got stuck somewhere. Maybe had engine trouble."

"Yeah, as a matter of fact, he does have a boat," he says. Interesting that his wife didn't know.

"Can I take a look at it?"

"If he took it out, it won't be there."

I stand up. "Let's go find out." I don't know why he's stalling. Or maybe he's just lazy and not really taking his friend's disappearance seriously.

"Let me go look up the slip number."

The boathouse is nothing fancy—a roof on stilts designed to keep the sun and rain from battering down on boats and their contents. This time of year the sun is weaker so it's cold in the shade under the roof. When we get to the slip, he points. "I guess he did take it out."

I stare at the place where apparently the boat is supposed to be. Something doesn't look right, but I don't know enough about boats to figure out what it is.

"If Wilkins took the boat out and hasn't come back, where would he likely be?"

Dooley and I look out toward the lake. He sticks his hands into his back pockets. "It's possible he decided to go up into one of the sloughs. Like you said, maybe he got stuck or had engine trouble."

"Wouldn't he have his cell phone on him?"

"Seems like he would," he says. "But you know how it is. Coverage can be spotty."

"Or he might have gotten hurt and couldn't get to his phone."

"I suppose." He sighs and frowns out at the water. It looks cold and uninviting. "Tell you what. I'll take my motorboat out and do a reconnaissance of the lake. Go up into some of the outlying channels and make sure he's not in some kind of trouble. Shouldn't take more than a couple of hours." He chuckles. "He'll be put out with me if he sneaked away for some peace and quiet and I roust him out."

"I'd like to cover that base, though."

"That's right. I'll get on it."

CHAPTER 3

Back at the station, there's nothing going on, so I look up Lewis and Margaret Wilkins on the Internet. It turns out there is plenty of information about them online. Although Dooley said Wilkins didn't have friends around here, it appears that he and his wife are in the social set in San Antonio. There are lots of photos of them at charity events and conferences. Newspaper articles tout Wilkins as a prominent orthopedic surgeon who is generous with donations.

Margaret looks like she is in her element, vivacious, with sparkling eyes and a radiant smile. She wears her hair fluffed out in a style that suits her, and her clothes look expensive. Something has changed her to the downtrodden, anxious woman I saw today. Lewis looks less comfortable, or maybe aloof. There's only one photo of him that looks as if he's engaged with the people around him. In it, he has his arm around a woman who is not his wife, and is leering at her, but it's a joke shot. If Lewis Wilkins is a ladies' man, it isn't apparent in these photos.

As a physician, it's always possible that Wilkins had to go home for an emergency call, although I don't know why he wouldn't tell his wife.

I look up his physician ratings on Yelp, and the reports are mixed. Apparently he doesn't have a very good bedside manner, but his patients think he is competent. Then I notice something odd. The Yelp reviews stopped over a year ago. That intrigues me, and I decide to probe a little further.

His office phone rings several times and then goes to voicemail: "I'm sorry, Dr. Wilkins is out of the office this week. Do not leave a message. If you have an urgent question, please contact Dr. Stephen Elgin. . . ." I jot down the number and dial it.

"Is Dr. Elgin in?"

"What is this in regard to?" His receptionist sounds unsure of herself, suspicious even.

"I'm looking for a doctor by the name of Lewis Wilkins. Dr. Elgin's number was on his message machine to call in case I needed to reach him."

Silence greets me. "Uh, I don't know exactly what to tell you. This is an answering service."

"Can I leave a message?"

"It's, um . . . Dr. Elgin died over a year ago. His partners only keep this number active in case one of his old patients calls."

She gives me the number of the office where Dr. Elgin's former partners practice, Drs. Evelyn Todd and Pradesh Singh.

I hang up and sit back. That's an interesting development. Why would Wilkins have the number on his answering machine directing patients to a physician who died a year ago? Is this simply an error, and out of carelessness the message wasn't updated? The Yelp reviews for Lewis Wilkins stopped over a year ago. So what happened in the last year? Has Lewis Wilkins not been in his office in all that time?

I dial the number for Drs. Todd and Singh. The office is closed until 2 p.m. I don't leave a message.

Suddenly I realize something that I should have thought of before. If Wilkins took his boat out, where is his car? Did he park it at the marina? I consider calling Dooley Phillips but decide to run out there myself and look around.

Before I can get out the door, I get a call from Lois Jenkins telling me that her father has wandered away again and she needs someone to go find him. Lois is in a wheelchair but still manages to care for her father, who has dementia. She has neighbors who look out for the two of them, but he's an adept escape artist.

I could call Bill Odum to handle it, but he has been working a lot of extra hours and I'd like to avoid disturbing him on his day off.

Jenks Jenkins is usually not that hard to find. It takes me only twenty minutes, but it makes me nervous when I find him walking on the dam road along the east side of the lake. I can imagine him thinking it might be a good idea to go for a swim, and that would be the end of him in this weather.

"I wasn't doing anything wrong," he says, when I tell him he needs to come with me. He's shrunk in the last several months. He used to be a towering man, well over six feet tall and hefty, but as his mind has slipped, his body seems to have hunkered down into itself. At least he's clean and his clothes are cared for. Lois manages to have someone come in every morning to get his day going. But he's only wearing shorts.

"No, you're not doing anything wrong. I thought you might be tired and want a ride home," I say. "It's chilly out here."

He tilts his head back and looks at the sky as if something might be written there that would answer a question for him. "I believe you're right. It is chilly." He climbs into the car.

When I deliver him home, Lois is effusive with her gratitude. She has battled MS for a number of years, and last year she had to give in to the wheelchair. The only time it seems to bother her is when her daddy goes off. She looks like she could cry. "I'm so sorry to bother you. I usually manage to keep an eye on him. I hate to think of putting him on a leash like a dog, but sometimes I think it might be the only solution."

I don't know what to tell her. She has no money to put him in a facility. The two of them live on Social Security, and that goes only so far. "Lois, don't ever hesitate to call on us down at the station," I say. "Somebody will always help you. It's no bother at all."

I drive over to the marina and cruise the parking lots that border the lake, but I don't see Lewis Wilkins's Suburban.

It's after two o'clock when I get back to the office, so I put in another call to Dr. Elgin's former partners. The receptionist tells me that they are busy with patients, but that one of them will get back to me soon. It's only ten minutes before Dr. Evelyn Todd calls. She has a brisk, bossy voice, but when I tell her what I want, she softens.

"Yes, Dr. Elgin was the nicest man. We miss him. He used to cover for Lewis Wilkins."

"Do you and your partner continue to cover for Dr. Wilkins?"

"Well, no," she replies stiffly.

"Do you know who does?"

"I don't think he needs coverage anymore."

"Why not?"

She hesitates. "After the lawsuit, his patient load fell off, and the last I heard he was going to close his practice."

"Lawsuit? What lawsuit?"

Her silence lasts a beat too long, "I guess I spoke out of turn."

"What kind of lawsuit was it?"

"I don't know much. But Dr. Elgin stood by Dr. Wilkins because he thought the verdict was too harsh."

"Dr. Todd, I'm asking these questions because of a police matter. Anything you can tell me would be helpful."

"I honestly don't know the details. All I heard is that Dr. Elgin said anybody could have made the mistake Dr. Wilkins made. But a jury awarded a large sum in damages, and apparently after that he lost most of his patients."

"Did he lose his license?"

"I can't tell you anything more than what I've already said. I'm sorry, I need to get back to my patients. Call the Medical Licensing Board. They'll have the details."

There was no reason for Margaret Wilkins to tell me about her husband's lawsuit and that he was no longer practicing, but it's curious that she kept it to herself when asking me to find him.

CHAPTER 4

I n the late afternoon, I call Ellen to find out what she wants to do tonight. She and I have been seeing each other for the past year. Our relationship is still more friendly than romantic. When I met her she was coming out of an abusive marriage. She had divorced her husband and moved to Jarrett Creek to open an art gallery and art workshop.

"I don't know. Maybe you don't want to do anything." She's got a snippy side that comes out when things don't go her way.

"What do you mean?"

"You sounded awfully busy when I asked if you could go to lunch."

"I was, but that doesn't mean I don't want to see you tonight."

This week she has been moodier than I've seen her in a while. Her feelings are hurt because neither of her kids is coming to her house for Thanksgiving dinner. Instead, they are spending the holiday with their dad "so he won't be lonesome." Although they say they have forgiven her for walking out on the marriage, they gravitate more to him than to her. She excuses them, saying that since he kept their house and still lives there, they want to go back home for the holiday. But it bothers her.

The kids are both grown, and you'd think they are old enough to understand that she left because she couldn't put up with being bullied any longer. Having had a few run-ins with her husband, Seth, I know he has a quick temper. He holds a grudge because of the divorce.

I suggested a mini-vacation for the two of us to get her mind off her disappointment—going to Houston to see some art, going to the coast, or maybe driving over to New Orleans—but I couldn't persuade her. It's just as well, since we're so short-handed at work, and now this business with Lewis Wilkins has come up.

When she doesn't reply, I say, "We've got a missing person."

"Who is it?"

"Why don't I pick you up and we'll go for something to eat and I'll tell you about it."

"Let's stay in. I want to watch *Blue Bloods*."

"Good. I'll run by Ranchero and pick up some food. We can figure out what we're going to do for Thanksgiving."

She protests that she doesn't mind cooking tonight, but I stand firm. Ellen's a good cook, but she's a vegetarian, and I don't really feel like I've eaten anything if I don't get some meat.

Before I leave headquarters, I put in a call to Dooley to find out if he's back from his reconnaissance of the lake. There's no answer at the marina, so I leave a message for him to call me as soon as he gets in. Then I call Margaret Wilkins. I figure if she had heard from her husband, she would have phoned me, but you never know. She answers after the first ring.

"Any news?" she says.

"No, I've been working on it. The highway patrol hasn't reported finding a vehicle like his. Have you tried him at your home in San Antonio?"

"He's not there." Her voice raises no possibility that she's wrong.

"I'll come back out in the morning and we'll talk again," I say. "Meanwhile, you have my number." I didn't tell her that Dooley is exploring the lake for signs of Lewis. She doesn't need to spend the evening imagining her husband drowned or dead from a snake bite.

After I pick up some enchiladas—cheese for Ellen and beef for me—some guacamole and chips, and a couple of pieces of flan, I stop by my house to change clothes. I've just finished buttoning my shirt when I hear my neighbor, Loretta, calling out.

"I'm glad you're here," she says. "I need to talk to you. Do you have a minute?"

"I always have time for you." I hold the door open for her.

I try to be extra nice to Loretta these days because she has been standoffish since I started spending time with Ellen. Or maybe I'm reading something into it. Ellen thinks that since Loretta started taking art classes, she has plunged into her "creative life" and doesn't have as much time for gossiping with me.

She refuses my offer of something to drink, and we sit down in the living room, since it's too nippy to sit on the porch. "I wanted to ask you if you've found out anything about Dr. Wilkins," she says.

"Not yet. I'm working on it. It's strange. Have you heard anything more?" It's valuable to have a conduit to town gossip, and I couldn't do any better than Loretta. She loves to be in the know, but she's a kind person and doesn't gossip just to be mean.

"No, I wondered if I should get some ladies or the preacher to go out there and check in on her or offer to keep her company. Since I'm leaving in the morning, I want to take care of it now."

"I wouldn't jump into anything. She's got a next-door neighbor who said she'd look out for her."

"What next door neighbor?"

I describe Glo Hastings. "You'd like her. She's friendly."

"You know we don't get a chance to meet those lake people." She cocks her head. "Where do you suppose Lewis Wilkins is?"

"Loretta, you know by now that I don't do a lot of supposing until I gather information. He could have taken a notion to go off by himself for some reason, or he could be stuck somewhere in his SUV." I throw up my hands. "Abducted by little green men in a spaceship."

She flicks a hand in my direction. "Don't be silly. You have to take it seriously. You ought to at least talk to Dooley, since he and Lewis are friends. Suppose he's hurt somewhere?"

"I did talk to Dooley and he said he doesn't know where Wilkins is. I have the highway patrol looking for his car, and Dooley was going out to explore some of the little coves off the main lake."

She looks at me sharply. "Did Margaret say where she thought he was? Did they have an argument?"

"No, but that doesn't rule it out."

She keeps her eyes on me, and I can almost hear the wheels turning.

"Maybe he *was* kidnapped," I say, laughing.

Her eyes narrow. "Who would kidnap him?"

"He's a doctor. They're well-off."

"Well-off, huh? That's not the way I heard it. Connie said they've had some money problems. Dr. Wilkins had a lawsuit against him."

Why do I even bother searching for information on the Internet when I can just ask Loretta?

"Do you know if they're friendly with anyone else in town?"

"She never mentioned if she is. Dooley is the only one I know of."

"Has Margaret Wilkins ever said anything that made you wonder if she and her husband get along all right?"

Loretta considers her answer. She has her hands folded into her sleeves, the way she does when it's cold.

"Are you cold? I can turn up the heat."

"No, I'll be going soon." But she sits there.

"All right, spit it out. Do they get along?"

"Samuel, it's not that I know anything for sure. But you know how you sometimes get a feeling that things aren't quite right between two people?"

I nod.

"I don't know how to say it, but I think Margaret Wilkins doesn't like her husband very much. Matter of fact, when she mentions him, I sometimes think she has something against him."

"You think maybe he's having an affair and she knows it?"

"Maybe. If he was involved with anybody around here, I'd have heard about it, I think. So maybe in San Antonio. It's under two hours to get there. If he's catting around, he could drive there and back in no time."

Later I tell the story to Ellen over enchiladas, trying to make it funny, but she isn't so easily drawn out of her funk. In fact, she seems irritated that Loretta gossiped about his possible philandering. "I think everyone should keep their gossip to themselves until they know exactly what's going on." It's an uncharacteristically curt remark. I'm almost relieved when her program comes on. We watch it in wary silence, and I'm home and in bed by ten o'clock.

CHAPTER 5

The night turned bitter cold, unusual for this time of year. By midday it could be in the seventies again, but I take extra time to make sure my cows have plenty of feed and that none are suffering from the cold.

It's nine o'clock by the time I get into work, and I feel guilty, thinking I should have called Margaret Wilkins earlier. I also wonder why I haven't heard from Dooley Phillips. I put in a call to him before I call Margaret, and reach him at the marina.

"Dooley, I thought you were going to call after you looked for Lewis."

"You know, Chief, I have to apologize. I should have called to tell you. I meant to go out, but something came up and I didn't get to it. I'll be on my way as soon as it warms up a little bit."

I'm surprised. It never occurred to me that he wouldn't go to the trouble of searching for his friend. "Why don't I go out with you? I'm going to talk to Margaret again, and then I'll stop by and we can get right on it." That way, he can't weasel out of it again.

"I suppose that will be all right." Once again, I hear that reluctance in his voice.

I call Margaret and tell her I'll be over in a while. But before I can get out the door, the phone rings.

"This is Chief Craddock."

"Oh, hello. My name is John Hershel. I hate to bother you. I don't want to be a nuisance. But I just had something happen that disturbed me, and I thought I ought to report it." He speaks slowly and politely, and I picture a careful man.

31

"Mr. Hershel, are you a resident of Jarrett Creek? I don't recognize your name."

"Of course you don't. My apologies. I have a vacation home on the far side of the lake. My wife and I come here every chance we get. We love the peace and quiet. My wife loves to watch the birds, and I do a little drawing in my spare time."

"What can I do for you?"

"Well, sir. I caught somebody trying to make off with my dog."

I've been lounging back in my chair, enjoying his easy way of talking, but at those words I bolt up. "You caught them?"

"I don't mean I laid hands on them. I mean I caught them in the act and sent them on their way."

"Mr. Hershel, I'm going to come and talk to you."

"Please don't bother. The dog is fine. I just thought it was worth a call."

"It's no bother. Now if you'll tell me how to find your place, I'll be there in twenty minutes."

"All right, if you think it's important."

I put the "Back in an Hour" sign with my phone number on the door and head right out.

This is the fourth dognapping, or attempted dognapping, this month. The first three were successful. One man lost a valuable hound, and the other two beloved pets. It makes me uneasy. I've heard that medical labs will pay for dogs, and it turns my stomach to think that somebody would take a pet and turn them over for a few extra bucks. If that's what happened, I want it stopped.

The Hershel home is past the Wilkins place, almost at the end of the road. It's one of the few two-story places with a nice porch and some big trees in front. The homes end where the land curves around into the water. It's nice that the builder had sense enough to keep the wooded cove. A couple of small rowboats are tied up on a dock at the end. With the trees and the inlet, Hershel's wife must have plenty of bird life to keep her occupied.

John Hershel is a thin, balding man of fifty, with a solemn expression and a courtly manner. The dog in question, a big-chested beast that looks like a cross between a shepherd and maybe a Rottweiler, sticks close to him.

"He's friendly," Hershel says. He looks down at the dog. "Maybe too friendly for his own good."

"What's his name?"

"Satch. Named after the greatest trumpet player of all time."

Satch allows himself to be scratched behind the ears.

Hershell invites me in and offers me coffee, which I appreciate at this time of the morning. We sit at a big family-style table in the kitchen, and the dog parks itself on the floor next to the table.

"I really thank you for calling me about this," I tell him. "I have reason to be concerned."

"Is that right?" He looks alarmed.

"We've had some dogs stolen, and you're the first eyewitness."

"Oh, my goodness. Satch really could have been stolen."

"Tell me what happened."

He crosses his arms on the table and leans onto them. "My wife and I were going into town to buy groceries. After we'd driven a couple blocks, I remembered that I'd left the coffee pot on. I told her to let me off and I'd walk back and she could go to the store by herself. I walked back along the shoreline. It was cold, so I didn't dawdle." He clears his throat. "I had just walked in when I heard a commotion out back. We usually leave Satch outside when we're gone. He was howling and squealing. I was afraid some kind of animal had gotten into his pen."

He gestures toward the back of the house. "You know, any kind of wild animal could be back there. I've seen a bobcat, and I heard that somebody saw a panther not that long ago. So I ran outside and there were two men, with a rope around Satch's collar, hauling him toward their pickup." His face is flushed. "I have to admit I lost my temper. I asked what the hell they thought they were doing with my dog."

"I'm not sure that was a smart move. If they were intent on getting the dog, they could have attacked you."

He looks embarrassed. "It didn't hurt my chances that I grabbed my shotgun on the way out. They backed right off when they saw that."

"Did you ask them to explain themselves?"

He chuckles. "I did, but, Chief Craddock, I'm in the insurance business, claims division. I've heard every excuse in the world for why somebody got up to something. They told me that somebody had told them there was a family out here who wanted to get rid of a dog, and that they could come pick it up. They claimed they got the wrong house." He raises his eyebrows at me.

"Can you describe the men to me?"

"Both of them young, in their twenties, I'd say. Neither of them tall. One was maybe five seven, five eight, the other a few inches taller." He looks down at the dog and reaches over to scratch his head. "I sure am glad I came back."

"Were they white men?"

"Yes, one of them with dark hair and the other had reddish hair. He was sturdier than the dark-haired one. Kind of seemed like the boss."

"Would you recognize them again?"

"You'd think I would, but I don't know. I was pretty flustered. I was mostly interested in getting old Satch here away from them."

"You didn't get a license plate, did you?"

"No, I didn't think to do to that. But I remember the vehicle. It was a faded-out black pickup, and the paint was all scratched up like maybe they drive through the brush a lot. And at one time it had those flames painted on the side, but that was pretty much flaked off."

I get up. "I'm going to put out a notice to people to be sure and keep their dogs close for a time until I run down whoever's doing this. Meanwhile, if you see any of your neighbors, be sure and tell them what happened so they'll take it seriously."

"I sure will." He gets up and the dog does, too. "Much as I have a fondness for this dog, it's nothing compared to my wife. She'd be awful upset if anything happened to him."

"And you'll be keeping him indoors?"

He laughs. "Either that or my wife will see to it that I sleep out in the doghouse with him."

There are a couple of cars in Gloria Hastings's driveway, next door to Margaret Wilkins's place. I'd like to have a word with Gloria's husband before I go to see Margaret. Yesterday, talking to him didn't seem so urgent, but with still no news of Wilkins, I'm increasingly concerned.

I rap on the door, but there's so much racket inside the house that I doubt anybody can hear me. When there's a lull, I knock again. The door is flung open by an unseen hand. Gloria is hurrying toward me. "Kids, settle down." She claps her hands together and two children, a boy and a girl, careen from somewhere in the room and plop onto the sofa, making motorcycle noises.

"Now stop that," she says, looking back at them. "This man is a policeman. I'd hate to have to ask him to haul you off to jail. I don't think they have pumpkin pie there."

They giggle but keep an eye on me.

"Remember the wild bunch I told you about?" she says, turning back toward me.

"So these are the culprits?" I say.

"Two of them anyway. My daughter's kids. That's Marcie, she's six, and the four-year-old is Chris. Say hello, kids."

The both say hello, darting glances at each other and suppressing giggles.

"My son Luke's boys are out in the woods. They pretend they're hunting squirrels, but I don't know what they'd do if they shot one.

They're older, but I wish they wouldn't go out there. Snakes and goodness knows what all. They're just like their daddy. I couldn't keep him indoors. What am I doing? These two have taken my sense. Come on in and have some coffee."

"Your husband home?"

"He's in the back bedroom. I'll get him."

As soon as she leaves the room, Marcie hops off the couch and stands in front of me. "Do you have a gun?"

"I own a gun, but I don't carry it. Not too many criminals around here. Have you run into any bad guys?"

She shakes her head solemnly. Her brother slides off the sofa and eases over next to her, watching me as if he's worried I'm going to grab him.

Gloria comes back out followed by a short, stocky man with ice-blue eyes and a sleepy smile. He shoves his hand out. "I'm Frank Hastings. Sorry I didn't get back to you. My kids came in last night with these hopped-up children and we haven't had a quiet minute since then."

"Can we go out on the porch and talk for a minute?"

"Glad to. Let me get us some coffee."

We sit on the padded chairs on the porch. Frank tells me he has had a successful career as a regional salesman for farming equipment. He's been headquartered in both Dallas and Houston, and is now close to retirement. "I'm hoping we can pull out of city living and move here. I never get tired of fishing." He looks out over the lake as if he owns the whole thing, but in a peaceful way, not like he's boasting. "You fish?" he asks.

"I never did go in for it much," I say. I tell him I was a land man with an oil and gas company for most of my working life. "I guess I never was around water enough to think of fishing."

"If you change your mind, let me know. I can take you to try your hand one day." He sits a little taller and takes a sip of coffee. It seems to me the Hastingses represent the best of the kind of people who come as visitors.

"I'll consider that."

"Glo tells me Wilkins, next door, is missing."

"I was wondering if you had seen him yesterday or even the day before that out on the lake."

"Tell you the truth, I don't think I've ever seen him out there. He told his wife he was going fishing?"

"That's what she said."

"Hold on. What's that?"

We both hear it at the same time, children's screams coming from behind the house. Not the screams of children having fun. Hastings seems like a laconic man, but the sounds bring him bolting up from his chair. "Oh, Lord, what if one of the kids got snake-bit?"

He hoofs it down the steps, with me right behind him. Two young boys come barreling around from the back of the house and almost run into him. Their faces are pale except that their cheeks are bright from their exertion. The younger one is sobbing.

"Here now, settle down," Hastings says. "Are you hurt?"

They have been running so hard that they have to catch their breath. The older one leans over with his hands on his knees, gasping and half sobbing. The younger one throws himself at his grandfather, arms around his waist, howling.

"Ethan, it's okay." He pats the boy's back. "Austin, tell me what happened."

The older boy straightens up, struggling to get his emotions under control. "We found . . ." He points back toward the woods. "A man back there."

"A man! Did he bother you?"

"No, Grandpa." His eyes get larger and he is momentarily speechless, but then he blurts out, "He's dead."

Frank meets my eyes. We're thinking the same thing. Frank hollers up toward the house, "Gloria! Gloria, we need you."

His wife comes to the door and looks like she's going to make a sassy reply, but when she sees the boys, she runs down the stairs. "What happened?"

"Take Ethan inside." The young boy has calmed a little bit, but tunes up again when he sees his grandmother.

"Is Austin okay? He's awfully pale."

"He has to help us. I'll send him inside when we get back."

She starts to say something, but a look from her husband deters her. She picks up the younger boy, even though he has to be heavy. "Come on, sweetheart, let's get you inside."

The older boy looks longingly at his brother and grandmother.

Frank leans down to meet Austin's eyes. "Listen, I know this is hard, but you need to show us where you found this man."

"Yessir," the boy whispers.

"Where are your BB guns?"

"We left them. You told us not to run with them, and . . ."

"You did right. We'll get them."

"Give me a second," I say. I walk back to my squad car and pull my weapon and holster out of the glove compartment, where it usually stays locked up. I strap on the holster under my jacket and go back to join Frank and the boy.

Austin is reluctant to start moving, so Frank grabs his hand. "We'll face this together," he says.

At his age, I imagine the boy isn't inclined to hold anybody's hand, but at the moment he doesn't mind.

We head off into the brush where there is a sort of path almost directly behind the Wilkinses' house next door. It's not much of a path, overgrown with bushes and vines. Hard to believe these boys were intrepid enough to plow through it. Of course, they never thought they'd see anything more exciting than a possum or a copperhead.

CHAPTER 6

We follow Austin for a quarter of a mile before he starts to slow and hang back. He stops next to a pile of rotten wood. "It's up there." He points.

"You sure?" Frank asks.

"Yessir. We had just passed this old stack of wood. I remember it because we wondered if snakes were living in it. We poked sticks in it, but nothing crawled out. Then we walked on and . . ." He swallows.

"I'll go on ahead," I say. "Stay here for a minute." I figure if the boy has been mistaken, we may have to go a little farther.

But I need not have doubted him. I smell the body and hear the buzz of flies before I see it. I flinch at the sight. It's easy to see why the boys were so shocked. The upper part of the man's body is streaked with black, dried blood, and strips of skin have been torn away from his face and arms. The face is barely recognizable as human, and the throat has been torn open. Flies surge around it so that it almost seems as if the body is moving. On closer examination I see that the scalp is torn away, with hair clinging to it. My stomach roils. I think of the story of the child being taken by a panther. It had to have been a big cat to do this kind of damage.

"You all right?" Frank calls out.

"Yeah. I've found him." I see the two BB guns lying where they were flung, and I pick them up and walk back. The boy has taken up a stick and is flailing at some of the brush. I hand him the guns.

"Say 'thank you,'" Frank says gently. Trying to normalize things for the boy.

He whispers a thank-you.

I take out my cell phone. The signal is weak, but I give it a try and am relieved when the sheriff's office in Bobtail answers. I tell them what I've found and where we are. "We need the medical examiner and an ambulance to transport the body."

"You need the highway patrol?"

"No, it looks like he got attacked by an animal."

"Animal? What kind of animal?"

"I can't be sure. I'll get the vet out here to see if he can tell me."

"It's going to be a while before somebody can get there. We had a wreck out south of town and everybody's busy."

"That's all right. He's not going anywhere." I describe Hastings's house and tell them I'll wait for them out front.

I go back with Hastings and his grandson and retrieve my crime scene kit from the car. As far as I know, what happened here isn't a crime, but I want to take good look around, and I may as well do it right. I tell Frank Hastings that if he can stand it, I'd like him to come back with me to see if he can identify the body. "His face is pretty torn up, but at least you can tell me if the victim is the general size of Lewis Wilkins."

"I'll help any way I can." He goes inside to turn Austin over to Gloria and tell her what's going on. While I wait, I call the vet, Dr. England, and ask if he can come out and identify the likely culprit. If the attack was made by a rabid animal, we'll need to hunt it down.

Although I figure the dead man has to be Lewis Wilkins, I don't want to jump to conclusions. But I also don't want his wife to have to view him in the condition the body is in. That's why I asked Hastings to see if he could identify the man. But when he sees the body, he recoils.

"Are you kidding me? Who can tell who that is? He could be a good friend and I wouldn't recognize him."

"Is he the general size and shape?"

He shudders. "I suppose. I do not envy you having to examine what happened here."

40

I go back with him to wait for Doc England, who said he'd come right away. The thought of a killing by a rabid animal has spurred him to a quick response. He comes roaring up in the van he uses as an animal control vehicle. He's a rangy, wide-shouldered man in his forties who mostly deals with large animals. We waste no time getting back through the brush.

When he sees the body, he lets out a loud groan. "I've seen some bad stuff, but this . . ." He bends down to look closer. "Whoa! No cat did this. These are bites, not slashes."

"Bites from what?"

"Canine. Dogs do this kind of damage. They rip into their prey with their teeth. Cats use their claws because their teeth aren't strong enough to do something like this."

"You think we're looking at a rabid dog?"

He grimaces. "Could be. But there's more than one animal involved in this. You see here?" He points to the right side of the face, and then the left, lower down on the neck. You've got two different bite patterns. That tells me it's not as likely to be a rabies situation. A rabid dog is a loner." He stands up and steps back. "I think you're looking at a pack of stray dogs that got riled up."

The two of us exchange a glance. We're both thinking the same thing. There have been rumors off and on that there are dogfights being held in the back woods—and that when dogs get too old or too lame to fight, their owners turn them out to fend for themselves and they end up running in packs. "You think it's some of those fighting dogs?"

"Could be. It's pretty unusual for dogs to do something like this unless they're vicious to begin with."

"Either way, we're going to have to hunt them down. Can't have them this close to those houses back here."

He shakes his head. "Terrible." He glances at his watch. "I better get on back. I left a waiting room full of sick pets. And I still have a horse to go see to at one thirty."

I ask him to stop by Hastings's place to tell Frank I'm going to stay with the body. If dogs attacked this man, they might return and drag the body away, so I need to stay with it. I don't relish shooting a dog, even if it's vicious, but if I have to I will.

"Also, would you ask him to escort the team from Bobtail back here when they arrive?"

After he leaves, I go back and crouch down beside the body, shooing away the flies and steeling myself against the putrid odor. I want to see if there's anything I can retrieve to take to Margaret Wilkins that might identify him to her. The medical examiner will have a fit if I mess with the body, but I would like to find something to spare Margaret. I put on some gloves from the crime kit and search his shirt pocket gingerly, but there's nothing in it. I look to see if he's wearing a wedding ring, and that's when I realize there's something I missed. Something important.

Anybody who was attacked by an animal would have thrown his hands up to protect his face. But this man's hands are untouched. No defensive wounds. And then I notice abrasions on his wrists from rope or twine. This man's hands were tied. If they had been tied in front of his body, he still could have raised them in front of his face to ward off the dogs. They have to been tied behind him, leaving him defenseless.

I sit back on my haunches, shaken. What could Wilkins have done to provoke this kind of cruelty? I need to start over and look at the scene in a different way. It's too late to worry about it now, but there has been contamination of the area around the body. First by the children who found it, then by Hastings and me, and then by Doc England.

I stand up and take stock of the surrounding ground. Weeds around the body are broken off and trampled, the kind of ripped-up vegetation you'd expect if someone was being viciously attacked. There are scuff marks in a patch of dirt near the feet of the body, but it's impossible to tell whether they were there before the boys stumbled onto the scene. Most of the area is covered with a thick layer of dead leaves and weeds, which won't show paw prints or shoe prints. The wind is coming up, sending clouds scuttling across the sky and whipping up dead leaves.

I notice a rust-colored spray on some of the weeds and crouch to examine it. The spray appears to be dried blood. I also see white fur sticking to some of the pricklier weeds. I pluck a few weeds with fur on them and bag them for the forensics team. When they arrive, I'll point out where I found the fur. I don't know what good it will do to know what kind of dogs did this, but at this point any evidence is good.

The body is a nasty sight, but I force myself to concentrate on it again. I need to get some sense of how this happened, how this man came to be tied up and attacked out in the middle of nowhere. There must have been more than one person involved; one to lead Wilkins and the other to bring the dogs. But it's also possible that the person responsible tied the dogs up here and then came back with Wilkins. However, if the dogs were tied up, it seems like they would have howled or barked if they were left alone.

This must have happened at night, or someone would have seen or heard them. I look back toward the homes, roughly a quarter of a mile away, wondering if anyone heard anything. I can't see any of the houses from here, so it's probably too far away for the sound to have carried. Still, we'll have to question nearby residents.

I wonder where the victim was before he was brought here. He's dressed in khaki pants and a shirt. No jacket. If it is, in fact, Wilkins, we'll find out where he was when the highway patrol finds his SUV.

I feel a sudden chill, as if someone is watching. I turn slowly and survey the clumps of trees and bushes surrounding the area. It's silent and I'm alone, but that doesn't make me feel any more secure. One thing's for sure. This was no random attack. Where did the dogs come from? Who would do something like that? And why?

I call the sheriff's office in Bobtail with an update on what I've discovered. "We need the highway patrol after all. And the medical examiner should get here pretty quick."

"He'll get there when he can. He's still out at the accident." I tell them to notify the Department of Public Safety to send out a forensic team, too. The longer I'm here, the more I worry that I should have Margaret Wilkins come out to ID the man. If this is her husband, I hate to have her continue to wait for his return. It's a toss-up what would be worse, having her see him like this, or thinking he's alive when he isn't. Once the patrol officers and the sheriff's team from Bobtail get here, she'll notice all the action and know something has happened.

I finally give in and call my deputy, Bill Odum, to come out and help. There's not enough of me to go around. Odum never acts impatient when I ask him to drop what he's doing and pitch in. He tells me he's glad to have an excuse to come to work. "My wife had it in mind that we ought to clean out the garage. Nothing I hate worse, and you know I don't mind hard work."

Odum lives nearby and is the first to arrive. After he gets over the shock of seeing the body, I tell him my dilemma about Margaret Wilkins. He shakes his head, contemplating the alternatives. He's a hardworking man in his late twenties, with a blond buzz cut and a lean body from working at his daddy's farm on his off hours. With a sigh, he meets my gaze. "I don't know what to advise. What do you think Maria would say?"

Despite the seriousness of the situation, we grin at each other. That's gotten to be the catchphrase around headquarters: *What would Maria think of this?* And as soon as I think of it that way, I know the answer.

"She would say women are stronger than men and you can't keep this information from her."

He nods.

"I'd like you to stay here while I go and talk to her. When the crew gets here from Bobtail or from the highway patrol, you can leave. I just needed an extra body until they arrive."

He tilts his head. "I'm not sure which one of us is drawing the short straw."

I stop by to tell Glo Hastings that I'm going over to talk to her neighbor.

"You want me to come?"

"I think it's better if I talk to her alone. The fact is we don't even know for sure it's her husband."

She gives me an even look. "What's the likelihood that you have a missing man and a fresh body and that they aren't one and the same?"

"Not much. How are your grandkids doing? That was a pretty traumatic thing for them to see."

"They'll be fine. The little one wants his mamma, but she'll be back before long. Children are resilient as long they know they are loved."

I knock on Margaret Wilkins's door, and like yesterday she opens the door so fast it's as if she was waiting for me. Her eyes are like pieces of coal sunk into their sockets. Not much sleep last night.

"You've found him?"

Her blunt question jolts me. I had it in mind to break the news gently. "May I come in?"

She moves aside silently, and I ease past her into the room. She remains by the door, as motionless as a mannequin. "Let's sit down," I say.

"If you've found him, just say so and get it over with," she says, with a catch in her voice at the end.

"It's a little more complicated than that."

At that she cocks her head. "Is he in jail?"

"No ma'am. Come and sit down."

I take the first chair I come to, and she perches at the edge of one facing me.

"There's been a body found. But there's no identification on it."

45

"A body found where? In the lake? Was he drowned?"

"He was found in the woods, back a ways behind the house."

She blinks and turns her gaze toward the back of the house. "It can't be Lewis. What would he have been doing in the woods?" I wait to give her a chance to understand that there's a good chance the man was her husband. "What happened to the man? Did he get bitten by a rattlesnake?" She chews the corner of her lower lip, turning back and watching me intently.

"Do you happen to recall what your husband was wearing when he left here?"

"No, I don't know. He usually wears khaki pants and a button-up shirt. But I didn't see him when he left. . . . I don't understand. You've seen his picture. Can't you tell whether it's him?" Her voice is shrill.

The khaki pants fit, but who knows what kind of shirt the dead man was wearing. It was shredded and covered with blood.

"The identification is difficult. The body was damaged."

She stares at me.

"The problem is, the man was attacked by animals. Dogs. And his face is . . ."

She puts a hand to her mouth, stifling a cry.

"I'm sorry. I think it's best that you not try to identify the body until the medical team has had a chance to clean him up a little bit."

"No. I need to see him now. It may not be him."

"Mrs. Wilkins, are there any identifying marks on your husband's body? A tattoo, birthmark, scars?"

"His little toe is missing on his right foot. When he was six, a neighbor child dropped a hatchet and cut it off."

I rise. "That's a pretty good marker. Let me go take a look, and I'll get back with you."

"I want to see him."

I sigh. "I can't keep you from it, but it's a bad idea. You'd be better off waiting."

A knock on the door saves me. The door swings open and young woman says, "Mother, what's going on next door? What are all the cop cars doing there?" She's willowy and attractive, looking very much like a younger version of Margaret Wilkins. She's dressed more for a board meeting than a day in the country, with a slim-skirted suit and white blouse, high heels, and expensive-looking jewelry. Her officious tone matches her dress.

"Emily, there's been . . ." Margaret's voice falters. "Oh God, you'd better come inside."

Eyeing me as if she doesn't welcome a stranger in the house, the young woman sweeps past me. "Why is it so warm in here?" she demands.

"Where's Daniel?" Margaret asks. "I thought the two of you were driving up together."

The girl shoots her mother an impatient look. "He's bringing in the luggage." The announcement is punctuated by a thud on the front porch.

A young man strides in, grinning. He looks much like his father, but cheerful. He goes straight for Margaret and flings his arms around her. "How's my little mamma?"

"Daniel . . ."

At the sound of her voice, he steps back, looking puzzled. He turns to me and extends his hand. "I'm Daniel Wilkins. What's going on?"

I introduce myself. "I was talking to your mamma. Something has happened."

"Kids, come into the living room," Margaret says. "Let's sit down."

Emily's gaze sweeps past me to the living room. She frowns as if she doesn't like what she sees.

"Come on, Em. The furniture isn't going to give you cooties," her brother says. He puts his arm around Margaret and walks her over to the sofa. "Sit with me. Tell me what's up."

Emily sits down across from them primly and crosses her legs. She still isn't catching on that there's a problem. Or maybe she's scared and this is her way of dealing with it.

I'm still standing. Quietly, I say to Margaret, "You want me to talk to them?"

She nods. I walk over to the fireplace, where I can see all three of them.

"Your mamma called yesterday and said your daddy was missing."

"What? Why didn't you call us?" Daniel says.

"I just . . . I didn't know what to do."

"Oh, for heaven's sake," Emily says, practically spitting the words.

"Em, give her a break," her brother says.

"If you'll bear with me," I say. "An hour ago, the body of a man was found in the woods back behind your house. He fits your daddy's general description. I came to ask your mamma if there is an identifying mark I can use to confirm if it's him. I'm going back out there now to make that identification."

Daniel gets up from the sofa. "Wait. I'm confused. Can't you tell . . . ?" His question dies away. He's caught on that this is an unusual situation.

"The man we found was attacked by animals. It's hard to identify his features."

"Animals! Like what?" he says.

"The local vet says it looks like he was killed by a pack of dogs."

"Oh, my God!"

"You better sit down," I say. He sinks down next to Margaret and buries his head in his hands. He's breathing hard.

Margaret grabs his hand. "Daniel, we don't know for sure if it's your daddy."

He looks at her. Sweat has popped out on his brow. "What could he have been doing in the woods?"

"I really have no idea," she says. "This whole thing is unimaginable."

He looks up at me. "Is there a problem with packs of dogs back there in the woods? It's the first I've heard of it."

"There have been rumors that there are dogs on the loose."

Suddenly Emily stands up, her chin tilted at a defiant angle. "So you don't know for certain the man you found is our father, right?" Her tone is brisk.

"True, we don't know for sure yet. Like I said, I'm going back there now to try and identify him. Your mamma told me your daddy is missing a toe. That gives me something to use to rule out if isn't him."

Emily grimaces and a whimper escapes her. Daniel stands up and looks down at Margaret. "I'll go with Chief Craddock to make a positive ID," he says.

"No, Daniel, I don't want you to see your daddy that way," Margaret says, getting up from the sofa. "It's up to me."

"Why?" Daniel says. "It will be hideous for any of us. Why should you do it?"

"I suggested to your mamma that whoever makes the identification waits until the medical examiner has had a chance to clean him up a bit."

"And I told you I'm going to find out now," Margaret says. She walks toward the front door with a firm step. "Let's go."

"I'm going, too," Daniel says.

"I don't think I can stand it," Emily says.

"You don't have to go. In fact, I rather you didn't. If it turns out not to be your daddy, there's no sense in you having to see him," Margaret says.

When the three of us go outside, I see that two squad cars—one from Bobtail PD and the other from the Department of Public Safety—have arrived. The medical examiner isn't here yet. None of the officers are around, so I assume they've gone back to the scene. As we walk past the Hastings house, Glo Hastings comes out onto the porch. "Frank took the troopers back to the woods," she says. "He's back here, but he said if you need him for anything, just ask." She walks to the bottom of the steps and reaches out to Margaret. "I'm just so sorry. Let me know if there's anything I can do."

"I'll be fine, Gloria." Her voice wavers.

We make a quiet procession. The path is already beaten down more than it was. As I thought it might, the temperature has risen and it's almost warm, although the wind is still coming in fitful gusts. As we near the scene where the body was found, I hear voices and I slow up. "Look," I say, turning to Margaret and her son. "At least let me examine the man's right foot. If it's intact, the body isn't your husband's and there's no need for you to view it."

"That makes sense," Daniel says, putting his arm around Margaret and pulling her close. Margaret nods.

Three men I don't know are hovering over the body—one from the Bobtail Police Department, and two Department of Public Safety officers who are dressed in coveralls and booties to avoid contaminating the scene. The Bobtail PD man is standing a little apart, because he won't be called on to do any forensic work—that's up to the troopers. They all look young and shocked.

One of the troopers takes the lead and introduces himself as David Bagley and his partner as Don Casey. "I know you by name," Bagley says to me. "I work alongside Luke Schoppe. He thinks the world of you."

I nod in acknowledgment. "I'll do all I can not to disturb the body, but I'm going to take a look at the man's right foot." I tell them why. The men part the way, and I pull on a pair of gloves and stoop down to take off the right shoe. I peel off the sock. There's something vulnerable about the man's naked, pale foot and I have a momentary impulse to put my hand on the foot, as if to comfort him. But my training says otherwise.

There was never any real doubt in my mind that the victim was Lewis Wilkins, and the missing toe confirms it. I stand up and peel off the gloves. "Well, that pretty much tells the tale."

I walk back and tell Margaret and Daniel Wilkins that the man is likely their husband and father.

"Well." Margaret's voice is matter-of-fact. "Let me see him."

"Mamma, let's don't," Daniel says, grabbing her by the arm. "There's no use in it."

She yanks her arm away. "I want to see. I need to. And you should stay back here. Chief Craddock will help me."

Daniel looks at me with anguish on his face, but stays back as I lend my arm to Margaret for support. As we approach the body, her step seems steady enough, but I can feel her trembling. When we reach the grisly scene, she makes a noise deep in her throat. "Oh, Lew." She grips my arm but seems unable to turn away.

"Come on, Margaret, let's get you out of here," I say, and turn her around so we can move away from the body of her husband.

"How in the world did dogs get to him like that?" Her voice is barely above a whisper.

"I don't know. That's what we have to find out." I haven't told her he was tied up at the time of the attack. There's plenty of time to bring that up once she's had a chance to come to grips with his death.

Even though the missing toe corroborates that the body is her husband's, I say, "Do you have any reason to believe this isn't him?"

"It's him. The clothes. His . . . physical structure, I guess you'd say. It's him."

"I'm real sorry, ma'am," David Bagley says, and the others murmur their condolences.

I hand Margaret over to Daniel and tell them I'll come back to the house as soon as the medical examiner shows up. I tell the Bobtail officer, "I know you had a big accident to deal with this morning, so no need for you to stay. I'd appreciate it if you could escort the man's family back to their house."

I watch him lead them away. The path is already trampled. It's going to be well worn by the time this thing is over. When they are out of sight, I turn to the two remaining officers and we discuss how to proceed. They've had a chance to examine the marks on the wrists and agree with me that it looks like Wilkins was tied up before he was attacked.

"Execution by dog," Bagley's partner says.

CHAPTER 7

It's up to the DPS officers to collect crime scene data, and they'll share it with me, but I hang around long enough to ask the medical examiner one question. He tells me that his rough guess is that Wilkins was killed around thirty-six hours ago.

"Last time his wife saw him was two days ago, so that's about right."

"It's a hell of a thing. Wonder what he was doing back here?"

"I'm fixing to talk to the man's wife and kids," I say. "Maybe they can tell me something that will help us find out what he was up to."

The two young Hastings grandsons who discovered the body are back outside, across the road, next to the lake doing that thing that boys always seem to do—chucking rocks into the water. Frank Hastings is with them, sitting in a folding aluminum chair and doing something with a fishing reel that involves a lot of unwound fishing line. I wave hello, and he gets up and holds up his hand for me to wait. He comes over and says, "Glo wanted me to tell you she's got some sandwiches for you, if you're hungry."

I'm famished, and I take her up on the offer. She's got pimiento cheese and tuna. I'm partial to pimiento cheese, so I take a couple. There's a smell in the air that I associate with Thanksgiving. She says she's cooking the sweet potatoes in advance so they'll be ready to mash up and top with marshmallows. "I can't stand it, but the kids would kill me if I didn't serve it."

While I wolf down a couple of sandwiches, we make small talk, but finally she says, "I need to know if there's any danger to my grandkids. Frank said it looks like maybe some wild dogs attacked Lewis Wilkins."

I don't know what's best, to let her go on thinking this was a random dog attack, or to let her know that there was a human element to it. Both are frightening in their own way. I err on the side of vague caution, "I'd keep the boys out of the woods until we have a chance to figure out exactly what happened."

"Frank will take them out fishing tomorrow so they won't sneak off. Even if I told them Godzilla was back there, they'd still head straight for it the minute our backs are turned."

"Even after what they saw back there?"

"They'll get over it. Kids are so resilient that sometimes they seem heartless. In a way, I'm glad. But I still don't want them back there."

Before I leave she fortifies me with fresh oatmeal cookies and a cup of coffee, after which I feel more capable of facing Lewis Wilkins's family again.

I stop by my car to put in a call to Dooley Phillips. He needs to know what happened and that he needn't look for his buddy. The kid who works in the marina shop says he's down at the dock working on a motor. "Does he have is cell phone with him?"

"I doubt it."

"Then you need to go down and bring him to the phone. It's important."

Dooley sounds out of breath and a little annoyed at being hauled away from whatever he was doing. I tell him that we found Lewis Wilkins's body, and where. "It appears he was attacked by dogs."

"Oh, my God. Dogs? How the hell did that happen? What was he doing out there in the back country anyway?"

"That's what we need to find out."

"Thank you for calling me. My God, that's a terrible thing. Does Margaret know?"

"Yes. I'm at her place now."

"You tell her if she needs anything, just give me a call."

Daniel answers the door and tells me that Margaret is lying down but that he'll go get her.

Margaret's expression is grim, but she's composed. She's even put on some makeup, probably for her children's sake. We go into the living room. Daniel follows us, but I say, "I need to talk to your mamma alone for a few minutes, and then I'll want to ask you some questions, too."

Daniel hesitates, but Margaret tells him she'll be okay and he disappears down the hallway. Margaret and I sit down. Her anguish doesn't show in her face, but her hands are twisted together in her lap as if she's barely hanging on.

"I'm glad you sent Daniel out," Margaret says. "I don't want the kids to hear any more than they have to."

"I'm afraid it will be hard to spare them."

She grimaces. "Do you know where those dogs came from that attacked Lewis? I mean, did somebody own them and fail to keep them properly fenced?"

"I'm not sure. We'll be looking into it."

"'We' meaning who?"

"It's complicated. In small towns the Department of Public Safety has jurisdiction when a violent death occurs. They'll get some officers to investigate."

"Should I talk to them?"

"Like I said, it's complicated. It usually takes them some time to launch an investigation. The local law—that would be me—usually starts looking into it, so that when the DPS assigns somebody, we've done the initial work. We know the local situation, so we have an inside track."

"I see. So you're going to start investigating? Like trying to track the dogs?"

"Something like that. . . . I know it's a hard time, but I'd like to ask you a few questions."

She takes a deep breath. "All right."

"You still don't have any idea who your husband was meeting for dinner Sunday night? Where he was planning on going?"

"No idea. I can't imagine what he was doing back there in the woods."

"I understand that your husband had a problem in his practice a while back that resulted in a lawsuit. You didn't mention that the other day. Any particular reason why not?"

"I didn't think it had anything to do with him disappearing."

"Have you had any contact with the person who brought the lawsuit?"

"No." She hesitates. "At least not that I know of. Lewis wouldn't necessarily have told me."

"Apparently your husband's practice is not active right now. So how was he making a living?"

"He fills in for other doctors sometimes, if they're on vacation." Her jaw tightens. "It's not much of a living. How did you find out about the lawsuit anyway?"

"I called his office, and they put me in touch with someone who told me." I wonder why she thinks it would have been hard to discover the information.

She hesitates, lips in an angry line. "I don't see why this has anything to do with Lewis being attacked by dogs."

"I'm afraid it's more serious than that."

Her pale eyes are wary. "What do you mean?"

"I hate to tell you this, but it looks like the attack on your husband was intentional. His hands were restrained. Behind his back."

"Restrained?" For the first time, her voice rises. "You mean tied up?"

"Yes, ma'am."

"Oh, my God." She brings a hand to her throat. "That means he couldn't fight back. So somebody . . . you mean somebody killed him?"

"I'm afraid so."

She clasps her arms to herself, trembling. "Who would do something so horrible?"

"Your husband's murder looks like some kind of revenge. That's why I thought of the lawsuit."

She slumps back with a weary sigh. "That woman should be plenty satisfied. She bankrupted Lewis's practice. And won a nice fat settlement that we'll never finish paying."

"You think that satisfied her?"

"Greedy bitch." Her voice is hard with fury. "Lewis made a mistake, and she made him pay for it big time."

"What prompted the lawsuit?"

She looks down at her clenched fists. "He misdiagnosed someone. It was a bad mistake, but it was a *mistake*."

"Your husband's malpractice insurance didn't take care of it?"

She glares up at me. "He was self-insured. He thought insurance was too expensive."

"I see."

"I told him it was a terrible idea, but . . ."

"Do you have any idea what your husband might have been doing out in the woods? You said the other day that he was going fishing and you thought he fished with Dooley Phillips. But I asked Dooley, and he told me he hasn't ever been fishing with your husband."

She frowns. "He's the only friend of Lewis's that I know. If he went fishing with somebody else, I don't know who it was."

"By the way, I called Dooley and told him what happened. He said if you needed anything, to call him."

She nods.

I get up. "I'd like to talk to your kids, too."

"I'll get Daniel. But Emily left. She said she had some things to do." She gets up and starts toward the hall but stops halfway and turns back. "You won't tell Daniel that Lewis was tied up, will you?"

"I'm afraid I'll have to tell him."

She closes her eyes and puts a hand to her mouth, fighting back tears. "All right," she whispers.

Daniel is quiet and sober, the opposite of the cheerful man who bounded through the door a few hours ago.

I ask him if he had a good relationship with his daddy.

We're sitting in the living room, and he stares at the fireplace, where the fire is now down to ashes. "It was good. He could be a little self-important, but I learned to live with that."

"When did you last speak with him?"

He uncrosses his leg. "It's been a few months. Why?"

"I hoped you could give me some idea of what he's been doing lately. It might lead to some answers about what happened to him."

"No, I don't know what he's been up to. We don't really keep up."

"Would your sister have any idea?"

He raises an eyebrow. "She would know less that I do. She and our daddy did not get along. I had to beg her to come for Thanksgiving."

"Where does she live?"

"She and her husband live in Houston. Or at least they did. They're separated. I'm not sure why you're asking these questions. How is that going to help you find out why Daddy was attacked by dogs?"

"Daniel, it looks like someone might have set dogs on him deliberately."

His mouth drops open. "What makes you think so?"

I tell him the basics. "Do you know if he had had any arguments with anyone? I know there was a lawsuit against him, and that he lost the judgment. Did he ever tell you anything about the lawsuit that he might not have shared with your mamma?"

"No. I was out of the loop on that whole thing. My folks didn't want to discuss it with Emily and me." He springs to his feet suddenly, as if the news of his daddy being murdered has spurred him to action. He paces to the window and then back to me. "I don't care what he had done, nobody deserves that."

"Of course not." I get up. "I'd like to take a look at your daddy's desk."

57

"I'll get Mamma." Daniel goes down the hallway and comes back with Margaret. She leads me to a small room containing a daybed, a small desk, and a straight-backed chair. The only thing on top of the desk is a laptop computer.

"Okay if I look in the drawers?"

"Sure. I don't think he keeps much here."

She's right. There are a few envelopes, a stack of paid utility bills for the lake house, and office supplies. To be thorough, I look for false bottoms and take the drawers out in case he has kept something hidden. But I come up empty.

"I'd like to take the computer with me. Do I have your permission?"

"It's fine. Sure. Go ahead."

"Does he have a cell phone?"

She frowns. "He always has it with him."

"I'll ask if it was on him, but if you find it, I'd appreciate a call."

CHAPTER 8

I stow the computer in the squad car and hike back out to the crime scene. It's late afternoon and the DPS officers are packing up.

"Find anything worth talking about?"

"No. It's pretty overgrown back here, and we didn't come across any evidence other than the drops of blood and dog hair you pointed out. We didn't go back into the woods very far, though."

"You know when somebody will be able to mount an investigation?"

He raises his eyebrows. "You know how it is. We're short-handed. When we get to the office, we'll put the case on the roster. We'll let you know."

"I'll talk to the neighbors, find out if they heard or saw anything in the night," I say. I look around at the dense growth of scrub bushes. "We might send a posse out to track down the dogs, although they're probably long gone."

After they leave I stand where the body was found and look all the way around to see if there's anything that makes sense as a reason for the attack being right here, but nothing strikes me. I decide to walk farther back into the brush. It's late afternoon and starting to cloud up. Thanksgiving is usually a bright, clear day, but maybe this year we'll have rain. The thought of Thanksgiving brings Ellen to mind, but I push away my uneasiness about her mood. I've got plenty to deal with here in the woods. No need to borrow more trouble.

Even though I am self-conscious doing it, I take my gun out of its holster and carry it loosely at my side as I move forward. If I run across dogs, I need to be prepared. As I get deeper into the woods, the path gets wilder. I have to push aside clumps of vines and thorn bushes to make my way forward. I'm glad I'm wearing my boots. If I come upon a copperhead or rattler, they're not likely to get through the leather. This time of year they are sluggish anyway, and I ought to be able to move past a snake before it reacts.

I'm surprised when the woods start to thin out, and after another quarter mile I'm in a clearing of sorts. Not that the brush is any thinner, but there are no trees. Suddenly I hear movement off in the bush. I tense and bring up my Colt and chamber a round. Whatever it is, doesn't sound like it's big enough to be dangerous, and it's moving slowly. Probably a possum. I keep my eye trained on the sound as it moves closer, and then suddenly I see the last thing I expected to see. It's a little gray-and-white puppy staggering toward me. From the look of him and the way he moves, I can tell he's not that old.

"Hey, boy, where did you come from?"

When he hears my voice, he lurches forward, his tail wagging, although it's hard for him to navigate through the brush. I walk over and pick him up. He's pretty, with a soft, gray coat with a few spots of white on his belly and some black around his muzzle. He mewls and licks my hand with enthusiasm. I notice he's thin. "Where's your mamma?"

He wriggles in protest, so I put him down. He sniffs my boots and then heads off in the direction he came from, looking like he's on a mission. I follow him. Before long, I start to smell something rank, the kind of odor that puts your hackles up, a visceral reaction to the scent of death. Surely we don't have two bodies to deal with.

A few feet farther and I come upon the source of the smell. It's a dead bitch with the same coloring as the pup, lying partly covered by brush. Her body is a mass of scratches and lacerations. The pup stumbles over to her and latches onto a teat but gives up fast and sits back on his rump, looking confused. He whimpers.

I don't know what could have happened to his mother. Besides the scratches, she looks thin. Maybe she got lost and couldn't find her way back. But what is the pup doing here? It occurs to me that there may be other puppies wandering around in the vicinity, or, worse, lying dead.

I pick up the pup and listen for sounds of others that might have straggled away. I whistle a couple of times, thinking if there's a puppy out here, maybe he'll follow the sound. I walk several steps in every direction. This pup is too little to have gone very far, so any other puppy should be close by. I pick up a stick and poke aside bushes and leaves in case one is lying too weak to move.

I'd like to go farther into the woods, but the puppy is wriggling and whimpering. He's so thin that I'm afraid that if I don't get him some food and water, he's going to be in trouble. After twenty minutes, I give it up and take him back to my car.

I consider leaving the pup with Glo Hastings. But I reconsider and think it might be best to take him to the vet. Doc England can determine if there is any kind of problem with him; maybe something that killed the bitch.

I drive straight to the vet, the pup lying quietly on the seat beside me. It's almost five and Doc England's office is ready to close up. His assistant who doubles as receptionist has already put her coat on, but she shrugs it off when she sees the puppy, grabs him up, and calls out for the vet. Doc England keeps the same kind of hours I do—the kind where you are available if you are needed. He takes the pup from her gently.

"Come here, little dude, let's get you something to eat. Chelsea, can you get one of the small feeders for me?"

"Yes, sir." Chelsea is a big girl, but she moves fast, rushing past him into the back room.

I explain how I found the puppy. Doc's face is grave. "This dog looks like he's got some border collie in him, though not purebred, because the color is off. They're good dogs. Wonder what happened."

I sigh. "It looks like he had been wandering around for a while. I searched for any other pups, but I didn't find any."

He looks at the puppy again and says, "Hang on, little guy. You're going to be okay. Chelsea's going to fix you up." Then to me he says, "You know, I think I have a note about this pup's mother." He goes behind the counter and takes a book out of a drawer. He flips the book open, and I see notations of various kinds. He sighs and slams the book closed. "People over in Burton lost a border collie mix a few weeks back. She was ready to drop her pups, and they thought somebody took her. Maybe she wandered off, or maybe somebody took her and she escaped and was trying to get back home."

"Why is there only one pup, though?"

"I'll go out there and take a look at her. Maybe I can figure out what happened. You say it was the same area where you found that fella's body this morning?"

"A little farther along. I'll go with you."

"No need. Just give me a good idea of where she is."

Chelsea is back with a tiny bottle. She commandeers the pup and sits down in the front room and starts feeding him. He takes a couple of cautious tugs at the nipple, but then goes after it fast.

"Slow down," she says. "I'm not going anywhere."

"He's going to be fine," England says. "Some pups with a trauma like that will refuse a bottle, but he's after it."

"I'm glad. How old do you think he is?"

He pulls the pup's mouth open. "Maybe four or five weeks? Could be a little older. Too young to be in such a tough situation, that's for sure. You're going to have to do some pretty intense feeding for a little while."

"Whoa. No, not me. I don't have time."

"You know that expression, 'finders, keepers'? Well, you found yourself a dog, and you should keep it."

"Wouldn't the people who lost the bitch want this pup?"

"They might." He opens the book again and jots down the address and phone number on a Post-It.

I look over and see that with a full belly the pup has passed out on Chelsea's lap, as loose-limbed as if he's expired.

"Chelsea, load up Chief Craddock with the goods to take care of this puppy until he can buy some supplies."

She hands the pup to me. He hardly stirs. He must be exhausted. Before long, she's back with a small box of bottles and nipples, a couple of cans of puppy formula, and a sample bag of dog food. "For the first couple of days, bottle feed him every couple of hours until he fattens a little bit. Then feed him four times a day. Get some goat milk. That's good for them. In a week you can start mixing some of this dog food with the goat's milk and it won't be long before he'll be gobbling it up."

I'm too stunned by the responsibility to protest, and before I know it, I'm in my squad car on my way home with a dog. I wonder how my cat Zelda is going to take this. She tolerates Ellen's dog, Frazier, so maybe she'll be fine with this pup for a couple of days, until I figure out what to do with him. Maybe I can persuade Ellen to take care of him until I get hold of the family. It would give her something to take her mind off of not getting to spend Thanksgiving with her family.

In my garage I find a sturdy cardboard box to keep the dog in until I can figure out what to do. From the bathroom, I get some towels that have seen better days and make him a bed in the box. They didn't say whether the puppy could drink water, but I figure I'd better put some in the box, too. The second I lay him down, he gets up and staggers around, as if to explore the box. He's whimpering, and it occurs to me that what goes in must come out, so I take him outside, where he promptly obeys nature.

Back in the box, he explores for a few more seconds and passes out again. To my great relief. I'm exhausted, not with the busy day I've had dealing with murder, but by the demands of a puppy.

I call Ellen's phone number, but she doesn't answer. I would ask Loretta Singletary to help me find someone to leave the pup with temporarily, but she left this morning for Brady to be with her relatives for Thanksgiving. I dial the phone number of the people who reported their bitch missing. I'll gladly drive out and take the puppy to them, but there's no answer. It's almost six o'clock and dark.

I remember that I haven't checked on my cows, so I go down to the pasture and spend a half hour working by flashlight, topping up their feed and making sure everything is in good shape. On the way back, I go by the mailbox and bring in the mail. Back inside, the puppy is busy trying to jump out of the box. He stands as tall as he can, which is three inches below the top, and does a little hop, then falls back. It makes me laugh to see how determined he is. I take him out and let him explore the carpet. About then Zelda stalks into the room. If she could talk, she'd be hollering something to the effect of *what the hell do I think I'm doing bringing that creature into the house?*

"Take it easy. He won't be here long." If there's such a thing as animal communication, the puppy will get a chance to tell Zelda what a cushy situation she has. She believes she is entitled to more queenly treatment.

I glance through my mail, surprised to find one envelope that is addressed to me by first name and no stamp, so it was delivered by hand. I turn it over. There's no indication of who it's from. I slit it open.

Dear Samuel,

I didn't want to tell you this way, but I heard that a man was found dead and figured you were busy. I have decided to go to Houston for Thanksgiving to be with my children. It means I will be seeing Seth, but he has been easier to deal with lately and finally seems to understand that I have no intention of going back to him.

It's important to me to maintain a good relationship with my children, and this seemed to be the best step. I'm so sorry we won't be together, but I suspect you will be busy anyway.

I decided to take Frazier with me so you wouldn't have to deal with him. I'll phone you when I get back, probably Sunday night.

Yours,
Ellen

My first thought is, where is she going to be staying? I don't trust her ex-husband, no matter what she says. I can't decide exactly how I feel. Not good, but it's hard to pin down what bothers me most. The main thing is that I'm annoyed. She could have made this decision a while ago and not left me high and dry over the holiday.

A squeaky sound grabs my attention. The puppy is tuned up. His little head is raised and he's doing what appears to be a puppy version of howling. I'll bet he's hungry again. Zelda has settled herself on a kitchen chair so she can keep an eye on him.

"You better be glad Ellen took Frazier with her, or you'd be dealing with him, too," I tell her. The fact is that she has taken to Frazier. At the beginning, he kept himself aloof and that seemed to appeal to Zelda. This wriggling puppy is another matter.

I fix a bottle that looks pretty much like the one Chelsea fixed up, and this time he grabs onto it and the formula is gone in no time. Then there's a repeat of before—the outside activity, then a nap on his belly.

"Okay," I say, pretty much to myself. "Looks like it's going to be the three of us for Thanksgiving. It's going to be steak, though, and not turkey."

That means a trip to the grocery store. If I'm going, it has to be tonight. Tomorrow will be busy and I won't have time to shop, and I need to get some goat milk anyway. Before I leave, I give the puppy's rightful owner another call, but still no answer, and there's no message machine. It occurs to me that they may be gone for the weekend. So what am I going to do with a puppy for four days? As I start to walk out

65

the door, I realize that leaving him alone might not be the best idea, so I haul his box out to the car. I'll have to hurry at the grocery store.

I'm checking out with the groceries I've managed to snatch up when my next-door neighbor Jenny and her boyfriend, Will, come in. They spy me and walk over to say hello. Jenny looks in my cart. "Goat milk?"

I tell her I'm saddled with a puppy.

"How is Frazier going to take to a puppy?"

"I won't know for a few days." I tell her about the note Ellen sent me.

"Then you'll spend Thanksgiving with us," she says. "Is that all right?" she says to Will.

"Of course it is," Will says. To me he says, "There are dishes Jenny has to have and ones I can't do without, so between us we have enough for half the people in Jarrett Creek."

"We only have a couple of people from work coming over," Jenny says, "and you're welcome to join us."

I hate turkey, but I don't want to spend Thanksgiving by myself. "I'd like that. What I can bring?"

"Just bring yourself," Will says. He's the cook.

"I'll bring a couple of bottles of wine."

"Could you make Jeanne's cranberry salad?" Jenny says. "You made that last Christmas and it was great."

"I suppose I could do that." It means I have to go back into the bowels of the grocery store, but I think I can remember most of the ingredients. "Oh, wait," I say. "Is it all right if I bring the puppy?"

"Oh God, you're like a new daddy," Jenny says. "Sure, bring the dog. Better than having to hire a babysitter."

CHAPTER 9

Hallelujah! I had to get up only a couple of times in the night to let the puppy outside, and once to feed him. He loves the goat milk and went after it with great enthusiasm. Doc England said he might sleep a lot because he was probably exhausted by his ordeal, and once he had a full belly, he'd likely be okay. I draped a towel over the box to keep him warm.

Despite the fact that it's the day before Thanksgiving, I take a chance that I can get some questions answered with a few phone calls. I take the puppy with me into work and hope I don't get called out on anything that will require that I leave him behind. I can always take him over to the vet's office if I have to.

There's a message from Doc England, asking me to call him back. Maybe he's heard from the people who the puppy belongs to. But no such luck. "I went out to the woods and took a look at the bitch you found. There's no telling what killed her, but it looks like natural causes. Even though she was all scratched up, there was no bad damage. She wasn't abused. Her belly was swollen. She might have gotten some kind of infection after the puppies were born."

"Puppies?"

"Yes, she clearly had more than one, but I looked around and didn't find any others. I'm wondering if somebody found them and took them, and your little guy had wandered off and they missed him."

"Wouldn't somebody who found a pack of puppies call you for help?"

"Not if it was somebody who knows dogs. There are a lot of questions. Could be somebody was taking care of her and when she died they took her out to the woods rather than bury her. Maybe your pup was a runt, so they thought he wouldn't make it. Hard to say."

"After Thanksgiving, I'll get somebody to talk to people in all the houses out there, see if somebody picked up the pups."

"That's a good idea. And by the way, I brought her body out of there. I didn't want any animals getting at it. I'll dispose of her."

Lewis Wilkins's computer is sitting on the desk where I plopped it down when I took it out of the car this morning. I should tackle it, but I dread it. I'm pretty good with mundane computer tasks, but digging deep into someone else's computer is a challenge. It'll take some time, and I'd rather get a few other answers first. Still, there might be valuable information on it. With a sigh, I draw it to me and open it up. Bingo. It's password-protected. I can call Margaret and ask if she knows the password, or I can wait. It's always easier to put off something you don't feel particularly good at if you have a good reason to. The password is a good enough reason for me.

Looking at the computer reminds me that I need to locate Wilkins's cell phone. I phone the medical examiner's office, but they say the phone was not in his belongings. There was also no identification on him. Just the clothes he was wearing.

I want to find out the details of the lawsuit against Wilkins. When I call the state medical board's office, they tell me to e-mail them with the information I want. They send their reply within the hour. Who knew any bureaucracy could be so efficient—especially the day before Thanksgiving?

The news is sobering. Lewis Wilkins operated on the knee of a fifty-five-year-old woman. The knee subsequently became badly infected and the leg eventually had to be amputated. But that wasn't the error that got him in trouble. He got in trouble because he operated on the wrong knee. The woman was too traumatized to go back and have the bad knee surgically corrected and therefore was badly disabled. She had been the breadwinner because her husband had been injured in an automobile accident a few years earlier. The case went to trial, and the jury awarded her a million dollars. Like Margaret said, Wilkins was self-insured, so he was out the money.

I once had a knee problem that had to be operated on, and I remember the helpless feeling of trusting someone to take care of your problem. The woman must have been devastated by what happened to her. It was Wilkins's job to get it right, and he screwed up. Although he probably felt bad about making such a terrible mistake, he also most likely balked at the idea that he would be financially ruined. Everyone makes mistakes. But operating on the wrong leg? And having the leg deteriorate to the point where it had to be amputated? I shudder.

I ponder this as a possible motive for Wilkins's murder. Of course, the woman and her family were angry, but would she have been furious enough to kill him after the big jury award?

The puppy is awake and squirming around, squeaking, so I take him outside, then back in for a feed, and then outside again. When I bring him back in, he's awake, making excursions from one side of the box to the other, investigating. It looks to me like he is bigger today than he was yesterday. I wish Ellen were here to see him. I phone the people who owned his mother again, but no answer.

Someone drives into the parking lot outside. It's Emily Wilkins. She's wearing jeans and a gray sweater. Big silver hoops swing from her ears. When she walks inside, her eyes immediately go to the puppy. For the first time since I met her, her face softens. "Oh, how sweet. Is he yours?"

"No. I found him and I'm taking care of him until I reach the owner."

She cocks her head. "Isn't he awfully little to be weaned?"

"His mother died, and he needs a lot of looking after, but he's a sturdy little dog. He'll be okay."

"Can I hold him?"

I hand him over and watch her demeanor change completely as she coos over him.

"Now what can I do for you?" I ask.

"My brother said you wanted to talk to me, and . . ." she hesitates. "I want to talk to you, too."

"Why don't you start? Have a seat. Can I get you some coffee?" I take the puppy from her and put him back in the box.

She sits down and shakes her head to the coffee.

"How is your mamma doing today?"

She looks as if she has tasted something bitter. "Mother? Trust me, she'll be fine. She and Daddy didn't get along."

It surprises me that she freely offers something like that to me. Sometimes people can seem unhappy with each other and still have deep-down affection. "What makes you say that?"

"After Daddy lost all his money in that lawsuit, she didn't have any more use for him. I know she's glad that he's gone. He had a nice fat life-insurance policy. She'll be all set."

"Did you get along well with your daddy?"

"I don't like to be around either one of them. I got sick of them pretending to have a normal life, when things went to hell. It was impossible to talk realistically to either one of them."

"What do you mean?"

"After the lawsuit, Daddy treated me like a child. He'd tell me everything would be fine, that he'd be back to work before long, when it was obvious that wasn't going to happen. As for Mother, she could have at least tried to get a job instead of blaming their situation on him. She couldn't have made enough to live high, but it would have helped."

"Did your daddy resent that she didn't help?"

She chews her lower lip. "I don't know. He was funny about it. He was so used to acting like a big shot that it might have been beneath him to have his wife go to work." She leans forward, jabbing the desk with a manicured finger. "The only reason I gave in and said I would come this weekend is because my brother begged me to. I told him I would come for forty-eight hours, that's all. I was planning to leave tomorrow evening, as soon as we had Thanksgiving dinner. Is that going to be a problem?"

"No, as long as I have some way to reach you." I can't help adding, "You're not going to stick around and help your mamma with funeral arrangements?"

She gives a bark of laughter. "Trust me, she'll be fine. I'm sure Daniel will stay. In case you didn't notice, he's the touchy-feely one in the family."

I lean back and contemplate her. I don't like her much. She's acting like a spoiled teenager, and she doesn't seem to be fazed by the fact that her daddy has been brutally murdered. Or is it possible that Margaret and Daniel didn't tell her. "Did your mamma or brother tell you the details of what happened?"

She catches her lower lip in her teeth and nods.

"Your daddy was murdered in a particularly vicious way. Do you have any idea who might have had enough of a problem with him that they would do that?"

Emily gives a little jerk of her head, as if someone has slapped her with information she didn't want. Her voice is more subdued. "Only one person."

"Who?"

"I want you to find out if my mother might have had anything to do with it."

"You mean you think she hired somebody to tie him up and set dogs on him? Wouldn't it be easier to divorce him?"

"Where would she go? What would she do? She hates it here in this little town, but that's the only place she could have afforded to live if they divorced."

"There's the house in San Antonio."

"Oh, didn't she tell you?" she spits out the words. "It's for sale and they can't afford to buy anywhere else. They're lucky to have that place on the lake. They were planning to move here as soon as the house sold."

On the surface of it, the idea that her mamma killed her daddy is ridiculous. It would take a fiendish planner, and Margaret didn't strike me as one.

She draws a card from her purse and thrusts it at me. "Here. This is where you can reach me."

"You work at the Contemporary Arts Museum? What do you do there?"

She frowns. "I'm an assistant curator. And when I say assistant, I mean low on the totem pole."

"It's a nice museum."

"You've been there?" Her look suggests that she wonders why a rube chief of police in a small town would ever have occasion to wander into a Houston art museum.

Not only have I been there, but before my wife, Jeanne, died, we donated a couple of paintings to them from her mother's collection. "Yes, many times. I like it."

"Oh. That's nice."

"What's your favorite kind of art?" I ask the question because I'm trying to figure out where this young woman's heart is.

She looks puzzled, as if she isn't used to being asked. "I really like cutting-edge. You know, video art. Some photography." She cocks her head. "What kind do you like?"

"Oh. I'm an old guy. I like abstract and modern art. I'm fond of the California school artists." I wonder what she would say if she knew I had a Diebenkorn and a Wolf Kahn, or maybe she would like the more current pieces like the Melinda Buie.

She blinks, reassessing. "Well, if you ever come to the museum, give me a call. I can show you around."

By the time she leaves, the puppy is at it again and I have to go through the routine. After he's fed, I put him on my lap and scratch him behind the ears and on his belly. Doc England told me that would help his digestion and help to socialize him. Besides, I'm getting to like him. He's a self-contained little dog, not afraid to tell me what he needs.

When he falls asleep, I put his box in the cell and head for Town Café. After lunch I'll go back and talk to Dooley Phillips again. This conversation will be a good bit more serious than the last one. I want to know what happened to Lewis Wilkins's boat. Why was it missing from his slip?

CHAPTER 10

I don't know why Town Café is always crowded before a holiday, but people are crammed in like they're afraid they won't get enough to eat on Thanksgiving. Everyone seems lively, although a couple of people avert their eyes when they spy me. It reminds them that they're whooping it up when someone has recently been found dead.

Some of the holiday decorations—colored lights and shabby tinsel—stay up year-round in the cafe. But Alonso Peevy, the latest owner, has gone all out this season. Besides a giant plastic turkey on the counter next to the cash register, there's a fake Christmas tree with flocking and miniature beer can ornaments, and a big red ribbon and bow across the front of the counter. Candy canes have been stuck haphazardly around the walls, and there are bowls of red and green M&Ms on every table. I suspect it's the same candy canes and M&Ms that he set out last year. I wouldn't exactly call it festive, but it's certainly colorful.

I join the table of men I regularly have lunch with. A local contractor, Gabe LoPresto, is there along with our former mayor, Alton Coldwater, and a few others. Both of these men at one time were in the community's bad graces for poor behavior. After Gabe had an unfortunate episode with a flirty young girl, his wife forgave him and took him back, and Coldwater had to climb back into society after he pretty much ruined the town's finances. But here they are, part of the gang again.

I order the cabrito enchiladas and coffee. Gabe is sitting next to a man I don't recognize.

"This is my brother-in-law, Virgil Brooks. He's from over in Beaumont. He's in town for Thanksgiving. Got about ten kids." The guy grins and Gabe slaps him on the back.

"Three, Gabe. It just seems like ten."

"Heard about that guy from the lake that was killed yesterday," Gabe says to me. "What happened?"

"Not sure yet. He was a doctor from San Antonio, Lewis Wilkins, a friend of Dooley Phillips. Any of you ever meet him?"

Everybody says no. "I know Dooley, because I keep a little boat in his boathouse, but I never met Wilkins," Alvin Carter says. He's a tall, muscular black man, a good friend of LoPresto's. They're both dedicated boosters of the high school football team.

"Somebody said he was set on by dogs," LoPresto says.

"Looks that way," I say, not wanting to discuss it but knowing I'll have to say a few words to satisfy curiosity.

"Dogs?" Virgil looks horrified. "You have a pack of wild dogs around here?"

"Not sure," I say. "I don't know. There have been rumors, but I've never had any evidence. Gabe, you know anything about that?" He's a contractor, and always scouting out land for possible building sites.

He frowns. "Just rumors. But even if there are, why would dogs go after a man?"

"Must have been a lot of dogs to overpower him like that," Coldwater says. He's probing for information.

I hesitate. I don't want everybody to get riled up with the idea that a pack of killer dogs is on the loose, and there's no compelling reason not to tell them what really happened. With the number of people who already know, it's bound to get out before long anyway. I'm aware that they're all watching me. "Thing is," I say, "Lewis Wilkins was tied up so he couldn't defend himself."

"Oh, my Lord," Alvin Carter says. "That's a whole different thing."

There are hushed exclamations. "You mean he was murdered?" Coldwater's eyes get big.

"Looks like it. He sure as heck didn't tie himself up. But how the dogs got to him, I don't know."

"Doesn't take a genius to figure out what's going on." Harley Lundsford is a leathery-skinned farmer who comes into the café every single day. He's a fierce gun advocate and gets up in people's faces about it, but he's a hardworking man and people respect him.

All heads swivel in his direction. "It's probably some of them fighting dogs that were let loose when they got too old or beat-up to fight, and they formed a pack."

"Come on, Lundsford, you don't know that for sure," LoPresto says.

"I sure as hell do. There's people all over rural areas that are into dogfighting, and that's what they do. They turn them out when they get used up. People right around here."

I've suddenly lost my appetite. If there's anything that jars me, it's dogfighting. I was forced to go to a fight once and it stuck in my memory like nothing else.

"Like who?" I ask.

"I don't mean I know anybody in particular, if that's what you're asking."

"Well, what did you mean?" Carter asks. He doesn't get along well with Lundsford.

"Don't tell me you don't know there are dogfights any place there's back woods," Lundsford says. "The law gets to them in one place and they move on to another. I wouldn't be surprised if they had an operation in these parts."

"And you know this how?" I ask. My heart is pounding.

"You know I like to go to the gun shows," he says. "When I'm there, I hear all kinds of things. Men who shoot for sport sometimes are into dogfights and cockfights, too. I don't know that we have any action around here, but could be."

Virgil looks like he's ready to run out of the café, pack up his family, and get out of town.

"Gabe, you and Alvin have anything to add?"

Gabe's expression has clouded up. I have a sinking feeling in the pit of my stomach.

"It's not the first time I've heard those rumors."

His brother-in-law glances at him, startled.

"Take it is easy, Virgil. Just because I've heard of it, doesn't mean I've gone to a fight."

"Lundsford, is there anybody around here who might give me more information?" I ask.

Alvin shoves his plate away. "If I was you, I'd let it alone. Those people are flat-out dangerous."

"You trying to tell me that I should let them get away with murdering somebody?"

Gabe clears his throat. "This is all speculation. You don't even know if that's what really happened to Wilkins."

He's right, but I'm annoyed at the idea of them suggesting that it's best to ignore dogfighting. And another thing, it makes me uneasy about finding one puppy when others are missing. Could there be some relationship between the missing puppies and these dog people?

"No, I don't. But I do know he was attacked by dogs." I shove my plate away. "Speaking of dogs, I found a dead dog out in the woods in the same area where Wilkins's body was found. I had Doc England out there to examine her, and he said she had had a litter of pups. Have you heard any rumors about somebody having a bunch of puppies in their possession?"

"How would we hear anything like that?" LoPresto says. The men are looking at me with wary eyes. I'm angry, and they know it.

"What kind of puppies?" Lunsford asks.

"Mixed breed. Doc says some border collie and maybe golden lab." Lundsford is frowning. He's got something on his mind.

"What is it Lundsford?"

"I hate to say it, but I heard a rumor that sometimes these people who train dogs for fighting will use a regular dog for bait."

"Oh, come on. That can't be true. That's hateful," LoPresto says.

I look around the table and see I'm not the only one sickened by the idea, but they most likely don't have the experience I have.

I've been here a good forty-five minutes. I need to check on the puppy, and I need to calm down. "Well, now that I've ruined everybody's lunch, I guess I'd better get on back," I say. I'm aware that I'm leaving behind a bad taste.

When I come in, the puppy is sleeping so hard that I watch to make sure he's breathing. I'm glad he's feeling secure enough to sleep soundly.

I sit down at my desk and put in a call to my pal Wallace Lyndall at the sheriff's office in Bobtail. He and I have worked together one time and another. He's no ball of fire, but he does keep his ear out for what's going on in the county.

"You hear about any dogfighting going on in our neck of the woods?"

"Craddock, I swear to God, you get up to the damnedest things. Can't you ever call just to pass the time of day?"

"Let's pretend that's what I'm doing and I just happened to ask the question."

He snorts. "I haven't personally heard anything, but I'll ask around. Is this connected with that man who was killed out at the lake? The guys that went out on the call said he was all torn up and that his hands were tied."

"That's right. It was ugly."

"Sounds like he got in with the wrong kind of people. You think it might be somebody in the dogfighting business?"

"If I knew the answer to that, I'd have somebody in jail and all the details tidied up. He has some other issues that could have gotten him killed, but this is a pretty particular way of killing somebody."

"What else could have happened?"

I tell him that Wilkins was sued for malpractice and lost the case and was in financial trouble. "Not only that, his family was mad at him."

"Mad enough to tie him up and sic dogs on him?"

"Probably not."

"Now, I said I don't know of anybody sponsoring any fights around here," Lyndall says, "but I'll tell you what sparks my interest. We've had a run of dogs reported missing. As I understand it, some of the old boys will get cats and dogs and use them for bait."

"Shoot. I heard that from somebody else. What kind of sick person would do something like that? That turns my stomach."

"What about the whole issue of dogfighting *doesn't* turn your stomach?" he says. "And I'll tell you something else, you don't want to be messing with them. From what I hear, them old boys are mean as rattlers."

I don't tell him that I already know this. "I don't want to, but I may have to."

"If you wait it out, they'll move on."

"That doesn't mean they won't come back."

No sooner have I hung up than a pitiful little wail emanates from the jail cell where the puppy is sleeping. I walk in and rescue him from starvation, and then take him out. I wish Maria was here. She loves dogs and she'd be tickled to death with this little guy.

I remember that I haven't told Ellen that I found a puppy, and I try to call her, but her cell phone is off. I don't leave a message.

After the puppy eats and does his business, I let him roam around, and I watch him while I try to push away the terrible memory that Lundsford's words has brought roaring back.

My daddy was a drunk and a coward. I knew the first part from the time I was old enough to know what drunk meant, but I was a teenager before I recognized him for a coward, prone to picking on those who were too weak to fight back. And in my early years, that meant me.

One day, when I was ten years old, he told me to get ready, that he was taking me somewhere to have some fun. I had long since stopped expecting that he intended anything good for my brother or me, but I guess every kid holds that little bit of hope. We drove way out in the country, a place I'd never been. It's only in hindsight that I believe I had a premonition that something terrible was going to happen. I probably didn't.

We drove down a road that was barely passable, rutted and overgrown, until we came to a clearing where there were other cars parked along with a fair number of motorcycles. At that age I was all for motorcycles, and wanted to stop and take a look at them, but my daddy hurried me along. He had brought a pint bottle of whiskey, and pulled from it frequently as we walked. I was used to that, and it didn't seem unusual. We walked at least a mile until we came in sight of a ramshackle wooden building with a barn-door opening. Men were gathered around outside, talking and smoking, but I remember having a sense that they were nervous and excited. Maybe it was in their voices or their jerky movements. I remember for sure, though, noticing that I was one of just a few youngsters my age.

It was only when we got inside and I saw the arena and the dogs penned around the outside of it that I had an inkling of what was up. I had heard about dogfighting from boys at school. Not that anyone had ever seen one, but the boys had plenty of speculation and opinion. One or two had older brothers who claimed to have seen them, though details were vague.

In my memory it's hard to pick out what was worse, the fury of the dogs, massive beasts with their ears clipped, who went after each other making hardly a sound, all their energy going into tearing each other to pieces; or the brutal whoops and hollers and snarls of the men who had bet on them. They screamed, urging their dogs to fight even after they were bleeding and torn. The rank smell of cigarette smoke blended with the odor of sweat and blood. Money changed hands out in the open, and more than one fistfight broke out over whether a dog had been pulled too early. After a couple of fights in which dogs were carried or dragged bleeding from the ring, I told my daddy I wanted to leave. He'd have none of it.

I managed not to disgrace myself by crying or puking, but I couldn't control trembling. It was the longest day of my young life, and the day I knew that my daddy did not have my best interest in mind. I hadn't even thought about why my brother was not included in the outing, but when I got home he was there, grinning. "What did you think? You ever think a dog could be that tough? I might get me a fighting dog one of these days."

He probably would have, too, if he hadn't been too lazy to follow through. Horace and I were always different from each other, but until the dogfight, I hadn't known quite how different.

It was weeks before I stopped waking in the night, drenched in sweat, shaking, not daring to make a sound in case my brother heard me.

I was a kid then, and there was nothing I could do about it, but now I'm chief of police, and in a position to see to it that such abomination does not happen in my territory. I have no idea if Lundsford is right and there is some link between a dogfighting operation and Lewis Wilkins's murder, but if there is, we're going to have a showdown.

I shake myself from my dark thoughts and see that the puppy has worn himself out and is lying near my feet, dozing. I put him in his box and take it outside to my squad car. I go back and leave a note on the door saying to call me if anybody needs me, and I head out to the lake to talk to Dooley Phillips.

CHAPTER 11

People from out of town come here to fish and camp out most weekends and holidays. The only time the weather is usually too bad for people to come is February, when it sometimes rains for days on end and has even been known to snow and sleet. Today, despite the chill and the threat of rain, there are boats zipping around on the lake and a lot of RVs hooked up in the campground.

Dooley Phillips's café is doing a brisk business, but the kid behind the counter, who is frazzled by all the customers, says with a resentful pout that Dooley isn't coming in today. "He's got family coming in for Thanksgiving and he's taking the day off."

I don't have to have Dooley here to take a look at Wilkins's slip again, but I don't remember exactly where it was. "Is there a ledger that tells whose boat is in which part of the marina?"

"Yes, sir." Eyeing two men who are looking at some fishing gear on the back wall, the kid pulls the ledger out of a drawer and plunks it down in front of me.

It takes me only a minute to find Lewis Wilkins's slip number. When I get to the docks, I'm confused. I recall that we turned to the left when we first went to check if Wilkins's boat was out. But the numbers clearly point me off to the right. I follow along until I find the number. It most certainly is not the same slip that Dooley showed me.

There's a boat in it, but it doesn't look like any fishing boat I ever saw. It's a sleek-looking, luxury powerboat with a cabin and a motor that looks like it could pull a skier easily. The most interesting thing about the boat, though, is that it looks like it has never been used. And there's a line of green algae around the waterline, which means it must have been sitting here for a while. Why would somebody have a big, new powerboat out here and let it sit? Did Wilkins intend to fish and he lost interest? Maybe it doesn't even belong to Wilkins. It could be the number in the ledger was wrong. I need to have another talk with Dooley.

I get Dooley's home address from the kid at the marina and head on over there. On the way, I think about when Dooley took me to the slip that supposedly belonged to Wilkins. I remember at the time thinking there was something odd about the scene. And now I realize what it was. There were no ropes on the cleats. The slip look unused. Surely Dooley would have known that. Was he lying to me? And if so, why?

Dooley lives in a modest house smack in the middle of town. He does a brisk business at the boathouse, and I would have thought he would live a little more high on the hog. But he might have kids to get through college, or maybe he's just thrifty. The other possibility is that no matter how prosperous he may seem, running a business is always a matter of worrying if you're going to be sunk by something beyond your control.

Dooley's panel truck, with the "Dooley's Boathouse and Bait Shop" logo painted on the side is in the gravel driveway next to a small Chevrolet. When I knock on the front door, a young man in his twenties opens it. He looks a lot like Dooley, with his head of bristly sandy-colored hair, bushy eyebrows, and a jaw thrust out so that it looks like he's inviting a jab. I introduce myself and ask if Dooley is at home.

"I'm Dooley's son, Bobby. You know anything about turkey fryers?" There's a glint of humor in his eyes.

"I'm afraid not."

"Too bad. Daddy's out back wrestling with the turkey fryer, and I think we might be having turkey baked in the oven tomorrow instead of deep-fried." He laughs.

"I expect you've heard some creative language this afternoon."

"I didn't even know my daddy knew some of those words. Come on out back."

We walk through the small house that smells of pumpkin pie and something tangy. From the kitchen off to the right I hear pots banging. "You home for Thanksgiving?" I ask.

"Yeah, me and my sister. She's not getting here until later this afternoon. She had to work this morning. My last class was yesterday, so I came on down this morning."

"Where are you in school?"

He opens the back door, chuckling. "I wish I was still in school. No, I'm a teacher at a high school in San Antonio." Seems like teachers get younger every year, but I keep that to myself.

We pause on the back porch and see a pitiful sight. Dooley is standing in the middle of a mess of parts that could be a turkey fryer, but could also be a small vehicle. He's thrown his jacket off on the side and his billed cap is set back on his head. With his hands on his hips, he is the picture of frustration. He looks up and spots us, and kicks one of the parts. Then he hollers, "Craddock, stop snickering and get down here and help me figure this out. My son has washed his hands of the whole thing."

I walk down the steps and eye the mess. "If I were to put my hand in, that would be a matter of the blind leading the blind," I say. "Don't you have any instructions?"

"We must have had some at one point, but they're long gone. Bobby, go tell your mamma that there's no way in hell I'm going to get this cooker together. We're going to have to cook that bird the regular way."

Bobby snorts. "You're not going to like it when she comes out here and puts it together in five minutes." He walks back into the house.

"Wouldn't you think a man who can fix any boat engine he ever ran across could figure this thing out?" he says to me.

"I never could understand why anyone would want to fry a turkey anyway," I say. "Hardly seems worth the trouble. Turkey is turkey."

"I suppose. Come on into my workroom. I have a little whiskey in there and we can get a pre-Thanksgiving sip in peace. I know you don't drink on duty, but the day before Thanksgiving, you can have a sip."

I follow him into the garage, which Dooley has set up as part workshop, part den. There are a couple of ratty easy chairs off in a corner on a rug whose color has long since melded to dirt gray, with a rickety table set in between. He walks over to a countertop that holds an array of tools in good order, opens a little cabinet, and pulls out a bottle of Jack Daniels.

"The good stuff," I say.

"I get a nice discount on account of my grocery business at the marina." He pulls out a couple of glasses and pours us each a hefty shot. We sit down in the easy chairs.

"You and your son have a good relationship." I'm particularly sensitive to that at the moment, having seen the difficulty Ellen has with her kids and Margaret Wilkins with her daughter.

Dooley grins. "The turkey fryer gave him a chance to make fun of his old man, which he sincerely enjoys." He laughs. "He's a good guy. We have good times together." He picks up his glass, takes a sip, and smacks his lips. "But you didn't come here to converse about my family."

"No, I didn't. I need to talk to you about your friend Wilkins."

He sighs. "I don't know what to make of that. Can you fill me in on the details? I sort of know the general idea, but anything you can tell me that might not be pure gossip?"

I tell him as much as I know. When I tell him that Wilkins's hands were tied when he was attacked, he draws a sharp breath. "Son of a bitch."

"I'd like to get your take on that. Do you have any idea of somebody who might have had it in for him? I know about the lawsuit he lost, and seems like the woman he injured had a lot to be upset about, but she did win a pretty tidy sum."

"Goose with the golden egg," he mutters. "That jury ruined his life. What makes people think doctors are supposed to be perfect? Everybody makes mistakes."

"I read the information about the verdict. It looked like he was pretty careless."

He runs a hand across his forehead. "I guess since he's my friend I didn't want to believe he could bungle something so bad. He didn't think it was all his fault."

"Loyalty counts."

We sit without speaking for a minute. He keeps his gaze on his whiskey.

"How often did you spend time with Lewis?" I ask.

He looks at the ceiling. "When he was down here, we tried to get together once or twice with the wives, and every now and then we'd have few beers together in the evening."

No use beating around the bush. "Dooley, I have to ask you something. You took me to a slip where you said Wilkins's boat was tied up, and when we saw the boat wasn't there, you said he must be out in it."

He holds up his hand. "I know, I know. I took you to the wrong slip. I thought about it that night and I almost called you to tell you, but I figure it wasn't that important." He chews on his lower lip. "How did you find out it was the wrong slip?"

"Since his body was found yesterday, I wanted to see if the boat was back in the marina, so I went out there this afternoon and looked up his name in your ledger. The interesting thing is, when I found the boat, it didn't look like it had ever been used."

He nods.

"Why would you tell me he took the boat out if you knew he had never used it?"

"I wasn't thinking. I'd been working on an engine all morning and didn't have my head on straight."

"Dooley, I don't want to push you, but that's hard to believe."

He sighs. "I don't know why. I guess I thought maybe he was up to something he shouldn't be up to, and I wanted to cover for him."

"Like what?"

He doesn't say anything. Finally I say, "Like maybe going to a dogfight?"

He looks surprised. "Not that I ever knew."

"You sure you'd know if he did?"

His leg is jiggling up and down. He shakes his head. "Of course I can't be completely sure. I don't think he would, but . . ."

"But maybe there were things about him you didn't know?"

"Yep."

"Dooley, what was he doing with a showy boat like that?"

He's slow to answer, but finally he shrugs. "Won it in a poker game."

"Are you kidding me? That's a hell of a nice boat to have at stake in a poker game."

He gives a deep sigh. "It was unusual all the way around. I play in some friendly social games from time to time." He waits for my reaction. Gambling for money even in private games is technically illegal, but if lawmen in small towns busted every friendly poker game, we'd lock up half the men in town.

"I understand. That's not unusual."

"Not too much money at stake. At least not normally. But that night things took a different turn. The guy who owned the boat is Jerry Bodine. You probably don't know who he is."

I shake my head.

"He lives over in Bobtail. His father-in-law was Chuck Flynn."

"Is that right?" Everybody either knew Chuck Flynn, or knew of him. He owned the only real industry in the county—a lawnmower manufacturing company that employed a lot of people. He died not long ago, but before he died he sold the company to the employees, which made him something of a local hero.

"Apparently Chuck bought the boat not long before he died. He took it up to Possum Kingdom Lake—don't ask me why he didn't keep it here. But at any rate he never got a chance to use it before he got sick and died. Jerry and his wife inherited it. Jerry said the last thing he needed was a powerboat. He had it brought down to the lake here to keep until he decided what to do with it."

Dooley is enjoying telling the story, and I figure he'll get around to the point eventually. "So it sat here for several months. And one night Jerry came for one of our poker parties, and Lewis happened to be here, too. Well, we were drinking a little"—he lifts his glass—"and one thing led to another, and Lewis and Jerry got into an argument over a hand that was played. Next thing you know, they're upping their bets—kind of aggressive-like. I knew Lewis was having money trouble and he shouldn't have been betting the way he was, but I figured I wasn't his keeper, and he could make up his own mind. Suddenly Jerry gets all huffy and says he's putting up his boat against Lewis's place out at the lake."

"You're kidding. Lewis was willing to bet his house?"

"I tried to talk some sense into Lewis, but he didn't want to hear what I had to say. Well, long story short, he won."

"How long ago was this?"

"This past summer. June, July."

"And Lewis never took the boat out?"

He snorts. "He didn't really want a boat. It was a matter of pride for him to win it. He and Bodine seemed to have some kind of bad feeling between 'em from the get-go."

"Well, that's some story. Was Bodine upset when he lost the boat?"

"Just the opposite. He laughed and said it was an easy way to get the boat off his hands."

That explains where the boat comes from and why it was never used, but it's still an odd story, and I wonder if I've heard all of it. I may have to look up Jerry Bodine and find out his version.

"I'm trying to imagine what Margaret would have said if Lewis had lost the house," I say. "It sounds like Lewis could be a little impulsive."

"I believe that's a fair assessment. When he was young, he was hot-headed, but he had calmed down a lot. I think the business with the lawsuit got under his skin and made him regress a little bit."

Operating on the wrong leg could have been the result of an impulsive act, too. Although you'd think someone on the operating team would have called his attention to it.

"Speaking of Margaret, I'd like to know more about his family. I talked to their daughter today, and it seems like she didn't get along with her folks."

"You got that right. That girl thinks the sun rises and sets on her say-so. I don't have a lot of affection for Margaret, but I feel bad about the way Emily treats her."

"Sounds like Emily was pretty upset about the lawsuit."

"She was like that before the lawsuit. Lewis spoiled her. I shouldn't say he did. Margaret did, too. It's funny, though, I think I spoiled my kids, but they turned out okay."

All of a sudden, I hear light steps running through the gravel. "Daddy! Daddy are you out here?" A girl's voice calls out.

He jumps up. "That's my Annabelle." A big grin splits his face. "I'm in here, honey!"

A slim young woman in jeans and sweatshirt darts into the garage and flings herself into Dooley's arms and hugs him tight. "Mmmm, mmm, I've missed you," she says, standing on tiptoes to kiss his cheek.

Dooley is the picture of delight. "Have you told your mamma you're here?"

"Of course! She'd have a hissy fit if I came out here first." She turns. "I'm sorry, I didn't mean to ignore you. I'm Annabelle Phillips."

I introduce myself and then say, "Dooley, your daughter is one lucky girl. She doesn't look a thing like you."

He laughs. "Naw, she's pretty like her mamma."

Dooley's son strolls in. "Why don't you all come on in the house? Maybe Mamma will get off her feet for five minutes."

"Daddy," Annabelle says, "she's making enough food for twenty people. Who all is coming tomorrow?"

"It's just us. Craddock, you have plans? You're welcome to join us."

89

I tell him I've got somewhere else to be. "Listen, I'll stop in long enough to say hello to your wife, but let me ask the kids something. You've heard what happened to Lewis Wilkins?"

Annabelle shivers. "Mamma and Daddy called me last night to tell me. That was horrible."

"You two are the same age as his kids. Do you know them?"

Their eyes flick to each other and back in an unreadable exchange. "Not really," Annabelle says. "We hung out with them a few times when we were younger, and once we all went on vacation together, but they lived in San Antonio and we lived here, so we didn't see them much." She may say they don't know each other well, but I notice a flush rises to Bobby's cheeks, and I wonder if there's more to it.

"They don't get on well with their folks. Do you have any idea why?"

"Hold it," Dooley says. "You're not suggesting that either of the kids had anything to do with Lewis's death, are you? 'Cause I don't see that at all."

"No, that wasn't the idea. I like to get family relationships straight. They can be complicated."

"It was no secret that Emily didn't think much of her parents," Annabelle says. "I always thought she was a little hard on them, but . . ." she shrugs.

"I don't know," Bobby says. He's frowning. "Dr. Wilkins could be awfully strict. He wasn't always fair, either. I mean, Daddy didn't let us get away with much, but we always knew where we stood." He looks at Dooley.

"You didn't think so when you were fourteen," Dooley says.

We have been walking slowly toward the house, and we file up the steps and in the back door.

"Mamma," Dooley calls out. "Come on in here and sit down for a minute."

"Dooley, I'm busy. What do you want?" Her voice precedes her, and she comes to the door of the kitchen wiping her hands on her apron. I know her by sight. She's a short, plump woman with a halo of brown curls liberally sprinkled with gray. She's so short that she has to cock her head back to peer up at Dooley and me. "Oh, hello," she says. "I didn't know we had company."

"Not company," I say. "Just the police chief."

"Oh, I know who you are," she says. "You're a friend of Loretta Singletary. She thinks you're a smart cookie."

"I think the same thing about her," I say, grinning.

"He's here to talk about Lewis," Dooley says.

She shakes her head. "That's awful. I tried to call Margaret, but I guess she isn't answering her phone. I'll have to go out there." She looks at her family. "I was thinking we ought to invite them for Thanksgiving dinner tomorrow."

The kids both grimace. Dooley walks over and puts his arm around his wife. "That's nice of you, Connie, but let's keep the holiday for us and invite them over later in the weekend."

She looks up at him. "I don't like to think of them out there in that house with nothing to do but stare at each other and grieve."

"If you think it's the right thing to do, then we should do it," Bobby says. His sister looks at him like she could strangle him.

Connie sees the look and sighs. "Let me think about it a little more."

I excuse myself and ask Dooley to follow me out to the squad car, where I find my puppy is awake and trying to jump out of the box. I put him on the ground, where he starts nosing around.

"Where in the world did you get that pup?" Dooley asks.

I tell him how I found the dead bitch and the puppy along with her. "It's a mix with some lab and some border collie."

"He's a pretty little dog. Too bad he isn't a hound, or I'd take him off your hands. We had to put our coon dog down in September, and I've been on the lookout for a new one."

"In your search, have you heard anything about dogs being stolen?

91

We've had a few incidents of dogs disappearing, and yesterday a man who lives down the street from Wilkins came upon some men trying to make off with his dog. It occurred to me—suppose Wilkins was walking in the woods and stumbled onto some kind of illegal operation? They might have killed him to keep him quiet."

He frowns. "What do you mean 'illegal operation'? You mean somebody stealing dogs and keeping them in the woods? Why would they do that?"

"I've heard speculation that a dogfighting outfit might be operating in the area. Have you heard anything like that?"

His face has gone dark. "No, but if I did, I'd sure as hell have something to say about it."

"Think back to the last few months. Did Wilkins ever give you any indication that he saw something that troubled him?"

"First of all, Lew wasn't the kind of guy who goes for a walk in the woods. He's a city boy." It's gotten colder out here, and he shoves his hands into his jacket pockets. "And if for some reason he did, he sure never told me he'd seen anything odd. But I'm still wondering why anybody would steal a dog."

"This is all pure speculation, you understand, but somebody suggested that if there's an illegal dogfighting operation around, sometimes they steal dogs to use for bait dogs."

"Oh hell!" He kicks at the gravel. "That doesn't bear thinking about."

"Well, you're in a position to run into a lot of different people. If you hear a rumor that somebody is into fighting dogs around here, I'd appreciate your letting me know."

"I sure will." He looks down at the puppy. "What are you going to name this little guy?"

"Oh, he's not mine. I can't keep a dog. Too much trouble. I'm trying to get hold of his owners."

CHAPTER 12

It's late in the afternoon, but I figure I have time to go over to the Wilkins house and check up on them. Plus I need to find out if Margaret knows that her husband had a fine new boat tucked away in the marina. The holiday has messed with my timing. I'd like to find out if anyone has spotted Wilkins's SUV, but on the day before Thanksgiving I'm not likely to get a lot of action out of anyone in the DPS office. Murder doesn't take a holiday, but the people investigating it do. If Ellen were in town, I'd be putting in less time, too.

As I park the squad car in front of the Wilkins place, I think how different it is to try to put together the information I need from scratch. When something happens here in Jarrett Creek, I have years of knowledge to rely on for background—and Loretta's grapevine. But with the Wilkins family, I'm running blind. They could tell me anything, and I'd have to believe it. I can check facts on the Internet, but that doesn't get under the surface of who they are.

"You stay put; I won't be long," I say to the puppy, even though he's asleep. I know the dangers of leaving a dog unattended in a car, but this time of year it's cool outside and I leave the windows open for plenty of ventilation.

Daniel Wilkins answers the door. His face is strained. He rubs his hands together. "Come on in. It feels like it's gotten colder out there."

Margaret Wilkins comes out of the kitchen, wiping her hands on her apron.

"I came by to see if there's anything I can do for you."

She shrugs. "I thought about going to my sister's for Thanksgiving, but that would mean driving all the way out to Amarillo. Daniel and I, neither one of us, felt like making that long trip. And then Gloria, next door, asked if we'd join them. Daniel said we should." He's standing next to me. She shoots him an uncertain glance.

"They seem really nice," Daniel says, "and I think it would be better if we're around people. They have grandkids. They'll keep our mind off things—keep us distracted."

"Emily isn't going with you?"

Margaret's expression closes up. "Yes, she'll go over with us, but then she plans to head home. Why don't you sit down." She gestures to the kitchen table. "I'm making a couple of pies to take over there tomorrow. I don't know how they'll turn out, but it was only way I could think of to get my mind off of . . ." She trails off and turns around to attend to her pies.

Daniel and I follow her into the kitchen area, where she has two pie tins lined with crust. She says she's making one pumpkin and one lemon meringue. My thoughts stray to Ellen. She makes a good lemon pie, and I wonder if she's baking one for her family—including her ex-husband.

Daniel sidles up to me and says, "Can I talk to you for a minute?"

Margaret looks surprised, but then turns her attention back to her work, as if shying away from whatever her son has to say to me.

I follow him into the living room, which is open to the kitchen, so he keeps his voice low. "Listen, if you've talked to Emily, you need to take anything she says with a grain of salt."

"In what way?"

"Ever since Daddy got into financial trouble, she's been mad. She thinks Mamma didn't stand by him the way she should have." He pauses. "I don't know what she told you, but I wouldn't put it past her to accuse Mamma of something."

"You mean accuse her of killing your daddy?"

He grimaces. "I guess she wouldn't go that far, but she can be judgmental, and sometimes she gets carried away."

"I'll keep that in mind."

He tells me he's off to buy groceries. "Wish me luck. The store is going to be a nightmare. We had planned to go yesterday, but . . ."

When I return to the kitchen, Margaret is slipping the pumpkin pie into the oven. She has poured the lemon pie filling into the other crust. "Come on over here while I finish up."

I lean on the counter, watching her while she whips the whites and piles the meringue onto the lemon pie and tucks it into the oven. "I have a couple of things I want to discuss with you," I say when she's done.

"Let's sit in here," she says. "I don't like being in the living room without Lewis here. Silly, I know." She washes her hands and pours us each a cup of coffee, then joins me at the kitchen table.

"I'd like to get a list of names of your husband's friends in San Antonio."

She looks down at her hands. "Lewis didn't have friends."

"Doctors he worked with?"

She shakes her head. "Everyone more or less deserted him after the verdict came down. Not that he ever had close friends. More like acquaintances. And after what happened with the trial, most of them slipped away."

"How did he spend his time after the verdict? You said he worked for other doctors sometimes, but he must have had spare time."

"When he was home he watched a lot of TV, spent a lot of time on the Internet."

"Doing what?"

She shrugs. "I don't know." Then she blinks and gives a self-conscious laugh. "I don't think he was into anything like pornography, if that's what you're thinking."

"Hadn't occurred to me." Although it had. "One other thing. I talked to your daughter this morning. She told me you and your husband had your house on the market in San Antonio and were planning to move here."

She bends her head and massages her neck so that I can't see the expression on her face. "That was Lewis's plan."

"He liked it here?"

She straightens. "Liked it? I don't know that I would say he particularly liked it. We couldn't afford to live in San Antonio anymore. He also said he wanted to get out of San Antonio because he was tired of being cold-shouldered by people who knew what had happened. And Dooley encouraged him to come here."

"How did you feel about moving here?" I understand that I'm asking her invasive questions, but it's necessary. I usually know a lot about the people in town, so I don't have to pry. It's harder to investigate when I have so little background on the Wilkins family.

She sighs. "I wasn't exactly wild about it. Not that I have anything against this place," she adds. "You have to understand. Before the lawsuit, I liked my life. I never had any burning ambition to be a businesswoman. We had friends, and I liked to entertain. I don't mean it was all frivolous. When the kids were little, I did events to raise money for schools. After that I got hooked up with hospital charity events." She grimaces. "Of course that ended when the lawsuit came up. Everybody was nice to me, but the hospital didn't want me involved with fundraising for the hospital when my husband was being sued."

"Why is that?"

"Because that woman sued the hospital, too." She gives a humorless laugh. "I could see their point."

"You could still settle here. It's a nice town."

"That would be fine if I didn't have to find a job. I'll probably go back to East Texas. I have family there. Cousins. I have my fingers crossed that one of them can help me get a job."

"Emily told me your husband had a life-insurance policy."

Again that mirthless laugh. "Emily thinks she knows more than she actually knows." Her voice is bitter. "We had to cash in that policy to have money to live on. Damn it!" Her sharp words startle me. She fixes me with a fierce glare. "I tried to convince Lewis to move somewhere like Houston or Dallas, where nobody would have known what happened. Of course information about the lawsuit is in the public record, but it wouldn't have been in people's faces. Lewis could have found a group of doctors to work with, but he was too stubborn. He said if we stuck it out, eventually people would let go of it." She draws a breath and I see that she's close to tears.

"So you were short on money and the insurance policy had to go. But your house is up for sale . . ."

"And mortgaged to the hilt. I'll be lucky if the sale covers the mortgage."

"Why didn't you tell your daughter the truth?"

Margaret struggles with her answer, her eyes welling with tears. "I may have been angry with Lewis, but that doesn't mean I wanted our daughter to hate him. I was hoping if she came here for the holiday that we might be able to piece together some family time. Now . . ."

My cell phone rings and I see that it's a Department of Public Safety number.

"I need to take this," I say, pushing the button to answer it. "Craddock."

"This is David Bagley. The trooper who was out there with you yesterday? Thought you might want to know we found Wilkins's vehicle."

"Where was it?"

"Somebody spotted it out on the road between Cotton Hill and Burton and thought it was abandoned, so they called the highway patrol."

"Did you haul it in?"

There's a moment of silence. "Uh, no, we figured you might want to take a look at it at the site before we have it towed away. Somebody went out there and ticketed it so everybody would know it was on record."

More likely no one wanted to mess with it on the day before

Thanksgiving. But that's all right, because he's correct. I do want to examine it where it sits. He gives me the details of where the SUV was found.

I get up. "Margaret, the troopers found your husband's SUV. I'm going to go take a look at it."

"Where was it?"

I tell her where it was found. "Do you know if he knew anybody out that way?"

She shakes her head. "Not that he ever said."

"Would you happen to have a spare key in case it's locked up?"

She gets a key chain from her purse and pulls off the key to the SUV. "Should I go with you and drive it back here?"

"No, it's going to have to be towed somewhere so I can give it a thorough inspection. It'll take a day or two. Do you have another vehicle?"

"I have a car in San Antonio. I can get Daniel to take me there to get it." She's twisting her hands. "It's claustrophobic in this house. I want to get out of here for a couple of days, so I might stay overnight. Is that all right?"

"Of course. Just be sure I can get in touch with you."

She drops her head into her hands. "I don't know what I'm thinking. I can't stay in the house in San Antonio because the realtor might want to come in and show it. And I can't afford a hotel."

She said Lewis had no friends, and I wonder if she was deserted as well. "Do you have someone you can stay with?"

"I do, but that would mean having to make small talk and have people fuss over me because of what happened. That doesn't appeal to me." She straightens her shoulders. "I'm tired of whining. I'll come back here. I'll be fine."

It's late afternoon, and I want to get out to see the SUV before it gets too dark, but there's the matter of the boat.

"Margaret, are you aware that your husband had a boat?"

"You mean like a little fishing boat?"

"No. I mean like a cabin cruiser."

"What? No. What makes you think he had a cabin cruiser? We didn't have the money for something like that."

"According to Dooley Phillips, he did. He won it in a poker game a few months ago."

"Are you sure? Wouldn't he have had to put up money to win something like that? Where did he get that kind of money?"

I'm not going to tell her that he was willing to bet the very place she's living in.

There's a commotion at the front door, and Daniel comes inside bearing two armloads of groceries. I go help him, closing the door and then taking one of the sacks from him. Margaret follows us into the kitchen. "Why did you buy so much? You're leaving Saturday."

"I figured you would need some things."

"Daniel, I have to ask you something," she says, as she starts taking things out of one of the bags. "Did your daddy ever tell you that he won a boat in a card game?"

He wheels around and looks at her. "What are you talking about? I didn't even know he liked boats."

"He kept it at Dooley's marina," I say.

"What kind is it?" Daniel asks. "Like, a rowboat? Motorboat?"

"Bigger than that," I say. "A cabin cruiser."

"Well, good, maybe you can sell it and make some money," Daniel says to Margaret. "That is, if it's really his. He'd have papers on it. Did you find papers?"

"I don't remember seeing anything like that."

I'm aware that it will be dark soon. "Margaret, I need to get on over to look at the SUV. Unless something urgent comes up, I probably won't talk to you until Friday. If you come across anything you think might be important, though, give me a call."

When I get out to my car, the puppy is awake and squirming around. I start to take him out, but it occurs to me that if the kids next door see him, they'll swarm all over him. I drive down to the end of the road to John Hershel's place before I let him out.

After I put the puppy back in the car, I knock on Hershel's door. When he sees me, he says, "If you're here about Satch, he's safe in the house."

"I'm glad to hear it. I'd like to ask a favor," I say.

"What's that?"

"If you run into your neighbors, ask if anybody has taken in any puppies."

"Puppies? What kind of puppies?"

"Come on out here and I'll show you."

I take him out to my car and show him the wriggly little bundle.

"He's a cute dog. Little young to be weaned, isn't he?"

"He sure is." I tell him how I found him. "The vet said it's possible that somebody found the other pups and took them in. I'd like to know where they are."

"I'll be glad to ask around. Gives me a mission. I take a walk every afternoon with my dog, and we run into a lot of folks."

When I start the car, the puppy yips to tell me he's ready for a meal. I tell him he'll have to wait a little longer.

The road to Burton is a two-lane country blacktop off the main highway that winds through rolling hills studded with the occasional farm. It passes through the village of Cotton Hill, which consists of a church; a service station with a country store; and, surprisingly, a new antique store named Old and in the Way, installed in a former roadhouse that had fallen into disrepair.

In the waning sunlight it's a peaceful drive. I imagine all the farms full of young people back home for Thanksgiving, the kitchens full of warmth and laughter. If I don't pay attention, I could start to feel sorry for myself. I remind myself that my nephew, Tom, invited me to spend Thanksgiving with his family, but I declined because I wanted to stay around to spend time with Ellen. That didn't work out so well.

Of course I'm aware that all the families on these farms aren't reenacting Norman Rockwell scenes. Some of them are probably more like the Wilkins family, people struggling to find common ground and to smooth over differences.

Past Cotton Hill, I am on the lookout for a rutted road off to the right that Bagley described to me. It's closer to Burton than it is to Cotton Hill. The ruts are deep and they jostle me and the puppy. I wish I had brought my truck instead of the squad car. A mile in, I come upon Wilkins's SUV. I wonder why somebody called it in. It isn't in anybody's way.

It's parked at an angle, sloping toward a deep ditch on the right hand side, bordering on deep woods. The other side of the road is open pasture. By my reckoning the woods are on the backside of the vast wild country to the west of the lake where Wilkins was killed.

I climb out and walk around the big, white Chevy Suburban, bending to peer at the surrounding area to see if there are any shoe imprints in the dust. The verge it's parked on is part gravel, part rutted dirt, and doesn't lend itself to footprints. If there was a struggle here, there's nothing to indicate it. A few feet back of the rear bumper there's a tire imprint, but it would be hard to say whether it was made recently. Did someone meet Wilkins here and they drove off together? Was he forced to stop? The tire print could even have been made by the highway patrol or whoever called in the abandoned SUV.

There are no farmhouses in sight, so, whatever happened here, there are likely no witnesses. I put on a pair of vinyl gloves from the crime scene kit and try the door handle. The SUV isn't locked. From what I've heard of Wilkins, he seems like the kind of man who would always lock the door of his vehicle. The light is waning, so I fetch a powerful flashlight from my squad car to peer inside. There's nothing to indicate anything but a peaceful exit from his vehicle.

I go back to my car for a pair of crime scene booties. I always feel like an idiot putting them on. Until recently I never felt the need for something so fussy, but when Maria Trevino came to the department last year, she brought the fervor of the newly educated and convinced me that it was the right procedure.

With the booties over my boots, I climb into the front seat of Wilkins's SUV and take a look from that perspective. Nothing unusual to see.

I lean over and open the glove compartment and am not altogether surprised to find a weapon—but I am surprised that it's a serious weapon, a full-size .44 Magnum. I take it out and examine it. This is a gun for someone who is expecting trouble. I sniff it and can tell that it hasn't been fired recently. Then I take a closer look and can't help laughing. I'll have to take it apart to be sure, but if I'm not mistaken this gun has never been fired. Like Wilkins's boat, this is mostly for show. For a man who is broke, he has expensive tastes.

Besides some random receipts in the glove box, which I put into a plastic bag, and an empty tote bag stuck up under the passenger seat, the front is clean. Same in the back seat. I open the voluminous trunk and find a half-case of bottled water, a blanket, and an emergency medical supply case. I lock up the vehicle and watch the dusk settle around me as I consider what might have happened here. He didn't lock up the car. Which means either he expected to come right back, or he wasn't given the opportunity. The one disappointment is that I don't see his cell phone. I stash the gun and the bag of receipts into my glove compartment and lock it up. "Just give me a couple more minutes," I tell the puppy.

An overgrown path leads off into the woods, and I walk a few yards in, but as soon as I get into the trees, it's too dark to see anything. I turn on my flashlight, but all I see is trees and brush. For some reason I'm spooked. The woods are too still, or maybe it's my imagination.

When I get back to the SUV, I crouch down with the flashlight and shine it around under the vehicle. That's when I find the cell phone, a big, important-looking one, in the gravel under the inside of the front wheel. I picture somebody grabbing Wilkins and the phone skittering out of his hand.

When I get back in the car, the puppy lets me know he's out of patience. I get out the bottle I brought for him, and it doesn't take him any time to finish it off. Then I take him outside and he does his business. Just as we're ready to go and he's settling down, he starts and whimpers, his head turned sharply toward the side window. "What is it, boy?" And then I hear what must have startled him. Far off in the trees somewhere, there are dogs barking.

I drive the rutted road back to the highway and start to turn back toward home, but since I'm so close to Burton, where the pup's mother was from, I may as well swing by and see if the people who reported her missing are home. I fish around in the glove box and find the address that Doc England gave me, and enter it into my phone's GPS.

The place is past Burton, in a neighborhood of small but well-kept homes. It's dark when I reach the address, but not so dark that I can't see the For Rent sign in the yard and the air of abandonment. There are no lights on, and no one comes to the door when I knock. The house next door is lit up, so I go over there and knock. A middle-aged man wearing overalls and a work shirt answers the door.

"Them people? They upped and moved out of here a week ago. Didn't give no warning. Nothing."

"You know where they went?"

"I don't, but my wife might. Darla!" He hollers over his shoulder. A woman wearing a housedress and fuzzy slippers plods into the room.

"You know where Patrick and Janet went?"

"Janet said they was going up around Arlington. I think Pat got a job up there. Is everything okay?" she says to me.

"They lost a dog a while back and I wanted to ask them about it."

"Oh my, yes. They lost Princess. She was a pretty dog, but a little skittish. It broke Janet's heart. The dog was pregnant and Janet worried over her."

I'm not going to tell them what happened to the pup's mother, but I take out my card and hand it to the man. "If you happen to hear from them, would you have them give me a call? I have a question for them. We've had some other dogs disappear."

"Sure. But I don't expect to hear from them," the man says. "They was renters and they seemed to have itchy feet. Nice enough, but not somebody you get close to."

On my way back, I stop by Margaret Wilkins's place. Daniel answers the door. I tell him I found his dad's cell phone and that I want Margaret's permission to examine it. She readily gives permission, and I ask if she has a charger, since the phone is out of juice. She brings me one. "What do you think could be on it?" she asks.

"Could be nothing, but I need to find out." What would be nice is if there was a call from someone who was planning to meet him just before he disappeared, but that would be too easy.

Back home I feed the pup and take him outside. Despite how much I like him, I resolve to take him back to Doc England on Friday. I simply don't have the time to put into raising a puppy.

It's early-morning hours and for a minute I can't figure out what woke me. When I come full awake, I realize it's the puppy whimpering. I haul him outside, then bring him back to his bed, but the second I turn out the light he starts up again. I get up and give him something to eat, but he doesn't seem interested. I hold him for a minute, wondering if he's got something wrong with him, but he seems happy enough when I'm holding him. I put him back in the box and he squeaks some more.

Finally I get up and put him on the bed. He settles right in next to me and goes to sleep. I know it's a bad idea. I really do. But I need to get to sleep.

CHAPTER 13

Thanksgiving Day dawns bright and clear. I stretch before I remember that the puppy is on the bed with me. He's down near my feet and only wakes up when I start moving around. We eat breakfast together—him with his bottle of goat milk, and me some toast and coffee. I take him down to the pasture when I go to check on my cows. First I set him down on the ground, but then worry that if he wanders into the pen he could get trampled underfoot, so I put him in a pan that I use to scoop feed. It's a little taller than he is, so he can't jump out, although he immediately starts trying.

When I get back, there are two messages on my phone—one from Ellen and one from Jenny. I check Jenny's message. She says, "Will is in charge of the meal, but he wondered if you'd come over early and help him cook. I'll be acting like a lady of leisure."

I call her back and she says to come over at one o'clock. "Will and I are going for a ride first." Who would have guessed that Jenny, who loves her horses, would be lucky enough to find a beau who also likes to ride?

I'm putting off calling Ellen, but that's foolish, so finally I make the call. She answers right away. "Samuel, I'm glad you called me back. I was afraid you were mad at me."

I'm not mad, I am puzzled; but I don't want to get into it on the phone. "I'm fine. It's been busy."

"I didn't mean to sneak off that way . . ." Her voice trails away.

"You didn't sneak off. You wrote a note. If you hadn't, that would be a different story."

"What are you doing for Thanksgiving?" She sounds plaintive.

I tell her I'm going over to Jenny's. I've resolved not to ask her any questions about her family. I don't want to know where she is staying or any other details. "How's Frazier?"

As soon as I ask, I'm aware of how lame the question sounds, and the only reason I ask it is because I've been so dog-oriented the last couple of days.

She sighs. "I should have left him with you. I forgot how much . . ." And then she pauses. I know what she meant to say.

"You forgot that your ex-husband doesn't like Frazier." And Frazier is terrified of Seth.

"Yes, but Seth is trying to be nice to him."

I should tell her about the puppy, but it'll be gone when she gets back anyway.

I'm finding it hard to talk to her since I don't want to bring up family matters or the puppy. She seems to be having no better luck than I am. We limp to a close in our conversation. She says she'll be back Sunday. "I'm glad I came, because I'm getting to be with the kids."

I put in a call to my nephew, Tom. He and his family are spending Thanksgiving with his wife's family in McKinney. I'm glad I didn't join them. Tom's wife is a wonderful woman, but her daddy and I don't agree politically, and he seems to have made it his business to convert me to his way of thinking. Now I understand he's thinking of running for the local school board, and I can't stomach hearing chapter and verse on his plans to change the school to fit his ideas.

Tom and his wife, Vicky, are in good spirits. They make their apologies that I can't talk to their two girls, who have gone to the park to play touch football with some neighbor kids. When I hang up, I promise myself to get to Austin soon to visit them.

Last night I plugged in Lewis Wilkins's cell phone, so it's all charged up and ready for me to find out what's on it.

I turn it on and, like the computer, it's password-protected. I have a hunch that Margaret doesn't know the password, but I call her anyway.

It's after nine o'clock, but I worry that it may be early if she is having trouble sleeping. She tells me I didn't disturb her.

"I wonder if you know the password on your husband's phone?"

"Let me think. At one time I know he used 1-2-3-4. But I think when he got this one it was maybe his birthday? Try 0919 or 1964."

The first one doesn't work, but the second does. "That was it. You happen to know what his computer password is?"

"I'm pretty sure it's the same."

"I'll check that later, thanks. You doing okay?"

"As well as you can expect. I'm glad the kids are here."

"Your daughter came home last night?"

"Yes, around midnight. She told me she had been to San Antonio to see an old friend."

When I get into Wilkins's cell phone, first I look at the text messages. There aren't many, but one catches my eye. "See you in a few days!" It was from Daniel. Odd, Daniel told me he hadn't had any communication with his dad in a few months. I read the messages and they seem off, as if they are talking about something other than Thanksgiving. And then I see the date on it. This was an exchange from last spring. There have been no texts between them since then.

Wilkins was not much for texting. There are only a few other texts, mostly from businesses.

I turn to the voice messages. I listen to one from Margaret telling him to pick up lettuce and milk from the grocery store. Then there's one from Dooley a couple of weeks ago asking him to call back with his plans for Thanksgiving. Other than that, there's nothing to raise my interest.

Finally I turn to the list of calls that were left without messages. It's going to be a tedious job to find out who made these calls. Just having the name or number doesn't tell me whether it's from someone Wilkins had a relationship with, or if it was a telemarketing call. Sorting it out will have to wait, though.

Now it's time to tackle the cranberry salad. I'm still feeling out of sorts because Ellen ran out on me, but I'm determined to make the best of the day. I like Jenny and Will, and we'll drink some wine and have some pie.

I'm glad I said I'd make cranberry salad. That keeps me busy for a while. I let the puppy wander around and explore the kitchen, although every time I move my feet I'm afraid I'll step on him. Finally the salad is in the refrigerator and the puppy has fallen asleep on the floor next to his box.

Before it's time to get over to Jenny's, I go to headquarters. Although I left a note on the door telling anyone with a problem to call my cell phone, I don't always trust that people will do it. Sure enough, there's a call from Loretta Singletary's next-door neighbor, saying she thought she saw someone sneaking into Loretta's house last night. I go over and talk to her and find out it was a false alarm, that the man who she saw in Loretta's yard came to her house looking for a house that was a block over.

I chuckle when I get back and notice that Town Café's parking lot is full. Women all over town have probably been saying something like, "You're driving me crazy being underfoot. Don't you have someplace you can go?" I park in the headquarters parking lot, stick the puppy in the jail, and head across the street to the café. Sure enough, the place is crammed, almost 90 percent of the customers being men who are drinking coffee rather than eating.

The only regular I spot is Gabe LoPresto, who is sitting by himself, looking moody. "Mind if I join you?"

"Be my guest." He indicates the chair across from him.

"You look like you lost your best friend," I say.

"In a manner of speaking." He tells me that the quarterback who has led the Jarrett Creek High School football team to lofty heights this season broke his leg yesterday.

"How did he manage to break it?"

"Football practice. They were clowning around afterward and he jumped off some bleachers and landed wrong. It's not a bad break, but he's out for the season."

"That puts an end to the district run."

"Don't I know it!"

We don't even mention the backup quarterback, who is a freshman with good skills, but the build of a ten-year-old. That's the problem with living in a small town, the talent pool for sports is small.

"Where's your brother-in-law?"

"Virgil and his wife went over to see her cousin in Bobtail. Anything new about the fella that got killed?"

"They found his SUV out on the road to Burton, but that's all for now. I'm looking into it."

"You thought any more about the dogfighting possibility?"

"'Course I have. What I need is the name of somebody who can give me an inside track. Somebody who knows somebody."

He shakes his head, smoothing the mustache he's so proud of. "Why don't you talk to that bunch of motorcycle fellows you were friendly with a while back?"

"They're good people. I don't think they'd be hooked up with dogfighting."

"Maybe so, but I was thinking that a lot of different types of people come through their shop, and it seems to me like your same guy who has a yen for dogfighting might have a love for speed on a motorcycle."

"Good thought. I'll go see Walter Dunn on Friday."

We chew the fat some more. LoPresto just finished up a huge project of a big shopping mall in Bobtail, and he says he ought to be happy to have some rest time, but he's bored.

"Well, don't get into any trouble," I say. He doesn't laugh. He's been that route and it still stings.

I'm at Jenny's at noon. She greets me at the door with her hair up in a towel.

"Uh oh, I'm early. I'll come back."

"No, come on in and sit down. Will is going to be in the kitchen in five minutes." She looks down at the box I've brought with the sleeping puppy in it. "Oh, look at the little sweetheart. He doesn't look very old. What kind is he? Or she?"

I tell her the pertinent details, and when Will appears she heads back to dry her hair.

I like Will Landreau, partly because he's got a good sense of humor, but partly because he seems to have made Jenny happy. In the months since they've been a couple, her defenses have broken down more than I thought might have been possible. I've seen her have some moments of real lightheartedness with him. He's a couple of inches taller than her six feet, and lanky, with hair he wears barely above his collar. With his wire-rimmed glasses, he looks like a throwback from the 1960s.

He leads me into the kitchen, which has changed significantly since I first met Jenny. Her main source of nourishment before she started dating Will was cheese and crackers, whatever she brought home from a fast-food place, or whatever I brought over for her to eat. Now there are bowls on the counters with actual food in them—one with onions and potatoes in it, another with fruit. Her cabinets now contain ingredients for making meals.

Will sets me chopping onions and celery for the stuffing while he gets the bird out of the refrigerator. The turkey he brings out looks like it weighs thirty pounds. He lowers it into the sink with a grunt.

"It's going to take until midnight to cook a bird that big," I say.

He laughs. "It'll be done by five, since I'm going to cook it before I do the stuffing."

"What kind of stuffing are we making?" I ask.

He groans. "Not you, too. Jenny and I almost came to blows. I like a good cornbread dressing, and she swore that the only kind she'll eat is bread dressing because that's what her mamma used to make."

"Who won?"

He grins and pushes the glasses up on his nose. "I reminded her that she told me her mamma was a terrible cook. She had to admit I was right and said she's willing to try my dressing."

"Why such a big bird?"

"Jenny ordered it. She didn't have the first idea how much to order for six of us."

"Six?"

"Didn't she tell you? We invited a guy I work with, and he's bringing his wife and mother-in-law. We've never met her, but she sounds interesting. She's a widow from College Station."

Will and I work well together, and before long the aroma of turkey fills the air. I may not particularly like turkey, but it smells good when it's cooking. Besides turkey and dressing, we're fixing green beans, corn, and sweet potatoes. At the last minute Jenny comes in and insists that it won't be Thanksgiving without mashed potatoes. So we work those in, too.

The three guests come before we're ready for them. Everyone crowds into the kitchen to talk to us while we put the finishing touches on everything. Wendy Gleason, the mother-in-law, has a lilting voice and a sparkle in her eyes. She tends to the skinny side except for a very nice bosom, shown off by a green sweater that matches her eyes. Her mass of blondish hair falls to her shoulders. It's untamed and makes her look like a free spirit.

She offers to help, but Will shoos her away. "Samuel and I are a team. We don't need any women butting in."

She has a hearty laugh. I can't help grinning. "All right. I know when I'm under-appreciated. We'll stand around and keep you entertained." She picks up the puppy and cradles him. "You're going to get stepped on with all these people in here."

By the time the turkey is done and we sit down to eat, the conversation has warmed up. I discover that, like me, Wendy's spouse died a while ago, but unlike me she hasn't wasted time getting back out into the world. "My husband was a wonderful man in some ways, but he never liked to travel. He went with me sometimes to please me, but it was never his passion. I love to go places." She has been to India and Bali, which make her seem very exotic. Most people I know who have traveled outside the state of Texas have headed straight for Europe. I ask what made her choose the East.

"I love Europe. James and I went there a few times. It feels safe to me, but I wanted adventure. I have a couple of friends who like to travel, and we go all together."

Her daughter, Jessica, is a quiet person who seems to be overwhelmed by her mother. When Wendy tells a racy story about a cruise in the Bahamas last year, Jessica and her husband Ron exchange alarmed glances. But I find Wendy refreshing. Maybe it's because of the wine I drank while we cooked, but I feel a devilish impulse to ask her questions that encourage her to tell wild stories. She cuts her eyes at me and then at her daughter with a little shake of her head. "Later," she says. I notice her watching me a couple of times.

After we've eaten too much food and drunk too much wine, nobody feels like moving. Typical Thanksgiving, with everybody stuffed. We've promised each other we're going to take a walk before we have any dessert, but so far nobody has followed through. "I can't wait to taste your lemon pie," Jenny says to Wendy. Lemon pie. Uh oh, my favorite dessert. I like the kind Ellen makes. What if I like Wendy's better? I already feel like I'm in trouble.

Now that we've eaten, the puppy has been allowed in to explore the dining room.

"You need a name for him," Jenny says.

"I don't want to name him," I say. "I'm not going to be able to keep him. I don't have the time to raise a dog."

Wendy bursts out laughing.

"What's so funny?"

"Do you have any idea what your face looks like when you look at that puppy? He's yours whether you like it or not."

Heat creeps up my neckline.

"Where does he sleep?" she asks, her eyes dancing.

"In a box."

"Really?" It's like she has seen right through me.

"Mostly."

She arches a mischievous eyebrow at me. "You let him sleep with you, don't you?"

"Just once," I plead, and we laugh.

"He looks like he's being rolling in the dust," she says. "You could call him Dusty."

"He's the color of stone," Jenny says. "Stony would be a good name."

"Or Ghost," Ron says. He has contributed little to the table conversation, but has perked up at the idea of naming the puppy.

"You could call him after one of your favorite artists," Will says. "Call him Wolf, or what's the name of the guy who does the cakes?"

"You mean Wayne Thiebaud?" Wendy says, cocking her head at Will. She turns to me. "You're interested in art?"

"You should see his collection," Will says. Will is one of the few people around here who knows enough to appreciate my art collection.

"Let's go see it." She gets up. "We need to take a walk anyway."

Everybody grabs a handful of dishes to take into the kitchen. "I'll stay here and get this cleaned up," Will says. "You all go get the grand tour."

Jenny argues that she'll feel guilty leaving him with a mess. But he prevails and the rest of us go over to my place to take a look around. I start to take the puppy with me, but Will says to leave him in his box and he'll keep an eye on him.

I'm curious to know how Wendy will react to seeing my art. Because I have lived with it for so long, I tend to forget how unusual it is for a man in a small country town to have a valuable art collection. When my wife's mother died, she left us some valuable paintings, but Jeanne and I gave most of those to museums. We preferred to hang the things we bought together—mostly work from the Cali-

113

fornia school, like Richard Diebenkorn and Paul Wonner. I also have a Frederick Remington that doesn't fit with the others, but which I liked from the minute I saw it a couple of years ago. But my favorite is still a Wolf Kahn that we bought a few years before Jeanne died and which I've never gotten tired of.

Wendy is uncharacteristically quiet as we walk through the spare bedroom, the hallway, the dining room, and back to the living room. It's her daughter and son-in-law who *ooh* and *aah*. But when we're done, Wendy slips her arm through mine as we walk out the door. "What a joy to spend your days with those paintings," she says quietly. "I thought someone said you had a Wayne Thiebaud cake painting."

I tell her that I gave it to the Modern Art Museum in Houston. "It was never my favorite, and I can go visit it whenever I want to. It sounds like you like his art."

"I do. All that food! But he also did some nice paintings of San Francisco. It's one of my favorite cities." For some reason I have an instant fantasy of being in San Francisco with her.

Back at Jenny's there is pumpkin pie and the dangerous lemon pie. I had a bad feeling that I was going to really like the lemon pie, and I'm right.

Without my realizing it, dusk has crept up and I get up from the table. "Sorry, I've got to look in on my cows and get Dusty taken care of."

"So it's Dusty, is it?" Will grins.

"Seems right. An uncomplicated name," I say.

"You need to take some leftovers," Jenny says.

Wendy jumps up from the table. "I'll carry the leftovers to your house so you can take the puppy. Dusty, I mean."

I'm not enthusiastic about taking a lot of turkey, but I'm fine with the big wedge of lemon pie that Wendy tucks onto a plate.

"I'll be back before too long," she says to her daughter as we leave.

When we get the food put away in my kitchen, Wendy says. "Can I come and see your cows?"

"You've already seen my art," I say. "You might as well see the cows, too."

While we walk down to the pasture, she slips her arm through mine again, and I wonder if it's so she doesn't trip on the uneven ground, or if it's a signal of some kind. I've never been good at reading those things.

It's almost dark, but the cows crowd over to the fence to see who I've brought down here. Wendy reaches over the wooden fence and scratches a couple of them on the forehead. "Herefords are such sturdy cows," she says.

"You know Herefords?"

"My daddy kept a small herd. I always liked to go with him to tend to them. I miss them." She shivers suddenly. "I should have brought my coat." She turns her back to the cows and leans against the fence, her arms crossed. It's almost dark, but her eyes shine at me. "I've had fun today. We should get together."

"I'd like that," I say, and I would.

"Good. Then that's settled." She steps toward me and slips her arms around my waist under my jacket, head tilted up in an inviting way. It seems like the most natural thing in the world to lean down and kiss her. Her lips are soft and taste like lemon pie. Or maybe it's my imagination.

"Mamma, we need to get going." The voice drifts from somewhere near the front of my house.

"Oh, shoot." Wendy chuckles and gives me a last hug before she pulls away. "Maybe you should come for dinner tomorrow night."

I tell her I'd like that. My heart is hammering as we walk up to the house, partly because I'm feeling guilty at how much I enjoyed that kiss, and partly because I can't wait to see her again.

CHAPTER 14

I wake to the sound of rain, and see that I've overslept. Dusty is snoozing at the end of the bed, which may be why Zelda has nestled in next to me. It looks like I have a dog. I'm not quite sure how I feel about that. I consider how I would feel if I got a call from the owners who lost the pup's mother. Would I be sorry to see him go, or relieved?

For now, the question is, how is he going to respond to going outside in the rain? As if he understands what I'm thinking, he puts his paws over his face and wriggles.

I'm thinking all of this by way of avoiding the topic of Wendy Gleason. I intended to take my mind off Ellen, but I didn't intend for it to happen that way.

Thank goodness the phone rings, and I have to get up to answer it. And then I wish I hadn't. "And what might your plan be now?" Jenny's voice is amused, but knowing her I suspect she isn't altogether okay with me sneaking around with Wendy behind Ellen's back.

"I don't have one."

"Is that why you've got a date to see Wendy Gleason tonight?"

"What time is it? News travels fast."

"It's eight o'clock. Jess was on the phone with me an hour ago, wondering if you were a good person. I wasn't sure what to tell her." She snickers.

"I just got up. Let me call in a while when I've had a cup of coffee."

"I'm on my way to work. Some of us have a sense of responsibility." She hangs up, leaving me laughing.

It turns out that Dusty doesn't care if it's raining. He takes care of business and gives himself a little shake as soon as he's inside, and promptly falls over from the motion. I get a good laugh out of it. I take him into the bathroom and towel him off.

Over coffee, I complain to Dusty because I'm eating plain toast since Loretta is out of town. I could use a piece of her coffee cake about now. Then I remember Wendy's lemon pie. Turns out it goes down well with coffee.

I remind myself that I actually have a job to do. Dusty and I get to the office at nine o'clock.

The first thing I do is call the garage to have Lewis Wilkins's SUV picked up. There are a few new, minor matters to tend to. Ollie Olson has left a message that someone painted his car with slogans. I go over to see him and can't help laughing. Ollie is something of a ladies' man, and apparently he has ticked off his current ladylove. The slogans have to do with his philandering ways. When I point out that the "paint" is lipstick, he grumbles, but I tell him unless he wants me to put his friend in jail, maybe it's best to just wash the car and not make too much of it.

Then there is a garden issue to deal with, which is mostly a way for Nellie Black to get some attention. She's always complaining that the neighbor's terrier digs up the garden. The garden in question is lying fallow for the fall, so there can't be much damage. But I spend a little time chatting with Nellie. It turns out her daughter didn't come home for Thanksgiving and she feels sorry for herself.

Finally, I have some free time to go over and talk to people at the lake whose properties border on the woods where Lewis Wilkins's body was found, to find out if they heard anything unusual the night he was killed. A couple of the houses are locked up tight, so it's unlikely that anyone was around to hear anything. Of the others that might have been in earshot, they've all heard about the body being found, but none of them has anything useful to add to the information I have.

One woman is here alone and wants to know if I think she should be worried. "Usually my husband comes with me, but he's on a trip and I wanted to come out here and get away from it all. I've always wanted to write a book, and that's what I'm doing."

I tell her to lock her doors. "And get to know your neighbors. Have their phone numbers handy in case you need help."

When I run out of people to talk to in the immediate vicinity, I sit in my car and stare at the lake through the rain-streaked windshield and consider my next moves. Lewis Wilkins made a terrible mistake with a patient and paid for it dearly after a lawsuit. Now he has been brutally murdered. I need to dig deeper to find out if the two things are connected.

In addition to the medical situation, his family seemed to have gone off-kilter. His kids were angry, his wife anxious, and he had become secretive. Was he having an affair that went wrong? His only friend in town, Dooley Phillips, claims that if he was, Dooley never saw signs of it.

To cloud the issue there's an abandoned SUV with a brand-new gun in it and a boat that has never been used, despite Wilkins telling his wife frequently that he was going fishing. I'm having trouble making sense of it all.

I've been putting off tackling Wilkins's computer. It's locked up back at the office. I know how to use a computer, but I'm not an expert, and I don't have much of an idea what to look for. Still, I can take a look at his e-mails, the history of what he looked at on the Internet, and see if he has any files that might tell me something useful.

First I drop by Town Café and grab a bowl of chili. Seems like the perfect meal on a rainy day. Everybody must be home eating leftovers, because the place is almost deserted, which is fine by me. Being alone gives me a chance to argue with myself about whether I ought to call Wendy Gleason and beg off going to her place tonight. The conclusion I come to is that I will go, but I'll tell her that I am involved with someone else. Even though Ellen and I don't have a formal understanding, I would consider it two-timing to see Wendy on the sly.

Opening up someone's computer is the same as digging into a woman's handbag. It feels like a personal violation. But of course this man is dead, and I'm going to look through the computer in order to get a handle on what he might have been up to that got him killed.

As Margaret suggested, her husband's computer password is the same one he used for his phone, and as far as I can see his computer setup is typical. He has icons at the bottom of the screen that show he has the usual array of applications. What I'm interested in is his e-mails. He has a number of folders set up for the usual—banking, receipts, personal e-mails, and so on. But the one that catches my eye is called "Mal," which I take to mean "malpractice."

It sounds innocuous enough, but what I find stuns me. It's a daily exercise in hatred. The woman who sued Wilkins was not satisfied with money. She wanted her pound of flesh as well. I scroll down day after day of e-mails from her describing to him the struggles she faces. Fury springs off every page. "You are not fit to be called a doctor. You are a devil who steals people's lives. I hope your life is one day as blighted as mine." This goes on, stretching back for months.

Why did he keep them? Did he feel guilty? I wonder why he didn't change his e-mail address, or delete the messages unread. It's possible that he reported them to the police or to an attorney and was instructed to keep them. It occurs to me that despite Wilkins's daughter's claim that he never took responsibility for his error, maybe he did feel guilty and those e-mails felt like proper punishment.

And why did she send them? Does a mistake and revenge have to be perpetuated forever? It's like some epic struggle between two people in hell. Such hatred can eat at a person. Did this woman finally break and decide the only way she could be satisfied was to know he was dead? Did she arrange for him to be killed?

I wonder if Wilkins ever told his wife about the messages. Surely she would have told me. Or maybe he did tell her, but she never saw them and didn't realize how venomous they were.

I go through other e-mails but find nothing else of note. Then I start on the Internet history. Lewis Wilkins seemed interested in guns and an odd assortment of online betting pools for sports. He looked up a lot of gun shows. Most gun shows are in big-city convention centers, but the ones he noted are in small to mid-size towns. And then I remember Harley Lunsford's comments about the connection between dogfighting and gun shows. The gun shows Wilkins looked up would be ideal places for illegal dogfighting sites. Was that what got him killed?

The phone rings. It's Doc England. "I heard from somebody else who had a dog taken. I think it's high time something got done. This poor woman lives by herself out on the outskirts of town, and that dog was everything to her."

"When did the dog disappear?"

"Last night. She left him out because she's had a problem with foxes getting into her chickens."

"She didn't hear anything?"

"I didn't ask her. She was feeling pretty bad."

"I'll go out and talk to her."

When I hang up, I want to kick something. Whoever has taken those dogs has got to be found.

I call the woman whose dog got taken and she says she'd rather wait until tomorrow to talk to me, that a neighbor has come over and she's too upset to talk now.

It's late afternoon, and Dusty is trying to climb out of his box and practicing a squeaky sound that will most likely become a bark one day. I'm ready to call it a day. It's raining hard, so I rummage around in the closet and find a piece of heavy plastic to throw over the box. I dash out to my truck and shove it into the passenger seat. By the time I climb into the cab, I'm drenched. Between the rain and Thanksgiving food hangover, the whole town is quiet as a tomb. I don't meet one car on the road on my way home.

I leave Dusty inside the house while I go down to the pasture to check on the cows. Several of them are huddled in the shed, out of the rain, with another handful standing under trees. There are always a few that don't seem the least bit bothered by weather.

While I get ready to drive over to Bryan to see Wendy, I admit to myself that I'm nervous. Nervous like I remember from when I was a teenager. I try to think if I've ever felt like this with Ellen, even when we first started seeing each other. I don't know what it means that I don't think I did. It always seemed like we just got along well.

I fuss over whether to wear jeans or khaki pants and what shirt I should wear. Once I turn to see Dusty watching me, and I swear he has a smirk on his face. "What are you looking at?" I ask.

He takes that as an invitation to rush at one of my boots that has fallen over. They're my fancy boots, black, hand-tooled. I bought them in Austin a few years ago and haven't worn them much. "You leave teeth marks on those boots at your peril," I say.

Wendy lives in a sprawling ranch-style house in an older part of town, on what I estimate to be at least a half-acre lot surrounded by a rustic crisscrossed log fence. The front yard, lit up by outdoor spotlights, is a grassy expanse dotted with pecan trees. There's a hammock slung between two trees with a table next to it. I imagine Wendy lying out there, reading with a glass of iced tea at hand.

When I ring the doorbell, the door is opened by a teenaged girl who appears to have been crying. She's short and a little pudgy, with a round face sprinkled with acne. For a second I wonder if I have the wrong address, but she calls out, "Aunt Wendy, he's here."

Wendy comes rushing in, wearing an oversized apron and holding a wooden spoon. As she approaches behind the teenager, she makes a "zip it" motion across her lips, nodding toward the girl and raising her eyebrows.

I hold my hand out to the girl and introduce myself. She hesitates and looks back at her aunt as if unsure whether she should shake hands with me "This is my niece, Tammy. Say hello, Tammy," she says.

The girl shakes my hand, ducking her head.

Wendy takes me by the arm. "Come on in. I hope you like lasagna. It's my specialty."

"I like Italian food." I've brought a bottle of wine, and I hold it out to her. "Red. I hope that goes with it."

"Perfect." Her eyes hold mine, and then she says, "Tammy, would you take this into the kitchen?"

As soon as the girl is gone, Wendy whispers, "I'm so sorry. She showed up on my doorstep an hour ago. She and her mom had a big fight. I couldn't turn her away."

"Of course not. But I have to tell you, the puppy is in the car. He can stay there if . . ."

The girl is back in a flash, as if she sensed that we were going to talk about her.

"Bring him in right now!" Wendy says.

Tammy looks suspicious. "Bring who in?"

"You'll see."

I bring the box into the entry, aware, as I set it down, that it's starting to look shabby. The puppy has been chewing on it and scratching at the bottom.

Tammy squeals when she sees the puppy. I tell her his name is Dusty. Wendy grins. "You like that name, huh?"

After that, Tammy carries Dusty everywhere and sticks to us like glue, as if she has been assigned to make sure Wendy and I behave ourselves. Wendy makes a couple of efforts to get rid of her, asking if she has homework (*I did it at school*), asking if she wants to use her computer (*nope*), and if she wants to watch TV (*there's nothing on*).

The meal is delicious, and Wendy manages to keep up a lively conversation, even though Tammy is not a happy child and complains about school and her teachers; about her mother (apparently her father is a saint); and about her conniving best friend. Once, when Tammy is rattling on about her math teacher, Wendy catches my eye and lifts an eyebrow. Then I feel her foot rub against my leg. After that, it's all I can do to follow what the girl is saying and make appropriate comments.

Finally Wendy says, "Tammy are you still seeing that same boy?"

Tammy's eyes flash. "You mean Duck?"

"The one your mother doesn't approve of?"

"She refuses to get to know him. He's really nice."

"Nice enough to get arrested for attempted burglary?"

Tammy's hands curl into fists. "She told you that? Did she also tell you it was a misunderstanding? He didn't intend to rob anyone. He went to the wrong house. He was looking for a friend of his." Her lower lip juts out.

"Honey, it's hard for me to believe that. What does your daddy say?"

She shrugs. "He goes along with whatever *she* says." She shoots a resentful glance at me. "Do we have to talk about it in front of a stranger?"

"Not if you don't want to. I thought it might be interesting to get Samuel's perspective on your friend Donald, since he's chief of police over in Jarrett Creek."

The girl sits up straight. "He's a chief of police?" Her lip curls. "He looks like a regular person."

"That may be the nicest thing anybody has said about me this month," I say, trying to lighten the mood. "Your friend's name is Donald?"

She shrugs. "Everybody calls him Duck." She says it without a hint of humor.

"Why don't you tell me Duck's version of what happened?"

Wendy does the footsie thing again, so it must have been the right thing to say.

"Well . . ." Tammy draws out the word, suddenly shy now that she's been given the floor. "Just before school started in the fall, him and his friend Gordy were supposed to hang out. Gordy told Duck where he was going to be, but when Duck got there nobody answered the door. Duck thought maybe Gordy was around back, so he went into the backyard." She looks uneasily between Wendy and me. "And then the cops showed up, and they were really rough on him." She's left a noticeable gap between Duck going into the backyard and the police arriving.

"What do you mean rough on him?" I ask.

With an injured tone, she says, "They handcuffed him and threw him on the floor." The floor. Not the ground. Which means he was inside the house.

"So he was inside the house?"

"The door was unlocked. He thought it was okay to go inside."

Wendy gets up and quietly starts taking dishes into the kitchen.

"Why wasn't his friend there?" I ask.

"He gave Duck the wrong address. It wasn't Duck's fault!"

"So when Duck's friend Gordy told the police that Duck was telling the truth, they released him?" I doubt this, but I want to ask the question in such a way that she can see it's a reasonable assumption, and maybe it will help her draw a more rational conclusion than she has.

"No. That rat Gordy said he didn't know anything about it."

"I see. Then they probably didn't charge Duck, because unless somebody has been in trouble before, police will usually give people the benefit of the doubt—unless he had broken into the house, of course."

"I told you, the door was unlocked! He didn't have to break in."

"Exactly where did they find him?" Wendy is standing in the kitchen door.

"You don't believe him, either. I can tell." She juts her lower lip out like a three-year-old.

"Just trying to picture exactly what happened."

"I don't want to talk about it anymore. Can I play with Dusty?"

"Let's have dessert first," Wendy says.

She serves chess pie. "It's been a long time since I had chess pie." If I see more of Wendy, she's going to fatten me up. The thought catches me up short. What do I mean *if I see more of her*? I have no intention of two-timing Ellen. It's unfortunate that Tammy is here, as I haven't had a chance to tell Wendy that I have a prior commitment. Well, not commitment exactly, but prior interest.

The phone rings in the kitchen, and Wendy says, "That will be your mother."

"I don't want to talk to her," Tammy says.

Wendy goes off to answer it, and as the minutes stretch on with a low murmur, I try to think of something to talk to Tammy about, but I come up empty. When Wendy comes back, she says, "Your mamma wants to come over and talk."

I get up. "That sounds like my cue to get on the road."

"You don't have to," Wendy says.

"I've got a lot to do tomorrow."

She sees me to the door and closes it behind her, even though it's chilly. "I'm really sorry we didn't have time to get better acquainted," she says, and puts her hands on my chest. "Do you suppose we could try again?"

"I . . ."

Before I can say anything else, she gets on tiptoes and slips her arms around my neck and kisses me. I pull her in close. And I tell her that yes, we should definitely try again. "But let me take you out." I name a restaurant that I've been to a couple of times when I had business here in Bryan. "Tomorrow night?"

She hesitates. "Let me make sure Tammy is gone by then. I can't leave her here alone."

CHAPTER 15

I'm up earlier than usual Saturday morning, having tossed and turned most of the night. Nothing like being confused about a woman to make it hard to sleep.

I swear Dusty has grown a couple of inches in the night. He wriggles up to me on the bed, tumbling over himself. When he gets to my face, he nuzzles me and does the squeak that passes for barking. From her perch on the adjacent pillow, Zelda judges him not fit for bothering with. I pull on jeans and a uniform shirt and take him outside for his morning constitutional. The rain has gone, leaving the air fresh and crisp.

I feed Dusty and put him in his box, but it's clear that in a few days, he'll be able to jump out of it. I wonder if I shouldn't get him a real bed. Or a sturdier box. Ellen keeps Frazier in a crate at night, but I never liked the idea, even though he seems fine with it. I wonder how Frazier is going to take to the puppy? And I wonder why I haven't heard anymore from Ellen?

After I feed the cows, I take Dusty down to headquarters. Bill Odum is supposed to be back at work today and Maria will be back Monday, so it won't seem so deserted.

On my way home last night, I passed by Walter Dunn's motorcycle shop out on the highway, and I remembered that I had planned to call him to ask whether he knows anyone who might be involved in dogfighting. When I call the shop, the answering machine says they won't be open until noon, which gives me time to go over and check in on Margaret Wilkins's family and ask her about some of the things I found on Wilkins's computer.

People are still on Thanksgiving time, and there's not much activity anywhere. Smoke is coming out of the chimney at the Wilkins house. Margaret answers the door. Her face is pale and bleak. She gives me a cup of coffee, and we sit in the living room, where she has a fire in the fireplace. There's no sign of her kids. She says Emily went back to Houston last night, and Dan has gone off to buy light bulbs and will be back soon.

"I looked at your husband's computer, and I wanted to ask you a couple of things. Were you aware that the woman who brought the lawsuit against your husband was writing him hate mail?"

She looks startled. "No, he never said a word about that." Red spots flare in her cheeks. "What kind of hate mail? Threats?"

"Not direct threats, but certainly she bore a grudge. Did she have a family other than her husband?"

"I know she had a son, because he came to some of the trial proceedings."

"How old?"

"She's in her sixties, so he's maybe forty."

"Do you know where he lives?"

"I assumed he was from San Antonio, since he came to the trial, but I could be wrong."

"Why did your husband decide to fight the case? Wouldn't it have been easier to settle?"

Her eyes flash. "He was stubborn. He thought he would win." She looks like she could say more, but she shakes her head and is done. It makes me wish I had met the man. It's hard to get a clear picture of him from what people say about him. One minute Margaret is a loving wife, and the next she's bitter toward him. His kids seem to have mixed feelings as well. Even as loyal as Dooley was, his description of Wilkins was sprinkled with negatives.

"The other thing is, your husband seemed to be into sports betting. Were you aware of that?"

"What kind of sports?"

"He did online betting."

"So that's what he was doing on the computer all the time! Did he make any money at it?"

"That I don't know. Did he ever play poker with friends when he was in San Antonio?"

"Occasionally. A few of the doctors would get together every now and then and play. Not recently though. Not since . . ." Since the lawsuit, which turned their lives upside down.

When I get back to headquarters, Bill Odum is there. He's pale and his eyes are weepy and his nose is red.

"Have you got a cold?"

"That or the flu. I never get sick, but I feel like hell."

"Well, don't stay around here and give it to everybody."

"I figured you could use a break." He looks at the box I'm carrying. "What have you got?"

I put the box down and put Dusty on the floor.

"A puppy? What are you doing with that?" His listless response tell me he doesn't feel good. Normally he'd be all over Dusty.

I tell him how I came by Dusty. "Now why don't you scoot out of here."

"I hate to flake on you."

"I'll live. I'm working on the investigation of that man who was killed out at the lake, so I'd be here anyway."

I'm relieved when he leaves. I don't want him giving me or Dusty his nasty cold. I phone High Ride Motorcycle Repair and ask to speak to Walter Dunn.

"A voice from the past," I say, when he comes on the line.

"I'll be damned," Dunn says. "It's been a while. You looking to buy a Harley and take off on a road trip?"

"Maybe next time. I need to ask you to help me with some information."

I don't like leaving Dusty in the box so much, so I call the vet's office and see if I can leave him there for a while. Chelsea says to bring him on over. "We're busy, but I can put him in a cage."

I don't like the idea of a cage, but I guess it's not that much different from leaving him in a box in the jail cell, and I suspect she'll give him as much attention as she can. When I get him there she makes a fuss over him. "He's grown!"

"It's only been a few days."

"At this age they grow so fast! Besides, he was undernourished and he has some catching up to do. Oh, he's going to be a beautiful dog. You never got in touch with those people?"

"I went over there, and they've moved."

"Well, you'll find somebody to take him after the holidays are over. We can put up a notice on the bulletin board if you want to."

"Maybe later."

I pick up Walter Dunn from the motorcycle shop at noon and we go over to the barbecue place nearby. First we catch up on news. He and his wife have had a baby since I last saw him. "A boy. His name is Jackson, but we call him Jack." His good friend Jack was killed a while back, which is how I met him. He digs his cell phone out and shows me a picture of a hefty baby.

"He's going to be as big as you," I say.

"Sure looks like it." Walter beams. "Now what's this mysterious business you've called me out for?"

"Walter, have you ever had anybody in the shop who talked about dogfighting?"

A long sigh escapes him. "Yep."

"Really?" Even though LoPresto said motorcycles and dogfighting might have some crossover, I hadn't really expected Walter Dunn to confirm it.

He leans forward and clasps his hands. "We run a business. You can't turn people away just because you don't like their lifestyle. But that doesn't mean you have to like everybody."

"Does it happen often?"

"No, but there are a couple of regulars who like to talk it up. What's this about?"

"It may be nothing. I'm trying make sense out of something that happened."

Our barbecue sandwiches arrive, piled high and slathered with barbecue sauce, along with potato salad and pickles. We're quiet for a couple of minutes while we tackle the food. After a couple of bites, I wipe my face and say, "When was the last time somebody mentioned dogfights?"

"Three weeks ago? A month? Let me tell you, having a new baby in the house takes away some of your ability to process time. My memory sometimes doesn't seem to be what it should. But I do know it wasn't that long ago."

"Did they say there are fights around here?"

"I couldn't tell you."

"Let me tell you what's going on. We had a man killed over at the lake a few days before Thanksgiving. He was attacked by dogs. His hands had been tied, so he couldn't defend himself."

He grimaces and takes a swig of his beer. "That's a nasty way to go. And you connected that with dogfighting?"

"I found some things that made me suspect he attended dogfights. And if he did, he was likely betting on them . . ."

"I know there are people who get into that big-time."

"The reason I was asking if there have been any dogfights around here is because some dogs have gone missing in the area recently, apparently stolen. Somebody told me people who train fighting dogs sometimes use stolen animals as bait dogs."

130

"I guess I shouldn't be surprised. I'll tell you something that may surprise you, though. The guys who come in and talk up the fights don't really look like the kind of people you would point to as trouble. Most of them dress like you or me and seem real friendly and easy to get along with. You wouldn't know they had a sadistic streak, which is what I think drives some of those people."

"Do you think you could arrange for me to have a talk with one of them off the record, see if I can find out more about it?"

He sighs. "You sure you want to do that? From what little I know these people live by a different code than the rest of us. And they don't think highly of the law."

"I don't have a choice." I don't tell him that every part of my being is repulsed and infuriated by the subject. "Dogfighting and having somebody sic their dogs on a man who can't defend himself is bad enough, and the idea of using pets for bait adds insult to injury. I can't let go of it."

Dunn finishes up and starts chewing on a toothpick. "Well, they may be tough guys, but, knowing you, I think they'd be better off holding those fights in another county."

"I wish it was that easy. Do you think you could set up a meeting for me?"

He's slow to respond. "Why me?"

"I don't know who else to ask. If you can't help me, I suppose I can hang around a gun show and see if I can't get a lead."

"Talk to one of your Texas Ranger friends. They might have a connection, or know something that will help you out. Anyway, I'll see what I can do from my end. It's a nasty business and I don't want to get too close to it."

A RECKONING IN THE BACK COUNTRY

Wilkins's SUV was towed into the Texaco service station down the block from headquarters, and I take my crime scene kit over there to inspect it more thoroughly. As I approach the vehicle, I notice something I didn't see the other night. It has what looks like a brand-new, substantial trailer hitch on the back bumper. It's larger than a standard hitch that people use for horse or cattle trailers. It looks like Wilkins was intending to take his boat somewhere.

The thing about an SUV is that it's wide open and there aren't many places to hide things. I pull on some gloves and go back through every place I looked the other night, with the same results. There is not so much as a piece of lint under the seats, and the items in the console compartment—lip balm, change for parking meters, pens, breath mints, and a small packet of tissues—are arranged neatly.

I don't know where the spare tire is kept. I flip the back seats forward and see the edge of the mat. I peel it back to reveal a square inset with a pull tab. I pull it up, and suddenly it gets interesting. Instead of a spare tire, the compartment contains a navy-blue canvas bag the size of a large grocery sack. I open it and peer inside. It's broad daylight, but I still have trouble believing what I see. I smooth the mat back over the place where the tire should be and gently shake out the contents of the bag onto the mat.

In neat stacks tied by rubber bands are ten bundles of cash. The first one I thumb through is twenties. There are four of those, two stacks of hundreds, and the rest are tens. I remember reading somewhere that one inch of hundred-dollar bills is a little under twenty-five thousand dollars. These stacks are about three inches each. I do a little mental math, and my rough estimate is that there is a little under two hundred thousand here. I'm startled by voices and glance behind me to see two men walking away from the service station. They pay no attention to me, but I become acutely aware of the casual way in which this money is lying in the back of the SUV. I scoop it up and put it back into the bag.

Then I peruse the rest of the items I had dumped out of the bag.

132

There's a flashlight, a handful of energy bars, a baseball hat with no logo, a large bottle of vitamins, and a passport. I shake the bottle, and it sounds like pills, so I open it and pour some out into my palm. The bottle contains a variety of pills—some over-the-counter acetaminophen and three or four other types of pills with no identification. The one item remaining, the passport, might hold the key to all of the rest of it. In the photo Wilkins looks like a thug, but it's unmistakably him. So why is the name on the passport "Leonard Wilson"?

"You find anything interesting?"

I jump as Alvin's voice speaks almost directly into my ear. He's the owner of the Texaco.

"Not sure," I say, palming the passport. "Car's pretty clean."

He peers inside. He's a scrawny guy with a wisp of a goatee and thinning hair. "I don't believe I've ever seen such a clean car unless it's right off the lot," he says.

We pass the time of day a little longer, and then he ambles back to the garage. I check for any other surprises, but it looks like one canvas bag is enough.

I'm extra careful crossing the highway back to headquarters since I'm toting a bag with two hundred thousand dollars with me. I carry it inside and take out everything but the money and put it into a plastic bag, and lock that in the top drawer of the file cabinet, something I rarely have the need to do.

Now I have to figure out what to do with a canvas bag full of money. It's Saturday afternoon and the bank is closed, but I can't keep it here. Finally I call Ed Patrick, the manager of Citizens Bank and tell him I've got a special deposit and he agrees to come down to open up and take charge of the money. I lock the canvas bag in the trunk of the squad car and drive down the street to the bank to wait for him. While I wait, it occurs to me that I might be dealing with a wad of counterfeit money, but once he gets there and examines the money, Ed assures me it's real.

"Where did you get this much money?"

"It's a police matter. I'll need to put it in a safe deposit box for Jarrett Creek PD."

He tells me that will take some paperwork, and it will have to wait until Monday. "Meanwhile, we'll put it on a special hold under your name as chief."

"I want to be sure if anything happens to me, it will be accessible to the Department of Public Safety."

He has me sign a paper to that effect and gives me a copy for the office files.

CHAPTER 16

Relieved when the money is safely in the bank, I retrieve my dog from the vet's office. He seems happy to see me, wriggling all over and making little huffing noises. On impulse, I buy him a chew bone that Chelsea says will be okay for him.

Back at headquarters I set him on the floor to attack the chew bone while I take stock of what I've found out in the SUV. It looks like Lewis Wilkins was intending to skip out. Money plus passport in a different name equals running. I wonder if the new trailer hitch could be part of the plan. Maybe he was planning to take his boat down south, put it in the water on the coast, and head for Mexico. Did he even know how to attach a boat to a trailer hitch? I recall seeing boats pulled behind vehicles, and he'd need a trailer, too. I can't help thinking that if that was Wilkins's plan, Dooley must have known. Without help, how would Wilkins have gotten the boat onto the trailer and away from the marina?

If he was leaving, was he running from something or to something? If his family knew of his plans, they've been awfully cagey. Did anyone know?

More to the point, I wonder where the money came from. He was a gambler, so likely it's his winnings. But did he win it at cards? Or was it from dogfighting?

While I'm mulling it over, the phone rings. I pick it up without thinking who it could be.

"Hi." Ellen sounds breathless.

For a few seconds I'm stuck for words, feeling a guilt that is like a kick in the gut. Followed immediately by my silent argument to myself that I have nothing to feel guilty for. She's the one who went away this weekend—and stayed at her ex-husband's house. For all I know, they were in the same bedroom.

"Samuel? Are you there?"

"Yes, yes. I was just doing something."

"Should I call you back?"

"No. I'm fine. How are you?" As soon as the words are out, they sound awkward. I can't seem to help being wrong-footed with Ellen.

But she seems not to notice. "Good. I'm good. How was Thanksgiving at Jenny's?"

Besides my getting bamboozled by a woman, like a teenager? "Um, Will is a really good cook."

She laughs. "Good thing. I can imagine what Jenny would have done to a turkey. Was it just the three of you?"

If only. "No. There was a couple there from Bobtail that Jenny and Will work with." *And the girl's mother.* "And the girl's mother."

"That's nice. Did you have fun?"

"I guess. When are you coming home?"

"Um, that's why I was calling. I decided to stay on a few more days."

Two thoughts hit me simultaneously. One is a jealous stab, wondering if she's going to stay on at her ex-husband's place. The other is that now I can see more of Wendy.

"I'm going to stay at my daughter's place," she says. "We thought it would be fun to do a little shopping together."

"Sounds good." Why am I having so much trouble coming up with something to say?

"Are you okay? You sound distracted."

At last, something I can hang onto. "This case I've got. It's growing tentacles."

"Oh, that's too bad. Or maybe not. It means even if I had come back tomorrow you'd be too busy for us to get together anyway."

I should protest and tell her that I'd surely find time, but instead what pops out of my mouth is, "You're probably right. There's a lot to it."

"Oh, well. Then I'll see you in a couple of days."

When I hang up, Dusty is busy tearing up a piece of paper he found on the floor, growling with his little pup growl. I watch him for a minute and remember that I still haven't told Ellen about him. Last time I talked to her, he wasn't going to stay.

It's mid-afternoon, and I haven't called Wendy to find out if her niece has gone home. "Dusty, I've got myself in a predicament."

Tired of the game, he plops onto his backside and cocks his head at me, as if he's waiting to hear more of what I have to say. He's starting to fill in a little and his legs are sturdier. He's going to have a brush tail and is getting some fluff to his ears.

"Suppose I don't call Wendy? What do you think would happen? I expect she wouldn't pine away."

He ambles over and attacks my boot, falling onto the floor and gnawing.

"Oh, no you don't." I pick him up. "My boots are off-limits." I sigh and turn on my phone. Wendy's number is right there and I dial it.

"Samuel, I thought you'd never call," she says. "I managed to convince Tammy to go home." She sounds practically giddy. "Oops. I guess I'm assuming you called to find out if I can go out tonight?"

"Yep. Shall I pick you up at seven?" My heart rate speeds up.

"Are we still going to Landry's?"

"If that suits you."

"Of course it does. What should I wear?"

"What do you mean what should you wear?" I laugh. "How do I know?"

Her laugh gets me. "Seven is great. See you." She hangs up, leaving me smiling at the phone.

It's three thirty, plenty of time to go over to see Margaret Wilkins and ask her if she knew her husband was clearing out.

The Hastings grandkids are out front, playing a game of croquet with Glo. She waves as I pass. There's no car in front of the Wilkins place, and I'm afraid that Margaret has gone out with her son, but she answers the door.

"Tell me what's happening. I feel so isolated here, and I wish you could get things cleared up so I can figure what to do next, but I don't want to bother you." Her words come in a rush, and I imagine her pacing before I arrived, waiting for some word. More guilt, although this of a different kind.

"Something else has come up that I need to run by you."

"God, what now?" She opens the door wider.

We sit in the kitchen over coffee. Every time I'm in the place, I feel trapped. I can imagine how oppressive it must be for Margaret. "Do you and your husband travel out of the country?"

"Out of the country? We used to. We went to Europe a few years ago. And we've been to Puerto Vallarta a few times. Not recently, though. Why?"

"Where do you keep your passports?"

She blinks a few times. "Hold on. Let me look. Lewis usually brings a case with him with important papers. They may be there." She goes into the back room and comes back carrying a metal case. She opens it and searches through the file folders, selects one and opens it. "Here they are."

I open Lewis's passport and it's the same picture as in the fake one. "Does the name Leonard Wilson mean anything to you?"

She looks into the distance, frowning, but eventually shakes her head. "No. Who is it?"

"I went through the SUV and I found a passport with your husband's picture in it, but the name in the passport was Leonard Wilson."

She brings a fist to her mouth. "I don't understand. Why would Lewis have a passport in another name?"

"That's a good question. Something else. Along with the passport, there was also a fair amount of money. Do you have any idea where your husband might have gotten it?"

"It's the same as that boat you told me about. I have no idea. How much money? You mean like ten thousand? Twenty thousand?"

"A good bit more than that."

She looks as if she could cry. "That makes no sense. We're broke."

"Did someone owe him money? Maybe somebody paid him back."

"Not that I know of."

"Did you have any other property he could have sold?"

She shakes her head.

"Did he ever say he scored big when he was gambling?"

She sighs. "Until you mentioned that he won the boat, I didn't know he gambled for more than a few dollars. You didn't say how much money he had."

I'm not ready to answer her question, and something else has occurred to me. I remember the assorted pills I found in the prescription bottle he had with him. "Margaret, is it possible that he was selling fake prescriptions for opiates?"

"I don't know. Wouldn't someone have noticed if he was writing a lot of prescriptions?"

"Possibly." It's worth a call to the branch of the Department of Public Safety that handles fraudulent drug prescriptions to find out for sure. "Or maybe he was performing surgery again, on the quiet?"

"He hadn't applied for hospital privileges anywhere. Or at least if he did, he didn't tell me." Margaret lays her hands on the table in front of her, but when she realizes they are trembling, she clasps them firmly. "I don't understand this. And you still haven't told me how much money he had."

"Around two hundred thousand dollars."

Her mouth drops open. "That's impossible. I can't imagine where that much money came from."

"Is your son around?"

"He went out to see a college buddy."

"When will he be back?"

"Late tonight."

"Are you planning to go to San Antonio tomorrow to get your car?"

"How long will it be before the SUV is released?"

"Given what I found in it, I'll want a more thorough investigation, so it'll be a few days."

"Then I guess I have no choice."

"One more thing. I'd like to examine that case." I nod toward the metal case that held the folder with the passports.

"Of course."

The metal case contains several folders, but they are all innocuous. They contain utility bills, wills, automobile papers, and insurance for auto and both houses.

"Does he keep files anywhere else?"

"At home. He has a big desk, and it's full of papers. I kept telling him he ought to clean it out. Not that it isn't neat. Lewis was always a neat freak. But it has patient files from years ago. He never threw anything away."

I'd love to get my hands on that desk, but I suspect that will be the job of whoever takes on this investigation. It's looking much bigger now than when I first started.

At home I feed Dusty and put in a call to Maria. She answers right away. "Hey, boss." There's a lot of noise in the background.

"What's going on?" I ask.

"One last party."

"How was the wedding?"

"Wonderful. Lupe looked so beautiful. Everybody was here. I saw cousins I haven't seen since I was a little girl." In all the time I've known her, I've never heard Maria sound so happy and chatty. I imagine her family as a large, close bunch, although she has never revealed much about them. "What's up? Is everything all right?"

"We had a man go missing. We found him."

"What happened?"

"I'll tell you the details when you get back, but he was murdered."

"Oh my goodness. Any idea who did it?"

"Not at all. He and his wife are from San Antonio, so while you're there I want you to look into something." I tell her the details of what I want done.

"That won't be a problem. Do you want me to call you as soon as I find something out, or wait until I get back?"

"Call me when you know something."

"Will do."

"Oh, and by the way. I got a dog. His name is Dusty."

I hang up before she can quiz me about him. I grin, thinking how excited she'll be when she sees the puppy.

When Maria first arrived last spring, courtesy of an apprentice program from the state of Texas, I wouldn't have figured she'd last. Besides having a gloomy disposition, she was prickly. Being sent to a small town for her apprenticeship wasn't what she had in mind. She was even pricklier about working with an old guy like me.

We surprised each other. I surprised her by having more to offer than she thought. She surprised me by exhibiting a sly sense of humor and making friends quickly. People appreciate that she is serious about her job. When her apprentice period was up a couple of months ago, she decided to throw her lot in with Jarrett Creek Police Department for another year. "I can't promise I'll stay here longer than that," she said, "but I like it here." She has made particular friends with Loretta, though a more unlikely pair you'd never meet. And I have grown to depend on her.

As I'm getting dressed to drive over to Bryan to see Wendy, I notice that once more I'm taking more care than I usually do. I'm wearing a jacket and leaving my ratty hat at home. And I'm wearing my new boots again. I have a moment in which I wonder if I should call off our date. But I don't really even consider it—I want to see her. That's the truth of it.

The harder truth is that as much as I like Ellen, the feeling of excitement I have thinking of Wendy is something I've never had with Ellen. It would be a lot more convenient if I had. Ellen lives down the street, and to see Wendy I have to drive more than a half hour.

I'm so caught up in my thoughts that I almost forget about Dusty. I wonder what he's up to, and go into the kitchen to find him gnawing on the chew bone. "Looks like I have to take you along," I say, picking him up. "You better behave yourself. I don't want you to embarrass me."

On the drive over I have misgivings. Have I built Wendy up too much in my mind? It's true she's lively and fun and pretty. But am I making too much of the chemistry between us? As soon as she answers the door, I know I'm not. She's wearing a low-cut black dress that fits her like skin. It makes me want to run my hands over it. We stand like fools, grinning at each other. I had thought my teenaged days were over, but apparently not. I'm tongue-tied and all I can think about is when I'm going to get to kiss her.

"Samuel." Her voice is husky, and without even thinking, I put my arms around her and draw her to me. She lifts her face and I bend down and kiss her. Her body fits against mine as if we were sculpted together. After a few minutes of this it's clear to me that we aren't going anywhere. She takes my hand and leads me through the living room and down the hallway. The only thing she says as we reach her bed is, "Darn. I went to so much trouble to dress right." I can't find the voice to tell her that she succeeded.

Later, we're lying in bed, her head on my shoulder. It feels like I've always known her. We're talking softly when suddenly I remember and sit bolt upright.

"What's wrong?"

"I forgot I left the dog in the car. It's cold out there." I jump up and pull my pants on.

"I don't think he'll freeze to death," she says, laughing. "It's not that cold. I'll fix us something to eat while you go get him."

Dusty doesn't seem any the worse for wear. The pickup has retained its warmth and he's sound asleep as usual. I let him out on the ground and then take him inside, where Wendy makes a big fuss over him. I swear he's grinning by the time she sets him down.

Over ham sandwiches, she doesn't seem inclined to chew over what just happened between us. Instead, she asks me to tell her about my wife. "I bet she was terrific."

"She was." I tell her that Jeanne and I had a good life together—that we couldn't have kids and that Jeanne ended up working for the school. "All the teenaged girls loved her and hung around our house." I don't dwell on her fight with cancer. "Your turn. What was your husband like?"

She tells me that he died several years ago in a freak farm accident. "James wasn't a farmer. He was helping his brother bale hay and the baler turned over and pinned him."

"What kind of work did he do?"

"I'm sorry to say he was never very successful. He tried his hand at several things. He went to college for two years and hated it. He got

143

out and tried being a salesman, and he was terrible at it." She laughs.
"He didn't actually like people very much, although you wouldn't have
known it. He could be absolutely charming." She could be describing a
long-lost cousin; someone she was once close to, but moved away from.
"Then we decided to buy a pizza franchise, but it went bust."

Her eyes are soft as she recounts this, and I have the feeling that she
regrets some things. Maybe over time I'll find out what those things
are. "How could you afford to keep going?"

"I think that was part of the problem. James had money. His grandmother left him with a trust. Not that we were rich," she adds hastily,
"but it allowed him to dabble instead of being serious."

"Any other kids beside your daughter?"

She sighs. "I have another daughter, Allison. She's the opposite of
Jessica. Something of a wild child. She adored James, and when he died,
she became . . . I don't know what you'd call it . . ." She looks off into
the distance. "A wanderer?" She grins at me. "Sort of like me. I love her,
and I think she loves me, and when we're apart we miss each other, but
when we're together we don't get along that well. Right now she's in
India. God knows what she's doing there. I get postcards from her." She
shrugs, but I can see the pain in her eyes.

"You worry about her."

"Of course I do." She kneads her hands. "The way I'm sure my
mother worried about me. I know she's strong and capable, but things
can happen."

"That's what you get for raising a free spirit."

She smiles. "How did your wife like you being a policeman in a
small town?"

"I never was a police officer. I started out as chief." I tell her the circumstances and that Jeanne didn't like it much, so I left after a couple
of years and spent most of my career as a land man with an oil and gas
company.

"But you're chief of police again? How did that happen?"

144

"You mean at my advanced age?"

"No!" She shakes her head firmly. "We're not going there. I'm determined to enjoy every minute of my life. I don't do 'age' for me or for anyone else."

I tell her that Jarrett Creek went broke a couple of years ago, and that the situation led to me getting back into the position of chief. "It suits me. But I won't be able to do it forever. I'm looking for someone to take my place." I tell her about Maria and her foibles. "She's a good officer. I hope I can entice her to stay." As I describe Maria, I realize that I've left out Bill Odum. He deserves a shot, too, but although he is a good, diligent officer, he doesn't have Maria's fire.

We talk until late, and it's only as I'm on the way home that I realize that I never managed to get around to the question of Ellen.

CHAPTER 17

It's Sunday, and I don't go into the office first thing. I wait until after nine to call Margaret Wilkins to see if her son is in, but there's no answer. They must have gotten an early start to San Antonio. I get a call from Gloria Hastings asking me to come over for a meal. "Let's call it a late lunch," she says. "The kids are leaving at noon, and Frank and I will be at loose ends with them gone. It would be nice to have company. Do you have a friend you'd like to bring?"

For a second I consider calling Wendy to see if she wants to come, but until I get the situation with Ellen straightened out, I'm going to keep a low profile. I tell her that I'll be bringing someone, but not a human someone. She says the puppy is welcome.

Before I leave for the office I call Wendy to tell her I had a great time last night. She doesn't answer her phone, and I leave a message, wondering where she is, and then reminding myself that it's none of my business.

As I'm stowing Dusty in the pickup, I see Jenny and Will leading their horses out through the side gate. I walk over to say hello and tell them how much I enjoyed spending Thanksgiving at their place. As soon as I say so, I feel heat creeping up my neck. All it would take is for Wendy to tell her daughter Jessica that we've seen each other twice, and Jenny would be after me to fill her in on the details. Not that she's a gossip, but we've been good friends through some tough times, and she likes to know what I'm up to.

But she and Will seem eager to be on their way, and I escape without incident.

At headquarters, I take a couple of calls that have come in on the landline. Although the answering machine directs people to call my cell phone, a lot of people still prefer to leave a message. One woman has called with her weekly complaint that kids have been "cutting up on a Saturday night," as she puts it, in the house down the street. I'll let Maria handle this one when she gets back. She turns out to be good with old people.

Someone has stolen a few bales of hay from John Lothrup's barn. I suppose he has a way of knowing that some hay is gone, and I suspect it's kids who stole it for a hayride. He says he knows I probably won't be able to find out who did it, but he thought he ought to call just in case I have time to deal with it. I call him back and he doesn't answer, so I leave him a message saying that if I hear anything I'll get back to him.

The last message is one I'm pleased to get. The woman whose dog disappeared has left a message that the dog had wandered over to her friend's house a mile away and the friend had been gone and got back to find the dog hanging around. "Last time I was over there with Scout, my friend gave him a whole pork chop. I guess Scout thought that was the place to be."

At least that's one fewer dog disappearance to investigate. But it reminds me that I need to find out where those other missing dogs are. The problem is, I don't have the slightest idea where to start.

I spend the next couple of hours doing paperwork, the bane of any police chief.

When I drive over to the Hastings home, Glo and Frank greet me like an old friend.

"Smells good in here," I say.

"It's not much," Glo says, with a mischievous grin. "Turkey hash."

"Sounds fine." I try to muster some enthusiasm. Glo pushes us out of the kitchen so she can finish cooking. It's chilly outside, but Frank and I decide to take a walk along the shoreline.

"Now don't you disappear on me," Glo says. "It's just like men to wander off when the meal is almost ready."

I grin, remembering that Jeanne frequently complained about the same thing. While we stroll, Frank asks how the investigation is going on Lewis Wilkins's death. "I don't mind telling you, seeing him all torn up like that was like a nightmare."

"I've got a few leads, but nothing substantial. It was good of you and your wife to invite his family for Thanksgiving."

He shrugs. "I don't know that we helped. Our grandkids are a handful, and Margaret and her kids didn't come out of their shell much." He shakes his head. "A terrible thing for the family, and I get the feeling they aren't happy with each other. Especially the daughter, Emily."

"No, they aren't happy with each other, but I do know they were glad to spend time at your place. It helped them get their mind off things."

Glo sticks her head out the door and calls us in. "Come on in the kitchen and fill your bowls," she says.

I get near the stove and see what looks like a big pot of chili. "This doesn't look like any leftover turkey to me," I say.

She laughs. "I was teasing. Even if I liked turkey hash, which I don't, I couldn't have made it because the turkey was picked clean at Thanksgiving dinner. When my grandkids get to be teenagers I'm going to have to get a fifty-pound bird."

We enjoy a good meal, and afterward sit drinking coffee and eating leftover pie.

"I must admit our reasons for having you over weren't entirely selfless," Glo says.

"Oh?"

"Frank and I have been talking, and the more we thought about it, the more we wondered if Lewis was into something . . ."

"Something dodgy," Frank finishes her sentence.

"Anything in particular make you ask?"

"It's Margaret. She seemed . . ." Glo looks at her husband to fill in the blanks again.

"Like a whipped dog. We never saw any evidence that he hit her or anything, but once or twice we heard him yelling at her. And a few times we heard him leave in the evening long after you'd think they should have settled down."

"Not that it's our business," Glo says. "I don't like being the nosy neighbor. On the other hand, I couldn't help thinking it was odd for him to leave her alone in the evening like that."

"Why didn't you tell me this before?"

They look at each other. "We didn't think of it, had both forgotten. We were busy with the family, and then it was Thanksgiving and we didn't have a chance to talk to each other. Then Glo reminded me."

"How often did he go out?"

"Only a few times. Although it might have been more often and we didn't see him."

It's not new information, but it adds fuel to my suspicion that Lewis Wilkins was up to no good.

I had hoped that Margaret or Daniel would be back by now, but no one answers the door, so I head back to the station. I'm restless. On the Sunday after Thanksgiving, even investigating crimes slows to a crawl as everybody takes a deep breath before the holidays start in earnest. Action will pick back up tomorrow, but the lull gives me time to think. On a whim I drive to the park along the lake. Although it's chilly, there's no wind and in midafternoon there's a weak sun. I sit on a picnic table and stare out at the bleak-looking lake. Clouds periodically cover the sun, giving the landscape a bare and gloomy look.

Dusty is delighted by the chance to waddle around in the wide-open spaces. Oblivious to the cold, he sniffs every possible blade of grass and clump of dirt and stops a few times to lend his scent to that of other animals.

A RECKONING IN THE BACK COUNTRY

While I watch him, I mull over my two challenges—the two women in my life and the murder—not necessarily in that order.

Lewis Wilkins could have been killed because of the damage he did to a patient. But the patient's family was receiving a lot of money, and the only reason to think someone would murder him was pure revenge. Still, I should follow up with the family to find out what kind of people they are and whether one of them was holding a grudge left unsatisfied by the monetary award.

He could have gotten himself into a gambling bind. But why would someone kill him if he owed them money? He couldn't pay them back if he was dead. Maybe his death would be a warning to someone else. Or, if he was gambling on dogfights, is there something I don't know about dogfighting that means he was more likely to get himself killed if he owed money? And if he owed money, surely it wasn't more than the two hundred thousand I found in his SUV.

I hadn't seriously considered the possibility that a member of his family killed him. After all, how would they orchestrate such a horrible death? It doesn't add up. Margaret might have been fed up. She seemed shocked by his death, but she wouldn't be the first widow to make more of a husband's death than she actually felt. As for his son, Daniel, he strikes me as an easy-going young man, considerate of his mother and angry at his sister for her lousy attitude. Emily is a different matter. She's obviously got issues with her parents. But there are a lot of ways to kill somebody—even if you hire someone else to do it. Why would she go to the trouble of finding someone to kill him with vicious dogs?

I even consider Dooley Phillips. I have a feeling Dooley is covering up something. The way he tried to misdirect me with the boat still seems odd. If there's a reason why he arranged for Wilkins's murder, though, it escapes me.

And of course there is always the possibility that Wilkins was into something I haven't uncovered yet.

I'm starting to get cold when Dusty wanders in my direction and plops down with a sigh. I scoop him up and head for the truck. He flops down in the box and is sound asleep by the time the tires hit the pavement.

I was hoping there would be a message from Maria telling me what she learned on the errand I sent her on, but it's still a little early.

I go home to wait for Maria's call. Dusty is tired out from his activities and as soon as I feed him, he's out. I didn't know puppies slept so much. I stow his box in the bedroom so if I'm doing things in the front of the house I won't wake him up.

I haven't been in the house five minutes when someone raps on the door. It's Loretta and she has a package in her hands. I'm happy to see her back.

She plops the bag down on the kitchen table. "I brought something for you from my sister-in-law." She pulls out a cloth-wrapped bundle and unwraps it. It's a dark, heavy fruitcake full of nuts, the only kind worth eating, as far as I'm concerned. "Isn't that a beauty? She makes a good fruitcake. Better than any I ever tried to make."

"I'm sure that's not true."

She snorts. "It is. And she won't tell me the secret ingredient."

I reach out to pinch off a piece and she slaps my hand away. "It will be ready to eat by Christmas. You're supposed to pour brandy over it once a week until then."

"How much brandy?"

She cocks her head at me, measuring me. "What do you mean 'how much'? Until it doesn't absorb anymore." At the look on my face she says, "Never mind, I'll keep it at my house and do it myself, and then I'll bring it to you. But you have to pay for the brandy."

"I'll pay enough for my cake and yours, too."

I make us a cup of coffee, glad to have her chattering in the background.

"I'm so glad to be home. I love to go to my cousin's house and see everybody, but there is no place like home." She pulls out a kitchen chair and settles herself down. "Tell me what's going on. Have you arrested anybody for that Wilkins man's murder?"

I tell her that the holidays make it hard to investigate a crime.

"You don't think Margaret killed her husband, do you?"

"I can be perfectly honest with you when I say I don't have a clue. But I agree with you that she's hard to read."

She brightens. "You want me to talk to Connie, find out if she has any ideas?"

"No, don't do that. Let it alone."

"Something's different," she says. "Did you get a haircut?"

"No. Same old me." Except for a sudden complication in the lady-love department, which I hope to keep secret from Loretta for a little while, anyway. I swear, Loretta should be in the Homeland Security Department. Potential terrorists wouldn't stand a chance of keeping their plans secret.

Suddenly Dusty yips.

"What is that? Sounds like a puppy."

I get up and head into the bedroom and come back with the wriggly little bundle. "This is Dusty."

For once Loretta is speechless.

"I found him and I've taken a liking to him." I hear the defensiveness in my voice.

"What do you mean found him?"

"Out in the woods near where Wilkins was found." I tell her the story of finding the bitch and the mystery of what happened to the other pups. "Keep your ears open. If anybody suddenly has unexplained puppies around, I want to know."

"As long as they're being taken care of, what difference does it make?"

I don't want to tell her I'm worried that whoever took them might be involved in some way with either dognapping or dogfighting. "I need to know, that's all."

152

"He is cute, but what in the world are you going to do with a dog?"

"What do you mean what am I going to do with him? Same thing everybody does with a dog. He'll be my companion."

She snorts. I tell her to hold on while I take him outside. When I come back she says, "What does your cat think about him?"

"She likes him. At least as much as she likes anybody."

"Dusty is a good name for him. He looks like he's been rolling in the dust."

"That's what I thought." Although I'm not the one who named him.

She gets up. "I better get on home. Travel is harder than it used to be. I'm tired and I need to get the laundry done." At the door she turns and says, "One thing you better know. I am not going to babysit for that dog. You better ask Ellen if you need somebody to do that."

As soon as she leaves, my cell phone rings, startling me. I'll never get used to having it ring in my pocket. "Maria, what did you find out?"

"There was an open house today for the Wilkins's home. The real estate agent said an offer might be coming in, but she confided in me that she didn't think the offer would cover the mortgage cost."

I smile to myself. One of the talents I've found that Maria has is that she can get anyone to talk to her. I'm not sure if it's because she intimidates them or makes them feel safe. And she keeps what she knows to herself unless it's relevant to an investigation.

"How much is it on the market for?"

"Just under a million. It's a nice house, but nothing grand."

"Do you mind staying there until tomorrow? There's something else I want you to check up on." I tell her I'd like her to look up real estate in Lewis Wilkins's name. "His wife seems to have let him take care of their business dealings, and didn't ask many questions. It's possible he had some holdings she was unaware of."

I'm surprised when Maria calls back within the hour. "Looks like you were right."

"About what?"

"Dr. Wilkins did own other property." There's triumph in her voice, and I imagine her fierce expression. "I figured if Wilkins was using the agent for one house, he might have used him to sell other property. So I went back and asked the agent if Wilkins had recently sold anything through him, and sure enough he had."

"What was it?"

"Land out near the river. Small piece of property. And get this: It was in his name only."

"How did that happen?"

"The agent didn't know that. He said he didn't ask; that it wasn't his business."

"How much did Wilkins get for it?"

"Fifty thousand."

Maria tells me that the deal was a quick one because Wilkins owned it without a loan, and that the buyer paid cash for it.

Maria will stay over until tomorrow to check if there was other property in Wilkins's name only. "And find out when he bought it," I say. And then another thought occurs to me. "Also, find out if there is property in the name of Leonard Wilson. I'll tell you who that is when you get back."

A few minutes later, I call her again. "There's something else I'd like you to do. This one will be trickier." I tell her about the woman who sued Wilkins and the e-mails I found on his computer. "I want to know if we should consider her a suspect. Or someone in her family."

She doesn't answer right away. "How am I supposed to do that? I can't just go over to her house and ask if she happened to kill her doctor."

"You'll figure something out. Poke around. Find out how she lives. Anything you find out is more than we know now."

CHAPTER 18

Monday morning dawns gloomy. It looks like it could rain again. I go down and spend an hour with my cows, taking the time to check their hooves and skin, which I do every Monday. Cows are more delicate than they look, prone to all kinds of exotic diseases that can bring them down before you know it. I've brought Dusty with me again and put him in an empty corncrib to keep him safe. A couple of the bolder cows go over to check him out. To my satisfaction, he doesn't seem perturbed, and neither do the cows when he yips at them in what sounds like excitement.

My plan this morning is to have a talk with Jerry Bodine, the man Lewis Wilkins won the boat from. I wait until eight o'clock and reach him at the number Dooley gave me. He sounds like a jovial man. He tells me he has an appointment at ten, but if I come over now he'll be glad to chat.

I stop by headquarters and there's a message from our new mayor, Lester Pierce. Although he has been in office for several months, I still call him the new mayor because he seems to have stalled out on learning the job. He might be in over his head, which is hard to imagine considering we're a town of only three thousand people and there are no unusual circumstances to make the job particularly hard. I call him back, wanting to get it out of the way.

"What can I do for you, Lester?"

"I've been getting some uncomfortable telephone calls from citizens, and I want to know where you stand on finding out who killed that man out at the lake." He has the high-pitched voice of an old man, though he's not even forty.

"I'm working on it. But you do understand the Department of Public Safety is responsible for the investigation." I say this not to duck responsibility, but to try to help him understand the way things work.

"Well what are they doing?"

"As far as I know, nobody has been assigned to it. It takes a while. So I'm doing what I can."

"That's more like it. How long do you think it will be before you arrest somebody?"

I can't help laughing. "Lester, I have no idea. With the holiday, I didn't get much done. Who is it that's bugging you for answers? Is it people out at the lake?"

"Them and others."

I doubt it's others. And it may only be one person. Nobody likes to be confronted by a frightened citizen, and Lester has proven to be skittish when someone is upset with him.

"Lester, I wish I could tell you I've got it all wrapped up, but I'm struggling. The man who was killed is from out of town, and I don't know much about him except what I got from his family and from Dooley Phillips. They were friends."

He grunts. "I'd like to have something I can tell people."

"I'll let you know as soon as that happens," I say. "I have to go now. I have an appointment with somebody."

"Suspect?"

"No. Just somebody who might know some answers."

I hang up before he can start quizzing me on the finer points of my job. Ever since he was elected, I've had the feeling that he has a mind to get a younger person on the job. And I may agree with him. But not yet.

Once more I have the problem of what to do with Dusty. I'll be glad when he's old enough to come with me and hang around outside or in the truck. On my way to Bobtail to see Bodine, I stop off at the vet and ask them to keep him for a while. I swear when Chelsea takes him away, he gives me an accusing look.

Following Bodine's instructions, I find the warehouse where the lawnmowers are stored before they are sent off around the country. It's a handsome building surrounded by a chain-link fence with barbed wire on top. There's a sign warning trespassers that the property is guarded by dogs, although I don't see any sign of them.

Bodine meets me out front. He's a big guy all around, tall and with extra pounds on him. He has an open expression, laugh lines crinkling around his blue eyes.

"You have a lot of security here," I say. "Dogs in addition to that fence? You have a problem with theft?"

He laughs. "We did until we put up the fence with that phony sign."

"You don't have dogs?"

"Not anymore. Tried that and they were more trouble than they were worth. I was afraid somebody would try to break in and get attacked and turn around and sue us."

He leads me to a small office, sparsely furnished and kept in good order. He tells me it was his father-in-law's office. "Chuck sold the business to the employees, but he had me stay on as manager. After he died, I'm proud to say the new board told me they'd be glad to have me continue."

I sit down in a metal folding chair in front of his desk. It creaks as I sit down.

"Sorry about the cheap chair. I thought Chuck took being frugal a little too far, but I guess it rubbed off 'cause I haven't bothered to replace the furniture." He settles into a more comfortable desk chair that may at one time have been more expensive, but the leather is cracked and the arms worn down. "Now what can I do for you?"

"I need to ask you some questions regarding a poker game you were part of."

"I bet I know which one you mean. It's about that Wilkins fella who was murdered."

I nod.

"That was a damn shame. He seemed like a good fella. Into gambling a little more than I was, but a good man."

"Dooley Phillips tells me you lost a boat to him."

His laugh is a short bark and his expression is hard to read. Rueful? "I couldn't wait to get rid of that boat, but I was a little hasty."

"How's that?"

"I didn't reckon on my wife's attitude. She was none too happy to find out I had unloaded it."

I chuckle. "I can imagine. It was a pretty nice boat to give up so easily. Must have been worth a lot."

He leans forward with his elbows on his desk. "Look, my father-in-law could afford that boat. He was one of those men who couldn't seem to touch anything without money coming from it. And quite frankly, I haven't done that badly myself, but nothing like him.

"He had always dreamed of retiring and having a nice boat to putter around in. Still, my wife and I were surprised when he bought it on a whim. Sometimes I wonder if he didn't know he wasn't long for this world and he decided he needed to jump on it." He shakes his head. "Shame he never got to use it."

"Why didn't you sell it if you didn't want it?"

He waves his hand at the office desk, full of papers. "I've got a lot on my plate. Putting the boat on the market was on the back burner. I thought it was more trouble than it was worth. Or at least it seemed so after a few bourbons and a good game of poker."

"Why did Wilkins want the boat?"

"I don't know. Listen, I'm the one who started the bet. I told the guys I wanted to wager the boat because I wanted it out of my hair. Wilkins jumped at the chance. He didn't say why he was so eager to get his hands on it, and I didn't ask. I think he just liked gambling."

"Dooley Phillips told me Wilkins put up his lake house against the boat?"

"Yes, it caused a little problem."

"What kind of problem?"

"Like I said, we'd been drinking. He got hot under the collar when I asked him whether he was sure he wanted to bet his house. He told me in no uncertain terms that it was his business, and I should let him worry about it." He raises his hands as if in surrender. "I backed off real fast after that."

Dooley Phillips said Wilkins hadn't seemed worried that he might lose his house in the poker game, so I ask Bodine if he thought the same thing.

Suddenly his jovial manner disappears. He lifts an eyebrow and nods. "Yeah, I wondered why he seemed so confident. In fact, I thought maybe he might know he couldn't lose because he had some kind of scam going on."

"And?"

He shrugs. "I watched him like a hawk, and as far as I could tell he didn't cheat."

"Did any of the other men in the game lose big that night?"

"No, they didn't get involved in the bet. That was between Wilkins and me. The other fellas and I had played together a lot of times, and this was unusual. It's a friendly game and we usually play for small stakes."

"There was one thing, though . . ." He strokes his chin.

"What's that?"

"Dooley never brought Wilkins around to play poker again. I wondered a time or two if he and Wilkins had put on a scam together." He pauses, looking uncomfortable.

"Have you played poker with Dooley since then?"

"You know, I don't believe I have."

I stop by the courthouse and go to the medical examiner's office to see if they have the autopsy results on Wilkins's body. They tell me the autopsy was done, but that they hadn't had time to write it up over Thanksgiving weekend. And the ME is not here today. He's gone to San Antonio to a daylong seminar. "Call tomorrow or Wednesday and we'll send it over to you as soon as he has it written up."

On the way back to Jarrett Creek, I drive by the Wilkins place. Still no car out front, and no answer when I knock on the door. Next door the Hastings's house is closed up tight. They told me yesterday that they were going back home and would get an early start.

I stop back by the vet's office and pick up Dusty, who rewards the sound of my voice with a little yodel.

Chelsea grins. "He's saying he's happy to see you."

Maria told me that the property he sold for fifty thousand was a quick deal. That's been nagging at me. When I get back to the station, I open his computer and search his e-mail folders to see if he has any correspondence pertaining to sale of property. Sure enough, there's a file titled "Property" in his e-mails. I look through the e-mails and find out that he tried to sell a parcel of land a couple of times without going through a broker, but nothing came of it. It also looks like he has another couple of parcels, but these are small and worth less than fifty thousand total. It's time I asked Margaret if she knew that her husband owned those parcels of land. It feels like by having them in his name he was cheating on her.

I'm ready to phone Margaret's number when my cell phone rings. It's Ellen. My face gets warm and I have an impulse to let it go to voice-mail. But I haven't spent my life being a coward. Besides, it's not as if we have an agreement. I'm not really cheating by seeing Wendy. Or so I tell myself as I answer the phone.

"Samuel?" Her voice sounds subdued.

"In the flesh. What's going on? When are you coming back?"

"I'll be back tonight. Are you going to be around?"

"I will. What time are you getting in?"

"Before eight. I don't like to drive after dark." I can't imagine Wendy saying something like that.

"Give me a call as soon as you get in. You want me to pick up something to eat?" It's so natural to ask.

"I guess." She sounds so forlorn that it bothers me. She's usually, if not bouncy, at least upbeat. It's as if someone has wrung hope out of her.

"What's wrong? You don't sound like yourself."

"I'm just tired." And on that note we ring off. Something's up, I'm sure of it. Has her ex-husband browbeaten her? Have her kids given her an ultimatum? Did Jenny call and tell her I had had dinner with Wendy? I'll find out soon enough.

I call Margaret and she tells me she's in San Antonio. "Daniel brought me here yesterday and I decided to stay over with a friend. I'm glad I did. She cheered me up." She says she's having lunch and heading back this afternoon.

"Call me when you get back. I've got a few more questions for you."

She sighs. "Always questions. Never answers."

"Unfortunately I'm at that stage of the investigation."

After we hang up, I phone the marina. I keep getting a sense that Dooley is holding out on me. For somebody who was supposed to be good friends with Lewis Wilkins, he didn't seem to know all that much about him. After my talk with Jerry Bodine, I want to tackle Dooley again. Bodine's hint that Wilkins and Dooley might have gone in together to cheat him out of the boat doesn't make sense: They would have to have set it up in advance, and by all accounts it was spur-of-the-moment. Besides, Bodine said it was his idea to make the bet. But I can't ignore the possibility that there's more to it than the mere luck of the draw.

Dooley tells me to come on down and he'll treat me to a sandwich. Before I can leave, the phone rings again. It's Wendy. "Hey, I got your message. Want to come over tonight?"

My pulse speeds up. I do want to see her. A lot. If I could run over to Bryan right now, I would. "I can't. But I'll take a rain check."

"Not a problem." And she sounds like it really isn't. "Call me when you can."

Now that Ellen is coming back, what does that mean for when I can see Wendy? What the hell am I doing? "I'll call you tomorrow."

Dooley greets me like we're old buddies, with a clap on the back and a hearty smile. With the gloomy weather, the place is deserted and we have the café seating area, four folding tables and chairs, to ourselves. He says he doesn't mind if I bring Dusty in. "Technically it's against the law to have a dog in a café, but since you're the law, I'm going to let you worry about it."

Dooley asks if I want something to eat, but I tell him I'm not particularly hungry. He gets us a couple of ice cream sandwiches out of the freezer, which tastes good.

I first tell him about the vicious e-mails Wilkins got from the woman who won the lawsuit against him.

"Poor Lewis. Seems like it would be enough for her to get the money." He stares out the front window, his expression full of regret. "I guess if you were damaged through someone's mistake, and the damage was permanent, that would be enough to make you bitter."

"Did he ever mention the e-mails to you?"

"No. I wish he had. It must have been terrible getting messages like that every day. It would drag you down." He gives me a speculative look. "You're not thinking she had anything to do with killing Lewis, do you?"

"Hatred like that, I don't know. Seems like an odd choice of weapon, though."

He winces. He's eaten most of his ice cream sandwich, and wraps the rest of it up to throw away. I hand him my wrapper, too, and he takes them to the waste basket.

"I had a meeting with Jerry Bodine," I say.

162

"Is that right?" He sits back down with a sigh and tugs at his waist-band. "This time of year I always eat too much."

"Always," I say. We laugh.

"You said you were going to ask Bodine about the poker game where Lewis won that boat. Did he have anything to add?"

"Not especially. Let me ask you something. After that business with the boat changing hands, did you ever get another card game together that included Lewis Wilkins but not Bodine?"

"I don't believe I did."

"Any particular reason you didn't?"

He shifts in his chair, frowning. "I'd be lying if I said the business with the boat didn't pull me up short. It was a side of Lewis I had never seen."

"Had you seen that side of Bodine?"

He shrugs. "I don't know Bodine the way I did Lewis. Or the way I thought I knew Lewis. It was a kind of uncomfortable situation. Lewis was . . ." he shakes his head sharply. "It was like he was on a mission, and when Bodine tried to back out of the bet by reminding Lewis that he was risking losing his house, Lewis got aggravated. Made everybody uncomfortable."

"Bodine said he thought Wilkins was awfully sure of himself when he made the bet. Did it ever occur to you he knew he'd win because he was cheating?"

He holds my gaze for a few seconds, before shifting away. He sighs. "Of course it occurred to me, but I didn't see any evidence of it, and no one called him on any of his play." I hear another "but," in his voice, although he doesn't say it out loud.

"Do you think Bodine thought he was cheating?"

"He might have. I was embarrassed by the whole affair. Lewis was a guest—my guest—and he was being contentious with fellows I had played cards with many a time."

"But you didn't bring it up with him?"

"I didn't know what to do. Put yourself in my place. Lewis was hurting financially, and he was a longtime buddy. I tried to persuade him not to put his house up against the boat, but he brushed me off." Color rises in his face. "Bodine shouldn't have challenged him with that boat. The money didn't mean anything to Bodine, and it meant everything to Lewis." He gets up abruptly. "I'm going to get myself a beer. You want one?"

I shake my head. "But if you have any coffee, I wouldn't say no."

"I do, if you can call it coffee. It's more like sludge by now. I can make a new pot."

"No, sludge is fine. I'm not particular."

He swallows half the beer on his way back to the table. "I'll be honest with you. You asked me if I thought Lewis cheated? I told you I had no evidence of it, but I had seen him cheat before. We used to play in college, and he was called out a time or two. He always insisted that he had made a mistake, and nobody ever pushed it. You know, we were playing for nickels back then." He puts the beer down with a thump. "Honest to God, it never occurred to me that he would put me in such a spot."

"Who else was at that game?"

He wipes his hand across his mouth. "There was a guy from out of town, Houston, who was here for the weekend and looking for a game. I'd played cards with him a couple of times, but I don't know him well. Name of Mike Vaughan. And then there was an old boy from Bobtail that I play cards with quite a bit. Lonnie Casper. And then I think you know Roger Olivera."

"You think it's possible any of them might have spotted a cheat?"

He taps his thumb on the table, thinking. "Roger left before all this happened. Vaughan and Casper were interested to see how it played out, but whether they kept an eye on the cards, I couldn't tell you."

"Did everybody keep on playing after the boat changed hands?"

He frowns. "No. It kind of took the wind out of everybody's sails.

At first we were all laughing and excited. But afterward I think people were embarrassed. Kind of like putting that boat up against a house was too much. The game wasn't friendly anymore."

I take a sip of coffee. It's gone cold. "Where did the game take place?"

"Right here. After hours."

I had been thinking of some dark back room somewhere. "Dooley, is there anything you've been keeping from me about Lewis Wilkins? Anything at all?"

Dooley downs the rest of the beer. "I'm not sure what you mean. I have to confess that after the business with the boat, I didn't like Lewis as much. It seemed to me that he had gone off the rails somehow. There was a time I would have trusted him completely, but that business with the lawsuit changed him. I kept hoping he would turn himself around, but . . ."

"Did he ever indicate to you that he was planning to haul that boat down to the coast and take off for Mexico?"

"What?" He gives a short laugh. "Where did you get an idea like that? Lewis couldn't have done that. It takes somebody who knows what they're doing to load up a boat like that. And driving it is not easy either. And then to put it in the water?" He's shaking his head. "No way."

"He didn't ask you to help him?"

"He certainly did not. Although I suppose if he had asked me, I would have tried to find somebody to help him."

"Could he have asked someone else?"

"Not without me being aware of it, since the boat was here in my marina."

"Would there be anybody around here he could hire to take it out of the water and hook it up on a trailer after hours so you wouldn't know?"

He answers slowly. "I suppose there could be, but what would be the point?"

I don't have an answer for that, so I move on to the last matter. Can I even trust Dooley to answer if he knows? "Dooley, Lewis had some property in San Antonio that was in his name only. Did he ever mention that?"

He looks bleak, as if the revelations about what his friend was up to have been hard to take. "What kind of property?"

"Acreage."

He finishes up the beer. "It's pretty clear to me that I'd lost track of Lewis. He told me was broke, but if he had property, why didn't he sell it and make himself and his wife more comfortable? I never cared much for Margaret, but I'm beginning to see that she might have had a harder time of it than I thought, being hitched to Lewis."

CHAPTER 19

I haven't heard from Margaret, and when I try her phone, she doesn't answer so I expect she's on the road. I head back to the station and am as pleased as I can be when I see Maria's car there.

When I walk in carrying Dusty, she grins and hurries over to me. "Look at this little guy!" She takes him from me and cuddles him. When she puts her face close to his, he licks her. She laughs.

"Dusty. That's a good name for him. How did you get him?"

I tell her the story.

"What do you suppose happened to his mother?" she asks.

"Doc said it was natural causes. But he also said there were more puppies, and I'd like to know where they are."

She frowns. "I'll help you look into that." She looks around the office as if noticing for the first time that it's deserted. Where is everybody?"

"Connor isn't back from training, and I sent Bill home with the flu. I didn't want him spreading his germs around. Besides it was a quiet weekend."

"Except for the murder investigation."

"Except for that. So. What did you find out about Lewis Wilkins's property?"

"Not much. Wilkins has owned a few pieces of property for several years. But I didn't find any others in either his name or the one you gave me. What are you thinking?"

I tell her about finding the money and passport in the SUV. "I thought maybe he had sold some property and that's where the money came from. I give her my other, less savory, explanations. The name I asked you to look up was the name on the passport I found in Wilkins's SUV. Looks like he was ready to skip town."

She thinks about it. "What kept him around here? You found all that money in his vehicle. Why didn't he take off as soon as he had it?"

"I think he was planning to go by water, and he had arrangements to make." I tell her how he came by a fancy boat. "He had a brand-new, big trailer hitch on his SUV. I think he was fixing to haul the boat out and take it down to the coast, but he had to get somebody to help him hitch up the boat. Plus, his family was here for Thanksgiving. Maybe he wanted to spend time with them before he disappeared."

"You don't think his wife knew anything?"

I shake my head. "She said she didn't, and I don't know why she would have kept it secret from me if she did know. But there are things that puzzle me. I'd like if you went out there with me to meet her. I want your opinion. She's supposed to be back this afternoon, and I'm going over there to talk to her about the land Wilkins owned in his own name. If you aren't too tired, you can go along."

She smirks. "Too tired! That's an old geezer talking."

I give her narrow eyes. "An old geezer who's your boss."

She flaps her hand at me, dismissing the threat. "I'll be ready to go as soon as you are."

"Before we go, tell me what you found about the woman who sued Wilkins. Did you talk to her?"

"You know me. I think the direct way is the best way. I didn't call. I went to her house. Well, her apartment. She lives with her husband."

"Had she heard that Wilkins was dead?"

"Yes, somebody apparently had seen it in the San Antonio newspaper and told her."

"What did she have to say about it?"

"Plenty. She said she was glad he was gone, that he deserved anything he got, that he was the devil, yada yada. I know I should feel sorry for her. What happened was terrible. But she was a whiner. I hate that."

"How old is she?"

"Sixties. Both her and her husband are in bad shape. It looked like the only thing they do is eat and watch TV. It's clear what they spend the lawsuit money on. They had the biggest TV I ever saw, and two big recliners. Her husband sat there like a lump watching football the whole time I was there."

"Did you ask if she ever saw Dr. Wilkins after she filed the lawsuit?"

"She said he tried to get in touch with her, but she wasn't having any of it. After the surgery, Wilkins blamed the mistake on the nurse. She figured all he wanted was to talk her out of suing him by saying it wasn't his fault."

"Is it just her and her husband?"

"They have one son, but she whined that he never came to see them." She shudders. "I can imagine why. The place made me claustrophobic. And she's so negative it would drive you crazy. How can you feel sorry for somebody who feels so sorry for herself? She uses up all the sorry in the room. I was prepared to think the worst of the doctor, but by the time I got out of there, I wasn't so sure."

"You might change your mind when you know more about him."

"Like what?"

"He was gambling, and it looks like he was hiding money from his wife. His kids were barely speaking to him. Even his friend Dooley says he went downhill after that lawsuit."

"Sounds like maybe he deserves what he got."

"Not the way he died . . . nobody deserves that."

She looks at her watch. "I'm going to go get changed. I'll be back in twenty minutes."

She's back in fifteen. I haven't heard from Margaret, but I figure she should be home soon, so we head out to the lake. If she's not home, I can show Maria the site where Wilkins's body was found.

On the way I tell Maria about the possible connection of Wilkins's death to his gambling on dogfighting. "Seeing how he was killed, and the fact that he was gambling, I can't help wondering if he got himself tangled up with some people in that business."

"That would sure give him a good reason to run," she says quietly.

I look over and see that her back is rigid, and she's staring out the side window so I can't see her face.

"You know anything about that?"

She turns back to me, anger in her eyes. "Unfortunately, I do. I have cousins who go to dogfights and cockfights. A few years ago at a family reunion, one of them was bragging about it. I was a teenager. He said he went to Mexico to a dogfight. It made me sick. I went home and cried. My papa said he was trash."

I could tell her about my own experience with dogfighting, but I've never told anybody, not even Jeanne, and I'm not going to start now.

Margaret Wilkins's car is in the driveway—a modest little Toyota. When get to the door, I see that it's slightly ajar. I knock, but there's no answer. "Maybe she went next door," Maria says.

"Maybe." But I have an uneasy feeling. Margaret Wilkins is not the type of woman to leave the door open. I rap on the door, and when there's no answer I push on it. "Margaret? Are you here?"

At first I hear nothing. Then a thump.

"What was that?" Maria asks.

"Margaret?"

Another thump. "We have to go in." I hope we find Margaret somewhere in the back, dragging boxes out of a closet, but I don't think so. If that's what it was, she would have called out. The sound comes again.

"You have your gun?" Maria asks.

Of course I don't. "It's in the glove compartment." From her giant handbag she draws the compact Smith & Wesson that she favors.

"What are you doing with that in your handbag?"

"I didn't take the time to strap up before I left the house, okay? I'll go in first," she says and steps in front of me, gun leveled. "Margaret!" she yells.

This time the thumps are frantic. We can't risk going in too fast, in case someone is holding her hostage, so we ease around the walls of the front room, heading toward the hallway. When we get there, I grab Maria's arm and pull her back. "Cover me," I whisper. I move along next to the hallway wall and peek into the first room I come to, a small bedroom. Maria scoots in and clears the room. The thumping is coming from farther back. The next room appears empty, and Maria clears it as well. Then we come to a bathroom with no places of concealment.

We creep up to the last door, at the end of the hall. "If there's anyone here, you need to come out," I yell. I jerk my head to Maria and she comes up behind me. The door is halfway open. I fling it back and there on the floor is Margaret tied up and gagged. I start to move toward her.

"Wait!" Maria says. She eases into the room, looks behind the door, and then moves to a closet and flings it open. Nobody there. Another door leads to a bathroom. "Clear," she says as she leans over to peer under the bed.

Margaret's gag is a scarf tied tight around her head, covering her mouth, and when I remove it, I see that she was hit from behind. There is a lump and matted blood. As soon as the scarf is gone, she gasps and words spill out. "Oh, God, I thought no one would come. When I heard you, I banged my feet on the floor. I was afraid you wouldn't hear me and you'd leave me here."

Maria crouches next to her, puts her hand on her shoulder, and looks into her eyes. "Take it easy, we're here now. You're okay."

I untie her feet while Maria gets her hands. They've been tied with scratchy rope, and her wrists are raw where she tried to wriggle out of it.

"Let's get an ambulance out here," I say.

"I don't need an ambulance."

"Sorry, it's procedure," Maria says, though it isn't really. But I agree that Margaret's head wound needs to be looked at. She sits with her knees up to her chest, crying quietly, while Maria steps into the hallway to call for the ambulance. I do my best to comfort her.

When Maria comes back, she crouches down again and puts an arm around Margaret's shoulders and talks soothingly to her. Finally Margaret quiets down enough that I can ask her to tell us what happened.

She insists on getting to her feet so we help her up. She's wobbly.

"Let's get you something to drink," Maria says.

We guide her into the kitchen and sit her down, and Maria pours her a glass of water. She's shivering, and Maria goes back and brings her a sweater.

"I was so scared," Margaret says. "They kept asking where the money was. I told them I didn't know what they were talking about."

"Did you get a look at them?"

"No. They had masks over their faces." Which is probably why she's still alive.

"Start from the beginning and tell us everything you remember."

She tells us that she had just arrived home when someone knocked on the door. "I thought it was Gloria from next door. When I opened the door, two men with hoods over their faces pushed me inside. It was too fast for me to even scream. One of them hit me on the back of the head and I blacked out. When I came to, I was tied up and they started telling me they wanted their money."

"What did they say exactly?"

She rests her head in her hands. "They said something like 'your husband has our money.' I realized they must mean that money you found in the SUV. I was afraid if I told you had it, they'd kill me. So I said I didn't know what they were talking about. They said 'don't play dumb, he must have told you.' I said no."

"What did they say to that?" Maria asks.

Margaret whimpers. "One of them cursed, I think. I don't remember."

"It's okay," Maria says. "You're doing fine."

"What can you tell me about the men?" I ask. "Were they tall? Short? Did they have an accent?"

"Both a little taller than me. One of them was wiry. The other one was a little heavier."

"What are you, five foot eight?" Maria asks.

"That's right."

"And an accent?" Maria asks again.

Margaret cocks her head as if she's listening. "Both of them had soft voices." I remember thinking that they were doing something so awful and yet their voices were soft. In a way that was almost scarier."

"Did they have long sleeves? Did you see their arms?"

"Yes, they had long sleeves, but . . . oh." She looks at Maria. "I do remember. I saw the hair on the back of their hands. One had light hair, the other was darker."

"Very good," Maria says. "I know it's hard to concentrate, but try to think of anything else that might have caught your attention. A limp, or a funny way of moving, or an odd phrase."

Margaret puts her head in her hands. "All I could think was that if these were the men who killed Lewis, were they going to turn dogs on me, too. I was so scared."

Maria had told the hospital on the phone that there was no need for an ambulance siren, but they use it anyway, which means we hear them come blaring up. From the car I hear a little yipping sound. Apparently Dusty doesn't like what the sound does to his ears.

Maria goes out to meet them, and when the medical team comes inside, Margaret looks panicky. She tells them that she doesn't think she needs to go to the hospital, but they take a look at her wound and tell her it's best if she has it looked at. "You might have a slight concussion," the older of the team says.

"I'll come to the hospital," I say. "Do you want me to call your kids?"

A shadow passes across her face. "No. Don't."

"Margaret, do you remember if either of the men touched anything while they were here?" Maria says. "I'd like to try to get some fingerprints."

She looks on the verge of tears. "I don't know."

Margaret insists that she doesn't need a stretcher, but they tell her that at least they want to take her in a wheelchair. When she gets up to walk, she wobbles and sinks gratefully into the wheelchair.

After she leaves, Maria and I gather up the ropes and scarf used to tie her up and look for other evidence, but we find nothing. We decide that I'll take Maria back to get her car, and she'll come back to dust for prints while I go to the hospital.

When we get outside, there are a few neighbors hanging around, wanting to find out what the ambulance was doing here. A man who says he lives three doors down says he heard about the murder. "Did somebody else get killed?" His wife is standing next to him, looking frightened.

"No, it was an accident," I say. Maria darts a glance at me. She probably thinks I should warn people that someone had broken in and attacked Margaret. I would do that if I didn't think this was something particular to the Wilkinses.

On the way back I have a chance to run my ideas by Maria. "I told you that when I found the money in the SUV, I thought Wilkins was planning to go on the run with it, but the fact that these guys who attacked Margaret asked her where it was suggests to me that he was supposed to give it to someone. So why didn't he give to them?"

"Maybe he was on his way to turn it over and someone else abducted him," Maria says. She has Dusty in her lap and is stroking him behind the ears. He leans his head to get the best angle.

"So whoever killed him didn't know he had a bag full of cash with him."

"That seems obvious," she says. "But if they weren't after the money, why did they kill him? Was it a grudge? A random attack?"

"It was too specific to be a random attack."

Maria is quiet, so I don't say anything. She's got her stern look on, so I know she's working on the problem. "Look," she says, turning slightly to face me. "It's an awfully big coincidence that he owed that much money to someone and that someone else had him killed."

"But still, if whoever killed him knew he had money to pay off a debt, they would have searched the car. The stash wasn't that hard to find."

She nods. "So we're looking for two suspects. One who killed him and one who was willing to attack his wife to find the money."

We arrive at the station, but neither of us makes a move to get out of the car. "I'm thinking the attack on Margaret was odd," I say. "Why tie her up and demand the money? Why didn't they begin by telling her that her husband had a debt to pay and they expected him to pay it, and they were there to collect? There was plenty of time to get rough if she said she didn't know anything about the money."

"Maybe they thought she killed him and took the money." Her dry tone says she doesn't really believe that, but we are no closer to solving the riddle.

Maria checks the back of the squad car to make sure the forensics kit is shipshape, and when she's ready to go back to Margaret's, I say, "Be careful. They left her tied up for a reason. Maybe they were planning to give her some time to think it over and then they were coming back to try again."

"What are you going to do with Dusty while you're at the hospital?"

"I'll take him. He's used to being in the box."

"Yes, but he needs to be out playing. Why don't I keep him while you're gone? No telling how long it will take you."

"He'll get in your way."

"No, I'll put him in his box in the kitchen while I work."

"I know a sneaky excuse when I hear one. I better look out, or before I know it you'll take him over."

On the way home from the hospital, I stop and pick up Dusty from Maria's. I tell her that I'm no wiser than I was when I went there. "Margaret swears she knows nothing about the money her husband had with him, and that she can't remember anything else about the two men who abducted her."

It's after eight when Ellen calls to say she made it back to town.

"Would you rather forget about getting together tonight? You sound tired," I say.

"I am, but I'd like to see you. We can tell each other Thanksgiving stories. I'll bet yours was better than mine."

Guilt washes over me, and my heart plummets, but I tell her I'll come over.

On the way home I had stopped and picked up some salads and cold cuts at a deli in Bobtail, so I tell her I'll bring them. Nothing exciting, but a little different from the Mexican food we usually end up with if Ellen isn't cooking.

Ellen usually holds back. She's cautious by nature, so I'm surprised when she opens the door and throws her arms around me. "I'm so happy to see you," she says, reaching up to kiss my check. Frazier is a terrier, and full of energy. He dances around at our feet, yelping. I bend down and ruffle his ears, and he suddenly takes a step back, sniffing. He must smell the puppy. I have to coax him to let me scratch his ears.

Ellen leads me into the kitchen. "I hope you don't mind; I opened a bottle of wine before you got here. I need a glass. In fact, I may need two glasses." She likes white wine, while I prefer red, so I'm surprised to see that she has opened a bottle of pinot noir.

I finally really look at her. There are dark smudges under her eyes, and she has the anxious look that she used to have all the time when I first met her, the result of being married to a bully. A bully that she has spent part of last weekend with. For all I know, she has spent the whole weekend with him, and maybe even in his bed. But it's also possible that I'm trying to assuage my guilt by thinking she's guilty.

She pours me a glass and drinks a healthy swig of hers. She's usually a sipper. She opens the bag of food I've brought and starts bringing out the items. "Oh good, egg salad," she says.

"While you dish it up, I have something else to get out of the car."

I go outside and get Dusty. Back in the house, I walk into the kitchen. With his ears perked up, Frazier eyes what I'm holding. Dusty takes the opportunity to yip sharply.

Ellen whirls around. "Look at him! Where did you get him? Can I hold him?"

"If you don't think Frazier will be jealous."

She takes Dusty from me and cuddles him. Frazier stretches up onto his hind legs to see what Ellen is up to, so I crouch down to give him a good scratch on the back and behind the ears. I tell Ellen the short version of how I came to find Dusty.

"Poor little guy." She nuzzles him. "Can I introduce him to Frazier?"

"Sure, set him on the floor. Let's see what Frazier does."

Frazier rushes over to him, and for a second my heart pauses. What if Frazier decides to take a big bite? The puppy is not big enough to defend himself. Frazier sniffs him all over and then steps back and gives a low growl.

"No, Frazier, be a good boy," Ellen says.

Frazier decides that being a good boy would be better accomplished if he backs away with a baleful look.

"Oh, Frazier, come back. You're my good boy." He stops at the doorway and pouts.

I scoop up Dusty. This is Frazier's territory after all.

"Tell me what you've been up to while I've been gone," she says once we're sitting down to eat. The two dogs have settled at our feet. "You told me you had Thanksgiving with Jenny and Will. Did you have fun?" It's almost as if she knows and is poking at me.

I wish I could confess to her that I've met someone, but seeing how tired she looks, I postpone the discussion. Plus, maybe I don't even need to tell her. It could be that Wendy and I aren't really going anywhere. It may only be a quick fling. The thought of which makes my stomach plunge. But if I feel that way about Wendy and not about Ellen, is it fair to keep seeing Ellen?

She's still waiting for my answer, and looking at me oddly.

"I did have a good time. I like those two. And what about you?" I had not planned to ask her, but I want to change the conversation away from dangerous territory.

She puffs out a sigh and looks like she's going to say something, but instead she takes a bite of her egg salad and chews thoughtfully. There are tears in her eyes. "Would it be okay with you if we didn't talk about it tonight?"

"Of course it is." She had wanted me to come over to talk about our Thanksgiving stories, and now she's changed her mind.

She forces a smile. "Tell me more about the case you're working on."

"It's been a tough weekend." I tell her some vague details about the investigation. It's too horrendous to share more. "There are all these loose ends that I can't fit together. I'm going to have to hand it over to the DPS or the Rangers. They've got a lot more resources than I do, and I'm floundering."

"There's no shame in that," she says. "The man was a stranger and you don't know details about his family or his life. How is the man's wife doing?"

I tell her about Margaret's ordeal today.

"Oh, the poor woman. She must feel vulnerable out there at the lake by herself. And to be attacked in her own home! Do you think she'd like it if I went to see her?"

Her generous words remind me of why I like Ellen. She's thoughtful and kind. She's popular with the people she teaches in her workshops because of it. "She'll be out of the hospital tomorrow. I'll ask her if she'd like to meet you. She has been to a couple of meetings of the lady's sewing circle that Loretta is part of. Loretta says she isn't particularly social."

"Just a thought. Let me know."

Frazier is keeping up a low growl at Dusty, and I can see Dusty is puzzled. "Look, I have to get an early start tomorrow, and I can see you're tired. Let's talk tomorrow."

CHAPTER 20

I'm a good sleeper, but last night I tossed and turned, worrying first about Ellen and Wendy, and then turning my attention to Margaret Wilkins. I'm not doing right by any of them. By morning, I've come to a decision I don't like, but which is the right thing to do.

As I walk up from the pasture, I hear a familiar voice calling out, and I walk around to the front of the house. "I'm here!" I yell.

"Good. Got something for you," Loretta says. I go up the front steps and hold the door open for her. Loretta bustles in, carrying a plate that wafts a welcome scent, and sets it down on the kitchen table.

"Cinnamon rolls?" I ask, peeking under the foil.

"I felt like baking this morning. It's that kind of weather. I had gotten away from regular baking, and I miss it."

"You couldn't have made me any happier if you had brought me a pot of gold," I say, snatching one of the rolls and taking a big bite. For a moment I concentrate on the taste of those rolls that I've missed. "This may be the best you've ever made."

"They did turn out pretty good."

I put some coffee on and we sit for a few minutes. She tells me stories from her Thanksgiving visit. "I love my relatives, but I swear they would try the patience of a saint." She tells me her Uncle Edgar, who is at least ninety, has stopped smoking, but has taken up dipping snuff. "If that isn't the nastiest habit, I don't know what is."

Eventually she brings up the attack on Margaret, which she heard about from someone whose sister is a nurse at the hospital in Bobtail.

"She wasn't hurt too badly, but they wanted to keep her overnight in the hospital for observation."

"I called Connie. She's going over there today to check in on Margaret. She said with the kids home at Thanksgiving, she barely had time to get out of the kitchen. She told me she wanted to ask Margaret and her kids over for turkey dinner, but her family vetoed it. Anyway, I guess Margaret's kids dropped by to see her kids Thursday night, so they did get to visit."

I tell her I haven't come up with any solid leads on the case, and that I'm glad Maria is back. "Maybe between the two of us we can come up with something." I don't mention that I'm likely to turn it over to the DPS today.

"That little gal is a firecracker," she says.

She and Maria have gotten along ever since Maria helped her figure out who was vandalizing her flowers.

It's nice to spend a little time with Loretta, but after a while I tell her I've got to get to work. She jumps up. "I don't know why I'm sitting here. I've got a hundred things to do, too."

The phone is already ringing when I walk into headquarters. I was planning to call the Department of Public Safety first thing, and they've beaten me to the punch. The man on the phone is my old pal with the Texas Rangers, Luke Schoppe. "I believe your ears must have been burning yesterday, and not in a good way," he says.

"Schoppe, I thought you were going to retire. Did they hire you to maintain the gossip channel?"

"Don't change the subject. Sounds like we're going to have to send somebody over there to solve the murder of that man out at the lake. Looks like you're not as up to the task as I thought you'd be."

"I'm not up to it as much as I thought I would be, either. I'm stumped. But I'm not going to let my ego run away with me. I was going to call over to the county this morning and ask for some help. It's taking more resources than I've got."

"Like what?"

"The man, Lewis Wilkins, lived in San Antonio. I don't have the manpower to send people over there to research who he is and what he might have been up to, although Maria Trevino did a little snooping around when she was there this weekend."

"Listen, I'm driving over to Bryan in a few minutes. It'll take me an hour to get there. Can you meet me at the DPS office there? We can talk it over."

"I sure can." I don't like it that the first thing I think of when I hang up is that since I'll in Bryan, maybe I'll have a few minutes to stop by and see Wendy. It's like I don't have control over my own actions. I haul out my cell phone and dial her number.

I can't help grinning when she answers. I tell her I have to come over there to talk to a Ranger about the Wilkins case, and she says, "What time?"

"I should be free by noon. You want to get some lunch?"

"I'll make us something here." Her chuckle is a like purr. "You think that will be okay?"

I tell her I think it will work out. She says she's pretty sure it will.

Bill Odum's wife calls to say that his cold has settled into bronchitis and he won't be in for a couple of more days. I phone Maria and tell her where I'm off to. She asks me if I want her to go to Bryan, too, and doesn't seem to notice that I'm awfully quick to say no.

Schoppe doesn't get to Bryan until 10 a.m. He suggests we walk down the street to a coffee shop. He looks suddenly older. I hope he's okay. We've been friends a long time.

"You mind if we drive?" I ask.

"It's only a couple of blocks. You getting old?"

"I've got a puppy with me. I'll have to leave him in my pickup, but I don't want it out of my sight."

"A puppy?" He laughs.

We find a place in a yellow zone in front. It's still chilly, but the sun is out and I leave the windows down. It only takes finding one dog that has succumbed to heat in a car to assure that you'll never make that mistake yourself.

When we're settled at a table in the corner, he says, "You told me you're thinking of turning over the Wilkins investigation. What have you got so far?"

"You know about Wilkins's hands being tied when the dogs attacked him?"

"Yeah, we got that in the officers' report. You said you were looking into his activities in San Antonio. Seems like a dog attack doesn't point to a city kind of crime, so maybe he was involved in something around here."

"You're right, and there is an angle I'm working on." I tell him there are hints that his murder might have had to do with gambling on dog-fighting. "I don't have any hard evidence to back it up, though. You know anything about dogfights being held in the county?"

He clears his throat. "Matter of fact I do, but you're not going to like it. We've had a few reports that there've been some matches in the last few months here and there. Not only Bobtail County, but Bartleson and Marris as well. The problem is, nobody is likely to pursue it."

"Why not?"

"You know anytime you ask 'why,' the answer is always money. DPS doesn't feel like it has the resources to put into investigating dogfighting."

"Why the hell not?"

"For one thing, dogfighting is a big business. A lot of money gets thrown around, some of it in the direction of the law." We both ponder that for a minute. Payoffs don't sit well with most lawmen.

"Another problem is that people who get the fights together move around a lot, so it's hard to catch them in the act. Catching them usually takes an undercover operation. That can take months, if not years, and it takes personnel off bigger cases. Plus, there's a lot of danger to investigating it. A few lawmen have been killed in undercover work."

"I never knew the Rangers to be timid when it comes to investigating dangerous situations."

He fiddles with his coffee cup, keeping his eyes on it, and looking annoyed. "It's not the danger. It's a matter of whether the reward is worth the effort. You're putting yourself in a position to be killed, but if you catch anybody, even if they're convicted the penalty is a slap on the wrist. So the DPS feels like it ought to concentrate on more high-profile crimes, ones that you can put people away for."

"What do you mean, slap on the wrist?"

"Fighting or training a dog to fight is only a Class A misdemeanor. And attending a fight is only a Class C. I mean what's the point of putting officers in such danger if the people they catch get a maximum of two years in prison. And I never heard of anybody getting that much."

"I didn't know that. But why would somebody kill a lawman if the penalty is so light?"

"A man who's willing to put a dog through all that is not exactly the salt of the earth. And I'm going to tell you something else. I once worked on one of those cases; and when we caught the guy, I talked to him. He was pissed off that dogfighting was against the law at all! He thought he ought to be able to do what he wanted to with a dog. He ended up getting a year, and was on probation in six months."

"One thing's for sure. If somebody involved in those fights killed Lewis Wilkins, they're going to get a lot more than a year in prison."

"That's true, but, Samuel, I got to tell you I don't like the idea of you going after those people single-handedly. I think you're right. You ought to wait until the DPS gets on it. Shouldn't be much more than a couple of weeks."

I picture Margaret Wilkins's face when I tell her the investigation of her husband's murder is being put on the back burner for two weeks. I can't let that happen.

"My problem is that I may be wrong about the dogfighting. There are other puzzles." I tell him about the boat and the money and the attack on Margaret Wilkins. I follow up with Wilkins's lawsuit and the toll it took on his family.

"Lordy, that man was into a lot of trouble. You're right, it might have nothing to do with dogfighting."

"Except that he was killed by vicious dogs. My question is, if the people who snatched Wilkins out of his van and killed him did it because of dogfighting, what was their point?"

"Money, I would guess."

"That makes sense on the surface, but he had the money with him in the SUV. So why didn't they take it? It wasn't hard to find."

Schoppe strokes his jaw. "They must not have known he had the money on him."

"Then why didn't he tell them?"

"You're right, that points to the idea that whoever took him did it for some reason other than dogfighting."

I sigh. "But then why did they turn dogs on him?"

He shakes he head. "You've got a real can of worms on your hands. Whoever gets assigned to this will be grateful that you have gotten this far."

I don't tell him that now I've talked this out with him, I've changed my mind.

❧

During the fifteen-minute drive to Wendy's I lecture myself and plan how it will be. As soon as she answers the door, I'll say that we have to talk. I'll tell her that I'm seeing someone and that I don't feel right cheating on her. No, not cheating. That sounds like words from a country and western song. I just need to tell her that I don't feel right seeing her until I've sorted out my feelings about Ellen.

I park, and when I'm gathering Dusty to take in with me, Wendy comes out onto the porch. I'm glad I've got a good, strong heart, because it's keeping double time. She runs down the steps, hair flying, and her laugh practically lifts me off my feet. I put Dusty down, and Wendy and I wrap our arms around each other. My resolve lasts no longer than it takes to get inside the house. There's not even any pretense that we're headed anywhere but the bedroom.

After a while, when we're lying in bed with her head on my shoulder, we're both quiet. I'm thinking that I have to get back to work, and I'm feeling guilty for coming here at all, much less failing in my resolve to bring up Ellen.

She moves away and lies on her side, propping her head on her hand. "Isn't it time we talked about Ellen?"

I freeze, wondering if I really heard her correctly. But I know I did. "So you knew I was seeing someone?"

"Yes. My daughter is always trying to fix me up with someone, and when she heard an eligible male would be at Jenny's for Thanksgiving, she jumped on it. Jenny told her you were involved with someone."

I sigh and glance over at her. Her look is serious. "I kept trying to figure out a way to tell you. Ellen and I were . . . are . . . having some . . . I don't know. Difficulties, I guess you'd say. But that's no excuse," I add hastily. "I should have said something."

"Is it serious between the two of you?"

"Serious?" I ponder the question. "We've seen a lot of each other. I like her. She's a good person. But it's not the same as with you."

Her smile is radiant. "I was completely surprised by you."

"In what way?"

She slips off the bed and starts dressing. "It's been a while since I was attracted to somebody so strongly. I didn't expect it."

"Me either." I get up and begin to dress, too. I stop with my pants on and shirt off. "It's not fair to Ellen or to you to go on like this."

She sits down on the bed again, her back to me. "I'd be lying if I said I didn't want to keep seeing you, but I wouldn't want you to be seeing her, too." She holds up her hand to stop me replying. "I know it's not right to say that, but I'm not into sharing."

"Yes." I feel helpless. I don't know what to say to make it better. I walk around to stand in front of her. "Look, I was completely taken off guard. I didn't expect anything like this."

She reaches her hands out and I take them. "Okay, so we're even." She smiles.

"All I know is I want to keep seeing you. But I have to work it out."

She stands up and moves into my arms. We don't say anything for a minute or two. Then she pulls away. "At least I can feed you before you go."

We had closed Dusty in the kitchen with his chew toy to keep him entertained, and he's happy to see us. While Wendy makes our lunch, I feed him and take him out.

The talk between us over lunch is easy and light. A couple of times I have to remind myself that we aren't a couple and that I may not see her again.

When we're finished eating, she says, "Listen, I've made a decision. A friend of mine asked me to go out to San Francisco with her. I told her I couldn't, but I've changed my mind."

"When will you be leaving?"

"She's leaving tomorrow. I'll follow as soon as I can get packed." She laughs. "Don't look so glum. It will give us a chance to think things over. Don't you think that's a good idea?"

"How long will you be gone?" In the question is my unspoken wish that she wouldn't go at all.

"I don't know for sure. A week? Maybe two?" We look into each other's eyes. "I'm not going to the moon. We can talk on the phone."

I'm in turmoil all the way back to Jarrett Creek. By the time I reach headquarters, the only decision I've made is that I can't let my personal life interfere with the investigation into Lewis Wilkins's murder.

CHAPTER 21

M aria is in the office when I get back from Bryan, and she gives me a funny look. "Where have you been?"

Is it that obvious that I took a detour? "I told you I was going to talk to Schoppe."

"What did he say?"

I tell her that he and I were in agreement that it might be best to turn the case over to the DPS, but that it could take a while for someone to step in.

"Then we have to keep going," she says. "Let's brainstorm."

We talk it out and decide to go back out to the area where Wilkins was killed, and where I found Dusty, so Maria can get the lay of the land.

"What are you going to do with Dusty?" She asks.

"We'll leave him in the car. He'll be fine."

We park down the street from Margaret's place. Her son's car is parked in front, along with hers. It seems sad to me that Margaret's daughter didn't come to visit her after her attack.

Maybe it's because Lewis Wilkins's body was found back in this desolate wasteland behind the homes, but it seems gloomier than ever back here. Overnight rain left muddy areas and puddles, and we slog through them silently until we come to the spot where the body was found. The area is trampled and strewn with remains of the forensic details—a stray glove, evidence markers, yellow tape, and cigarette butts.

"I don't see why people don't clean up after themselves," Maria says.

"It was a gruesome scene. I expect people wanted to get out of here as soon as they could."

"Still." She pauses, hands on her hips, and takes a good look around. She looks behind her. "How far in does this thicket go?"

"It's several miles to the Burton highway, over to the southwest, but I don't know how far back it goes before you hit pastureland. You know this all used to be swampland before the dam was built that formed the lake."

"Gives me the creeps," she says.

To tease her I tell her the story of the child that was supposedly dragged away by a panther in the 1930s.

"Oh, thanks, I really needed to hear that," she says. She stops abruptly. "Listen. What is that?"

I listen, but don't hear anything, and I tell her so. "You're just spooked. What do you think it was?"

"It's a dog howling."

Goosebumps rise along my arms as I remember the dog howls I heard the night I went out to check on Wilkins's SUV and found his cell phone. I'm glad we left Dusty in the car, so I don't have to worry if a pack of dogs comes our way. Although the dogs that attacked Wilkins didn't do it at random, there's still the possibility that packs of dogs roam back here.

Maria must be thinking the same thing, because she unsnaps her gun holster so she can get to the weapon fast. She rests her hand on it. "How far to where you found Dusty's mother?"

"Right up the way here. The body isn't there anymore. The vet took her away."

We forge on. I hope to goodness we don't find another body, or dead puppies. I'm glad there's some sun today, though it keeps dipping behind clouds, and chilled shadows take over. Another three hundred yards, and I recognize the area where the dog's body was. "Right over here." Broken and stomped weed mark where the body was. Again, Maria looks around intently.

"Let's go farther," she says. "We need to see what that dog was howling about."

188

We've walked a half mile farther when the brush gets thicker. The rough trail we've been following almost disappears. I go first to push aside branches and stomp out a path. We're not talking. Circumstances seem to call for quiet. The going is tougher here. We scare up a copperhead that spooks both of us, even though it slithers away into the brush.

"Snakes!" Maria says under breath. "I'm ready to turn back."

"No, we need to keep going. Smell that?" I don't know how long I've been aware of a foul smell, but a shiver of breeze brings a strong whiff. Something dead. There's a body of some kind around here.

"Wait a minute," Maria says. She digs around in her pockets and comes out with a tube of hand cream. She squirts a little on her finger and rubs it under her nose. She hands it to me and I do the same, though I'm not sure which is worse, the sweet citrus smell or the citrus combined with rotting meat.

We round a corner and come upon a large, dilapidated shed, with the door hanging open. It's the source of the foul smell. As we approach, a mangy mutt comes slinking out the door and when he sees us he takes off through the brush. Maria jumps. "What the hell!"

Maria and I exchange glances. "I'll go check inside," I say. "You stay here."

"Take this," she says, and hands me the Smith and Wesson. I hold it at my side as I approach the shed.

"Anybody here?" I call out.

A few steps from the door, I hear a familiar sound. Flies have found whatever is inside. "Hello!" Nothing.

I peer in the window, but it's so crusted with grime that I can't see anything. I ease over to the door, get out my penlight, and shine it inside. It takes me a minute for my eyes to adjust, and when they do, I recoil. Two large animal carcasses lie inside the shed. I take out my handkerchief, hold it to my mouth, and move closer. I'm looking at the bodies of two of the biggest dogs I've ever seen. Their hair is white, like the tufts of hair I found near Wilkins's body.

They have been here some time and are bloated, but I can make out powerful chests and backs. Their heads are massive, with muscular jaws, which is where the flies have settled—because the jaws are black with blood. I'll put my money on the blood being Lewis Wilkins's.

I back out of the shed and find myself a little unsteady from the sight and smell. I give my head a hard shake and go over to Maria.

"Whoa," she says. "You need to sit down?"

"No, I'm all right. It's putrid in there. Let's get back, away from the smell."

I tell her what I found. "Doc England is going to earn his stipend on this one." He is paid to examine animals in suspicious circumstances.

"Yeah, what is it the state gives him in their generosity, forty bucks?"

"Something like that." I look at my cell phone. "No coverage. Let's get on back and call him."

"You want me to stay here?"

"I don't see the point. They've been in that shed a while. If someone was going to clear them out, they would already have done it."

When I call Doc England to tell him about the dogs, he says he needs to finish up a couple of things and he'll meet me at the site as soon as he can. "I'll stay here and meet him," I say. "Then he can take me back to the station. No need for both of us to traipse back out there. And there's something I haven't gotten around to I'd like you to take care of."

She gives me "the look." "It's something annoying, isn't it?"

"Tedious. You're better at things like this than I am."

"That's what men always say when they're foisting off a job on a woman. It's like Tom Sawyer."

"Would you rather go back to that scene?"

She wrinkles her nose. "I guess not."

I tell her where to find Wilkins's cell phone in my desk, and tell her I haven't gone through his phone calls to figure out which were legitimate calls and which were telemarketers. "Anybody who called Wilkins and didn't leave a voicemail, I'd like to know who they were."

"You think somebody called intending to say, 'Meet me here so I can kill you?' and didn't bother to leave a message?"

"Very funny. It's got to be done, that's all."

"All right, boss." She calls me that when she's feeling sulky. "But it's already four o'clock and I'm leaving at five."

"That's fine. An hour ought to give you plenty of time." To appease her, I tell her I'll leave the puppy with her, and that cheers her up. "I'll come by and get him at your place."

When England arrives, he grumbles about having to walk a mile back into the brush to examine dead dogs, but when we get there, he's all business. "These are cane corsos! I wonder what they were doing around here."

"What are cane corsos? All I know is they're as big as a bear."

"They're about the most dangerous dog you can get. They've been bred as guard dogs and attack dogs, and as a result they aren't good pets unless somebody really knows what they're doing when they train them. I wouldn't trust one myself."

"Kind of like pit bulls?"

"Worse. I don't know why anyone would keep one, and I sure don't know what these are doing around here."

I've brought a powerful flashlight and a battery-powered lantern back from the squad car, and I set those up for light. Doc crouches next to one of the dogs and has his own flashlight that he shines on the muzzle where blood has dried, and then moves the light to examine the head. "Look at this." He points to a matted area behind one dog's ear. "This one was shot." He lifts the dog's head. "Shine your flashlight here."

I shine it on the underside of the dog's head.

"No exit wound."

"Probably small-caliber, maybe a hollow-point. I'm going to have to ask you to try to retrieve it for a potential match if we get a suspect with a weapon."

"I understand," he says. He stands up and gazes down at the dogs. "Nasty business." He retrieves his case from outside. "You might want to stay outside for this. I'm not going to try to make it a delicate job. In and out."

It takes him ten minutes. He comes out and has the flattened bullet in a plastic bag. "Bullet looks like a flower," he says.

"Hollow-point," I say. "Probably a 9mm. It could be from a lot of different weapons, but likely a handgun."

"That would be your area," he says. "I can tell you it looks like whoever did this shot the dogs at pretty close range. There's gunshot residue around the bullet hole." I wonder how he knows this, but he seems to know all kinds of things from being a country veterinarian. "I could send somebody to haul the carcasses out of here."

I ponder for a minute whether I ought to get a crime scene investigation out here. Whoever shot these dogs likely had a hand in Wilkins's murder. They might have left a footprint, but between the rain we've had, and Doc England and me tromping through here, there's likely nothing left to find.

I notice that England has taken a device a little larger than a cell phone out of his bag and is approaching the dogs. "What are you doing?"

"It could be that whoever owned them had a microchip put in them. I'm going to scan them to find out."

He turns on the device and starts moving it around on the dog's head and neck. Suddenly the device pings. "Bingo. The microchip will tell you where the dogs came from." He gets up and shows me the device. There's a number on the small screen. "With this we can find out who registered this dog, and where they live."

"Is it a national registry?"

"Every company has a different way of doing it, but they're all on a national database. You'd be surprised how many dogs go missing. This makes it a lot easier to find them. I was going to suggest you get that pup of yours chipped when he gets old enough to start wandering around."

I feel a flutter of excitement. This feels like the first real lead in the case.

On our way back to headquarters, as we pass the marina, Dooley's truck pulls out in front of us. Dooley's son, Bobby, is in the truck with him. Loretta told me that Margaret's kids had gone over to visit Dooley's kids Thanksgiving night. It might not be a bad idea to ask Bobby what they talked about, in case they said something to their friends that they may not say to me.

Maria is still in the office when I get back, because she wants to know what I found out. I fill her in, and she has the same feeling I did, that this may finally give us a lead.

Dusty and I get in my pickup and head for home. I'm grateful that I don't have anything to do tonight, and I'm looking forward to spending an evening by myself. But it's not to be. Apparently Jenny Sandstone has been watching for me, and before I'm even up the steps she calls out from her yard.

I meet her halfway. It's dark by now. She still has on her work clothes. She's a lawyer over in Bobtail, and always wears suits. "I want you to come over and have a glass of wine with me," she says. "We need to talk."

I know what she wants to talk about, and I don't want to get into it. But she's a good friend, and if I'm going to confide in anybody, she's the best candidate. "Let me get some fresh clothes on. I've been dealing with . . . well, I'll tell you when I come over. Want me to bring anything?"

"Just bring yourself. I opened a fine pinot noir."

For the first couple of years Jenny lived next door, we were strangers. She keeps a couple of horses, and I refused to let her use my tank to water them because I didn't care for horses and didn't like that she had taken it for granted I'd say yes. That kept us estranged.

Now I think with embarrassment of how stubborn I was. We've been good friends for a while. I helped her through a hard time after her mamma passed away. One of the things we share is that we both like good wine. She introduced me to a wine club, and we get together every so often to share a good bottle of wine and gossip. I bought a sausage the other day and I'll take that over to add to our usual snack of cheese and crackers.

It's been a while since we spent an evening together, so first we catch up on small talk. She tells me about a case she's working on that's driving her crazy, and I bring her up to date on the Wilkins case. But finally, two glasses in, she says, "I guess you know I didn't call you over here to discuss our jobs."

"I figure you want to talk about my relationship with Wendy Gleason." I find it hard to meet her eye, so I take a sip of wine. "I don't know what to say. I've gotten myself in a situation."

"According to my friend Jessica, that's exactly what you've gotten yourself in."

"You know I really like Ellen."

"So do I." She pauses, looking aghast. "You mean that's all there is to it? You just like her?"

I feel antsy being pinned down. "What do you want me to say?"

She sighs and shakes her head. We're sitting in her living room, the site of many difficult scenes between us several months ago as she wrestled with her past. I'm used to being the one to give advice, not get it. "This is a small town, Samuel. You can't play fast and loose with the ladies without it getting around. I think you should figure out what you're up to before you hurt Ellen."

"I'd like to do that. Figure it out, I mean."

"I don't care which one you choose. I thought Wendy was a hoot the other night. It was the first time I met her. She seems like a free spirit, and I like that."

"Jenny, that's the problem. I'm really attracted to her. She's easy to be with. She's impulsive and funny and . . . all right, I'll come out and say it. She's sexy."

"All the things Ellen isn't."

"Yes, but Ellen has a lot of qualities I value. She's generous and warm and she's . . ." I sigh. It's not enough.

Jenny's eyebrows are up to her hairline. "That's it? That's all you can say for Ellen? How about that she's been through a lot and has managed to make a life for herself? That's admirable. How about that she is an artist? Even if you don't like the work she does, you at least ought to value that. It gives you something in common." She laughs. "Listen to me. I said I wasn't on either woman's side, but I'm making a case for her."

"I'm listening. The thing is, what you said about Wendy, that she's a free spirit. That's what appeals to me. But I feel protective of Ellen. She is steady and . . ."

"Unexciting, is that it?"

I nod, feeling like a schoolboy in the principal's office. "I know I need to tell Ellen that I met Wendy and that I'm not sure what my plans are. But she's been gone and she just got back." I'm not used to feeling wrongheaded, and it makes me defensive. "I only met Wendy last week."

"Does she know about Ellen?"

"Yes. We talked about that. She's actually going away for a couple of weeks to give me a chance to work it out."

"Ahhhh." Jenny's eyes narrow. "She's a sly one."

"What do you mean, sly? She's giving me space."

"Oh, listen to you, all hip psychology." She primps her lips. "*I need some space.*"

"You're right. I promise I'll discuss it with Ellen right away."

"And you don't need to look like a scolded dog. Man up!"

CHAPTER 22

At headquarters the next morning I call Dooley's place and he tells me his son went out fishing early, but that he'll be back by ten o'clock. I'm just hanging up the phone when it rings.

"Craddock? This is Harley Lundsford. You better get on out to my place. I've caught me a couple of criminals."

"What kind of criminals?"

"The dog-stealing type."

"Where are they now?"

"They're tied up in my barn. Now are you going to come out, or not?"

"I'll be there in fifteen minutes. Don't hurt them." Lundsford talks a lot about his love of guns, and I don't want him to get any ideas about shooting whoever he's got tied up.

Maria is walking in the door when I leave. I tell her where I'm going. "How are you getting along with those phone numbers on Wilkins's cell phone?"

"I think I'm done. I went back three months. How far back did you want me to go?"

"Three months should be plenty. Did you find anything?"

"I don't know for sure. He didn't make many phone calls. There were a few calls from his son and his wife, and one from Dooley. And some business calls. There were a few I couldn't identify. I thought maybe I'd listen to voicemail messages. Listen for anything odd. Are we legal here?"

"His wife gave me the okay."

"I'm going to finish that now unless you want me to go along with you."

I hear the reluctance in her voice. She's met Lundsford and finds him offensive. He made it clear he doesn't have much use for "ladies" in law enforcement. "No, I'll be okay. I'll call you if I need you."

"All right, you go off and have fun while I'm stuck here playing with this cell phone. And good luck with Lundsford."

Lundsford's place is in the middle of nowhere. Not that Jarrett Creek is "somewhere," but it's at least on the map. To get to Lundsford's you have to go out past the cemetery, north of the lake, and keep heading west. But when you get there, you'll never find a tidier farm. He raises turkeys, ducks, and chickens, and although he will never get rich, he seems to make a good living. His wife is his bookkeeper, and he has a disabled son whom I've met only a couple of times, but who Lundsford says is "the duck whisperer."

A couple of big, frisky dogs of indeterminate breed greet me when I get out of squad car, and they seem to sense that Dusty is in the car. They stick their heads in after I get out, sniffing with great interest.

"They're friendly," Lundsford says, as he ambles across the yard.

"You think they'll be all right with my pup?"

"They're gentle as lambs. They have to be, around the poultry."

I take Dusty out and set him on the ground so the dogs can sniff him. Their tails whip back and forth and they dance around him.

"He's a nice little pup," Lundsford says. "I like a dog. That's why I was so put out when I caught two boys trying to lure Tippy and King into their truck. See, it's parked over there by the side of the barn."

I look over and recognize the pickup with the faded flames that John Hershel described as being driven by the men he caught trying to steal his dog. This makes it twice these men have been caught. Not exactly brilliant criminals.

"How did you catch them?"

"They thought they'd sneak up in the night, but my boy, Jimmy, has ears like a bat. He come running into the bedroom and says, 'Daddy, somebody's outside creeping around.'" Sure enough, I go out with my shotgun and catch them dead to rights. They had some meat and were trying to lure my dogs into their car."

"Harley, that's more words than I've heard you string together at once in all the time I've known you."

He has a fierce gleam in his eyes, and I have a feeling I know just what he's going to say. Sure enough he says, "I'm riled up. Now people won't be so quick to think I'm nuts for keeping guns for protection."

"Nobody thinks you're nuts," I say, although that isn't entirely true. It's not that he keeps guns that bothers people, but that he seems to be obsessed with them.

"Come on out to the barn and take these thieves off my hands."

The barn is a fine, sturdy structure. The dogs follow us, with Dusty struggling to keep up.

As soon as Lundsford opens the door, someone yells, "Let us out of here!"

"I'm going to close the bottom part of the door so the dogs stay out," Lundsford says. He does so, and then he motions to a door at the back of the barn and we walk over. He picks up the shotgun that he has leaned against a wall before he unlocks a door. "They ain't going anywhere, but I like to be careful," he says.

Inside, he has two men in their twenties tied up with barely enough play in the rope so they can reach a bucket that he has positioned for them to relieve themselves in.

"Who are you?" one of them says. He's a burly youngster with fire-red hair, small eyes, and a bristle of red beard.

"I'm Samuel Craddock, chief of police in Jarrett Creek. I don't believe I know you boys."

"You gotta let us go," he says. "We didn't do anything. This man's crazy. Him and his retard son." He jerks his chin in Lundsford's direction.

Lundsford flinches and tightens his grip on his shotgun.

"Can I get your names?"

"I'm Cal," the red-haired one says, "and my pal is Pete."

"What were you doing out here?" I ask.

"We were lost," Cal says. Pete, a dark-haired, dark-eyed man with a furious look in his eyes, hasn't said anything.

"You was lost and you thought maybe you'd use my dogs to lead you out of here?" Lundsford says.

I hear somebody come in, and turn my head to see his son, a stocky man with a moon face standing behind us. I nod to him. "Hi, Jimmy."

"They're bad men," he says. "They were trying to steal Tippy and King."

"What would we want with two mutts like that?" Cal says.

"They ain't mutts," Jimmy says, with a hitch in his voice. "They're good dogs."

"I'm going to take you boys back to the station and have a chat with you. Lundsford, you can come down to the station, and I'll take your statement whenever you want to."

"Goddammit!" Pete snarls. "You can't run us in. We told you we haven't done nothing."

"We have connections," Cal chimes in. "We can have your job."

"And welcome to it. We'll sort all that out when I get you down to the station," I say. "Unless you want me to leave you here so Mr. Lundsford can figure out what he wants to do with you."

They decide they'd prefer to go with me.

I untie Cal and put cuffs on him and take him to the squad car. Lundsford waits for me to come get Pete. When they're locked inside the car, Lundsford says, "I'm going to follow you to the station. Jimmy, can you take care of things while I'm gone for a while?"

"I sure can."

"Remember your mama is here, if you run into trouble, but I know you'll do fine." With that interaction I see Lundsford in a different light than I've seen him before. The boy is full of pride that his daddy trusts him to take over in his absence.

"I want you to know, I've been looking for these two," I say. "I don't know what they're up to, but they've stolen more than one dog, and I'm going to get to the bottom of it."

Back at the station, I give Maria their driver's licenses to check if they have any open charges against them, and then I lead them into the back room to lock them into a cell.

"You've got a female cop working here?" Cal says, as soon as Maria goes back into the office.

"You got a problem with that?"

"I guess not." His sneer tells me that he does.

When Lundsford arrives a few minutes later, I poke my head into the office and ask Maria to take his statement while I talk with the criminals.

As soon as I walk back to the cell, they start up. "We ought to be fed," Cal says. "That man kept us tied up and didn't feed us anything."

"I'll get you a sandwich in a little bit. First I need some answers." I settle myself in a chair outside the cell. "Talk to me," I say.

"About what?" Cal says.

"What were you two doing out there?"

"Told you, we were lost."

I wave my hands back and forth. "No, no, that doesn't fly. Lundsford found you trying to lure his dogs into your pickup. Now we've had several cases of dogs disappearing around here, and I want to know what you're up to. I'm having your truck towed in, and I'm going to go through it with a fine-tooth comb. If I find evidence that one of those dogs that have gone missing has been in your truck, you're going to jail."

Pretty much nothing of what I said is true. For one thing, what would I charge them with? At most, a misdemeanor for stealing a dog.

I can't prove they hurt the dogs, even if they did steal them. And I'm probably not going to waste a lot of time examining their vehicle. The question is, will they take the bluff?

"You can't haul my truck in!" Pete says.

So this is Pete's vehicle. "Sure I can. But I might be inclined to back off if you tell me what you did with the dogs."

Cal looks sidelong at his buddy, and I know I've nailed them.

I wait, while Cal gives his chin a good scratching and Pete tries to kill me with a laser stare. Finally Cal says, "We're going to sell them."

"You need to be a little more specific. Sell them to who?"

"A guy told us he'll give us good money for them."

"What guy?"

"I never met him. He called me and told me there was money if I picked up a few dogs."

"How much money?"

"Fifty dollars per dog."

"Pretty generous."

"It would have been if we wasn't sitting in this cell."

"Any dogs in particular?"

"No, he just said random dogs."

"Has he paid you?"

"Not yet. He said we'd get paid when we round up a dozen dogs. We only have eight. You'd be surprised how hard it is to find dogs to steal. People keep their dogs pretty close."

"It must be tough on you. Where are the dogs now?"

"In a shed out in the woods on the road to Burton."

"And you leave the dogs there? Is there somebody there to take care of them?"

"No, we're not mean. We leave water for them. And we feed them. It's not cheap. Dogs eat a lot. I don't know if it's going to be worth it in the end."

Does he actually think I'm going to sympathize? "But the dogs are okay?"

"Yeah. They're a little stir-crazy from being penned up, but they seem okay. I don't want to hurt a dog. I kind of admire them. They're all shitting in one corner, kind of like they got together and figured out that's where the potty is." He snickers and nudges Pete, who doesn't join in the laughter.

It's a relief that the dogs are okay, if in fact he's telling the truth. "When was the last time you took a dog over there?"

"A couple of days ago. We was supposed to take another one, but the guy caught us and we gave it up for the day."

"How will you get paid when you have enough dogs?"

"The man gave me a phone number to call."

"I'm going to need that phone number."

"I've got it here," Cal says. He takes out his wallet, fishes around in it, and through the bars of the cell hands me a filthy piece of paper with a number scratched on it.

"And you don't know what he was going to do with the dogs? You didn't ask what he wanted them for?"

"No sir." Cal shrugs.

"It never occurred to you that the dogs might be used in ways that they may suffer, and that you're causing suffering to the people you stole pets from as well?"

Pete has continued to fume silently. "They can get another damn dog," he says. "What's the big deal?"

"If causing suffering isn't a big deal to you, maybe it will be a bigger deal that you've been stealing someone's property and you're going to jail if anything has happened to any of the dogs."

"I swear they were fine the last time saw them," Cal says. Pete may be immune to threats, but Cal is nervous.

"All right, I want you to show me where the dogs are, and if they're okay, then we'll call it quits. Were any of the dogs you picked up a pregnant bitch?"

They look at each other. "I don't think so. If she was, not far enough along so you'd notice."

"One more thing. Did you steal a couple of cane corsos?"

The two look at each other. "Cane what?" Cal asks.

"Big dogs. Vicious."

Cal shakes his head. "I'm not exactly afraid of dogs, but I won't have anything to do with a vicious dog. I don't want to get bit."

Maria has checked to see if either of the boys has a criminal record. Calvin Madigan has a couple of misdemeanor driving offenses, but neither of them has any outstanding charges.

I tell Maria I'm going over to get some sandwiches for the two guys and ask if she wants anything, but she says it's too early for lunch. When I get back, I hand the criminals their sandwiches and tell them they can eat in the car. I want to get out to where the dogs are being kept.

I hate to do it, but when we leave I lock Dusty up in the empty cell again. He'll probably sleep the whole time we're gone, and I don't want to get in a situation with him where there are a bunch of dogs around that I don't know anything about.

CHAPTER 23

As soon as Cal gives me directions, I suspect I know where the dogs are being kept. We travel south of town and onto the road out to Burton. Maria is with me, and to be on the safe side we have handcuffed the two men in case they have some kind of nefarious ideas. But they seem almost cheerful now that we're getting close to where they left the dogs.

Sure enough, Cal guides me straight to the area where Wilkins's SUV was found. I remember hearing dogs barking when I was leaving the scene the night I first examined the SUV. If I had investigated then, it would have saved the poor dogs some time being locked up and their owners some distress. It might also have brought me closer to figuring out what the dogs have to do with this case.

We park and I hear the dogs in the distance.

"They make a racket," Cal says. "I imagine they're tired of being cooped up."

"Do they fight each other?"

"Not that I saw. These are pet dogs." Again I think of what fate might have awaited them if they had been turned over to use as bait dogs.

"It's off that way," Cal says. "Over to the right." He points to the path I took before I decided to turn back because it was dark.

Maria and I leave the two men in the car and head off on foot in the direction of the barking. The vegetation is overgrown with weeds, and droopy vines hang off the trees.

Pretty soon we come to the big shed. It's much bigger than the shed where we found the two dogs shot. The racket is fierce. The shed isn't locked, and we pull open the door. The stench is terrible, and we both cough. There's fencing across the door so the dogs can't get out. They leap up, tails wagging and barking like crazy. But I have to admit, they don't look abused. Like Cal said, there are eight dogs. Over by the wall there are several bowls lined up and a big washtub with water in it.

"I wonder whose property this is," I say, "and whether they knew what this shed was being used for. Surely they could hear this commotion."

"What are we going to do with these dogs?" Maria says. "We can't leave them here. Suppose whoever paid those guys to steal them comes to take them away?"

"One of us needs to stay here and guard the place. I hate to ask you, but I think you should stay so I can come back with my pickup. That way we can get all the dogs out of here at one time."

She looks around nervously. Maria is not one to be afraid, but the place doesn't have a good atmosphere. "You're right. I'll stay."

"I'll tell you what. I'll leave you the shotgun."

"I appreciate that."

We hate to close the dogs back up, but there's nothing more to be done until I come back with my pickup. I go back and bring the shotgun to her, and we scout out a place for her to keep an eye on the shed without being out in the open.

On the way back I drive a lot faster than I did on the way over. I tell the two boys that when I return with the dogs, I'll take them out to Lundsford's place to pick up their truck, but until then they'll have to hang out in town. "As long as you can behave yourselves."

"We're not criminals," Cal says. "We needed some cash."

"You're still criminals in my book," I say. "You're lucky I don't have the time to fool with petty criminals at the moment."

As soon as they're on their way, I jump into my pickup and floor it back out to where I left Maria. I didn't like leaving her out there alone, not knowing who might be lurking around the shed. She's fine, though, except for the dogs driving her crazy with their barking.

To move the dogs to the pickup, we use rope for leashes, and then lash them to the bars inside the pickup so they won't jump out. Bringing out two dogs at a time, it takes two trips, thirty minutes total. The dogs are wild with excitement.

When we show up at Doc England's with eight dogs, he comes out to take a look and starts laughing. "I have to say I'm laughing partly out of relief. I hate to see a family dog disappear, and there are going to be some happy people. I recognize at least three of them right off the bat. We'll get them sorted out. I have a pen I can put them in around back, and Chelsea will make phone calls to the owners and to other vets in the area to see if they have any reports of missing dogs."

I tell him to be sure and call Bobtail, because my friend in the police department there said they had had reports of missing dogs.

"How did you find them?" he asks.

I tell him that Harley Lundsford is responsible for capturing the boys. "The boys had a phone number for somebody they were supposed to call to sell the dogs to. I'll try the number as soon as I have some time." I have my doubts that it's going to be useful. I suspect whoever has this scam going will have security in place so he doesn't get caught.

"After we get the dogs settled, I have something else to tell you," he says.

We get the dogs penned up with some food and water, and then I go in to talk to England.

"I heard back about the dead dogs we found. They were registered, but the registration address wasn't up to date. The folks at the registration office said people sell dogs sometimes, and the new owners often don't bother to change the registration."

"Did you get the original owner's information?"

He hands me a sheet of paper with a name, address, and phone number.

I tell him the story the boys told me. "They said they were getting paid fifty bucks per dog."

He grunts. "Well, you can tell them they were being short-changed. If these dogs are going to medical labs, they're paying well over five hundred dollars a dog."

"Why didn't I know that?"

"It's an awful business, and every few years you'll get an article written about it and everybody gets stirred up, but then it goes back to normal. It's hard to police that kind of thing." It makes me think of what Schoppe told me about dogfighting not being high on the list of priorities for law enforcement. Dogs going to medical labs or to dogfighting. Both do a brisk business and the dogs suffer either way.

By the time I get Cal and Pete out to Lundsford's to retrieve their pickup, leaving them with a warning not to show their faces around here any time soon, it's past lunchtime.

"I'm going to treat you to a fancy lunch," I say to Maria when I arrive back at headquarters.

She gives me her eye roll.

"I'm even going to let you choose the place."

"Let me think. Town Café or the Mexican restaurant? Hard to decide."

"You forget there's also the DQ."

She perks up. "We could get hamburgers there." Her favorite food.

That's what we do, her a plain hamburger, and me a chili cheese-burger, and we bring them back to the station so we can talk while we eat.

"I'm trying not to jump to conclusions," I say right off, "but it seems like an awfully big coincidence that dogs have been stolen and that dogs killed Lewis Wilkins. But I'm damned if I can make the connection."

"Maybe there's no connection. Maybe it really is nothing more than coincidence."

"There's something else, though. Remember what Margaret said about the two men who attacked her—that one had light hair and the other dark?"

"You think they could be the ones who did it?"

I hesitate. "I don't have any real reason to think so, but that's a second coincidence. One coincidence I can ignore, two not so much."

My phone rings. It's a number I don't recognize.

"Uh, is this Craddock?" Whoever he is sounds furtive.

"Yes, this is Chief Craddock."

"This is Randy Coyle." He's mumbling and I have to strain to hear him. "Dunn, down at the motorcycle place, asked me to give you a call. Said you had some questions?"

"Mr. Coyle, I appreciate your getting in touch. When can we meet?"

"You understand this is off the record. Dunn told me you were a man of your word, but I have to be careful."

"You have my word. I need to get a general idea. I don't have to hear specifics."

Maria is watching me with curiosity. She's not used to hearing me pussyfoot around.

He tells me where I can meet him. "I don't want to be seen with the law," he says.

When I hang up, I tell Maria where I'm going.

"I hope he isn't planning to ambush you," she says.

"Why would he do that?"

"I don't know, but I don't trust people who are into something so awful."

I haven't spoken to Margaret since she got out of the hospital, although Maria called her earlier this morning. Margaret said that aside from a headache, she's okay and that her son is taking good care of her. She also tells me that Connie called and is going to bring some food to her.

I've got some time before I have to meet Randy Coyle, so I run out to Margaret's place. It's time I bring her up to date on the investigation, although I dread it.

Daniel meets me at the door, and before I can say anything, he puts his finger to his lips and steps out onto the porch. He looks grim. "I want to talk to you before you go in with my mother. Do you have any clues about who attacked her?"

"She wasn't able to give a description. I've talked to the Department of Public Safety about getting more people on the case, but they said it could be a week or more. So until they take over, I'm pursuing a couple of ideas."

"Like what?"

"I'm not at liberty to say."

"What do you mean, 'not at liberty'? Don't give me that small-town cop BS."

I blink, not having expected him to lash out. "You think you'd get more information out of a big-city cop? I sincerely doubt it. We're not in the habit of discussing our suspects with civilians."

Now it's his turn to blink, and he shakes his head as if to clear it. "I apologize. I'm on edge. I need to get back to work, but I don't want to leave Mamma here by herself after what happened."

"I understand. What kind of work do you do?"

"I'm in commercial real estate. Just getting started. It's a tough business to break into."

"You in San Antonio?"

"Actually, I've just moved to Houston. The opportunities are better there. I got hired on by a big company."

The door opens and Margaret peers out. "Daniel, why don't you invite Chief Craddock inside?"

Margaret has a haunted look that I've seen before in people who have been assaulted, but as usual she has herself under control. "I can't stay long, but I wanted to check on you and update you on the case," I say. I tell her the same thing I told Daniel, that until the DPS sends out a team, I'll continue to investigate. We sit down in the living room. She sits in a chair that is surrounded by signs that she is cared for—a stack of books, a footstool, and a lap blanket—and Daniel sits where he can keep an eye on her.

"Have you remembered anything else about the men who attacked you?"

"It was so sudden." She kneads her brow with her fingers. "I've gone over it again and again, and I don't remember anything I didn't already tell you. One of them did most of the talking, and he wasn't brutal. He almost sounded apologetic."

"You said you were afraid they would kill you."

"Yes, I was. I didn't know what they were going to do. And then when they left me tied up, I was afraid nobody would come to find me."

Daniel groans.

"Give it some more thought. Either of them use an unusual phrase or mention the other one by name—you'd be surprised at the number of people who get caught because somebody forgot and used a name."

She bites her lip as she tries to recall the incident, and at one point she shivers.

"You really think this is going to do any good?" Daniel says sharply.

"Daniel, I don't mind, if there's any chance of catching these people."

"I want to know what they were after," Daniel says.

I'm startled. I look at Margaret, and she has her hand over her mouth. She drops her hands into her lap. "Go ahead and tell him."

I fill him in on the money I found in Wilkins's SUV. "I don't suppose you know what your daddy intended to do with that much money."

"Not a clue." His eyes are blazing and he blurts out, "But whatever it was, he clearly didn't intend to let my mother know he had it. From what you've been finding out about him, it was probably to pay off gambling debts."

"Daniel, we don't know that. Don't jump to conclusions."

"The guys who attacked you weren't kidding around," he says to her. "They were thugs. Dad was associating with thugs." He's practically shouting. He gets up and shoves his hands in his pockets. "You have the money now?" he says to me.

"It's in a safe deposit box. At the moment, it's evidence. Eventually it will go to your mamma, unless it's stolen, and then it will be up to the state to figure out where it goes."

CHAPTER 24

I follow Randy Coyle's directions to a trailer park out between Jarrett Creek and Bryan. At his request, I've changed into civilian clothes and I'm driving my own truck, so people won't recognize me as a lawman. All the way I work to tamp down my memory of that terrible fight my daddy took me to. It's not like I haven't gotten over it; I hadn't thought about it in years. The events of the past week and a half have dredged it up.

The "trailer park" is a collection of RVs and Airstreams in a clearing off the road that seem to have gotten together with no central idea. It reminds me of a haphazard wagon train in a western movie.

Coyle's trailer is not the worst of the lot. It's reasonably clean on the outside but looks abandoned. The curtains are drawn and there's no car around anywhere. But when I knock on the door, it opens and a man says, "Get inside."

I go in, alert, ready to pull my weapon if I have to. The light is dim, but when my eyes get accustomed to it everything looks fine. The man in front of me is slim, dressed in well-pressed khaki pants, a plain white T-shirt, and a jean jacket. His brown hair is cropped short, and he's clean-shaven. He's a nice-looking guy, and as Dunn mentioned, he looks like he is a regular citizen, and not someone into a horrible pastime.

He doesn't offer to shake hands, and neither do I. I've brought a six-pack of beer as he requested. He asks me if I want one, but I tell him no so he puts the whole pack into the refrigerator without taking one himself either.

He motions for me to sit at a small dinette table next to the kitchen, and he sits opposite me. "What is it you want to know?"

I've figured that he's not going to give me long, so on the way over I prioritized my questions. "I've heard that people who fight dogs use pets for bait dogs."

"Bullshit. That's a stupid rumor. Why would a person who respects dogs do something so awful? I've heard that rumor before and it pisses me off."

Respects dogs. Right. "I assume that dog matches bring out heavy gambling."

"It's like any other sport."

"Sport?"

"Damn right, it's a sport. How is it any different from getting someone in top form to box or wrestle? Or getting a horse in condition for a race? You think a racing horse has a say in the matter?"

"They're running a race, not trying to attack each other. And the man who's boxing has a say-so in the matter. The dog doesn't."

"Of course he does. If he doesn't want to fight, he sits down."

"And gets torn to pieces?"

He slams his hand down on the table. He may look innocuous, but he has a short temper. "You see, that's why I don't like to talk to outsiders. You don't get it. People who have a dog they've raised and trained don't want to get them killed, or hurt too bad. A dog is no good to you dead. If they get too badly injured, they'd have to be put down. So if they're getting the worst end of the deal, you pull them. With a fighting dog in top shape, you patch him up and in a few weeks he's good to go."

He sounds reasonable, but I have trouble with the concept. "I assume most of the dogs you fight are pit bulls?"

"A good number." He looks at his watch.

"Ever heard of a cane corso being fought?"

He holds his hands up like I'm holding a gun on him. "Every now and then you'll hear of it, but that's a dog you don't want to mess with. They're trouble."

"More than a pit bull?"

"Your pit is loyal. Your corso has the reputation of being unpredictable. Not that I know from personal experience, and I don't intend to."

"Would anybody ever put a cane corso into a fight if it wasn't trained?"

"Oh, hell no. Fighting dogs have to be trained right from a pup. You can't just go out and find a dog and say, 'get in there and fight.'" He glances at his watch again.

"A couple more questions. I understand that people who set up dogfights move around. Have there been any in the area recently?"

"I can't answer that." He gets up. "I'm going to have to call this quits."

I get up, too. "I appreciate your information. One quick thing. If somebody bets on the fights, how deep in debt can they get before they're in big trouble?"

He squints his eyes, thinking. "That's hard to say. Depends on who you're in debt to and how much they think you can get your hands on."

"As much as two hundred thousand dollars?"

He blows out a breath. "That's some serious debt. I was thinking more in the fifty-thousand range. Two hundred thousand? I never heard of anybody getting close to that, and I think I would have heard. People would talk."

I'm getting into my truck when my phone rings. It's Wendy, and for once I don't feel excited to talk to her. It's hard to shift gears after what I've just heard.

"Wendy? Where are you?"

"I'm leaving for the airport and wanted to say good-bye. That's all."

"Which airport are you leaving from?" I want to feel some connection because she's leaving, but I'm numb.

"I'm driving to Houston. The best flights leave from there."

"I wish I could have driven you there."

"It's best this way. I'm glad I didn't get your voicemail, though. At least I get to say good-bye for real."

"I hope you have a good time," I say, but it still feels wooden. How can someone like Randy Coyle exist in the same world with Wendy?

I'm out of sorts when I get back to the station, but I feel marginally better when I walk in and find Maria playing with Dusty. She's tied a knot in a length of rope, and he's worrying it and yipping at it.

"Glad you made it out alive," she says. "Did you get any useful information?"

"As a matter of fact, I did. He said he didn't know anybody who would fight cane corsos, so those dogs that killed Wilkins were probably not fighting dogs."

"Then why did they attack Wilkins?"

"He told me the reason people don't fight them is that they're too unpredictable. They're dangerous."

"That makes sense."

"There's more. It seems unlikely that Wilkins was in debt for dog-fighting." I tell her my informant's opinion that the amount of money in question was too rich for the dogfighting world. "At least around here. He said in rural counties, fifty thousand is a lot."

"Good to know. Looks like we've been . . ."

"Don't say it."

She can't help herself. ". . . barking up the wrong you-know-what."

"Dusty, she's asking to get nipped." He's gotten tired of the rope game, so I pick him up and set him in my lap. "What did you find out about the property where the dogs were being kept?"

"It took some digging. I found the owner's name and address out in Burton. I went out there, and the house was all closed up. But a neighbor told me the old man who owned it has gone into a nursing home and his family hasn't decided what to do with the house. They gave me the phone number of the man's son."

"I wonder if the man who had those two boys stow the stolen dogs there knew the property was vacant?"

"I wondered the same thing, so I phoned the man's son. He said he didn't know how anybody would be aware that his daddy wasn't living there. He said his daddy pretty much kept to himself. But he also said that if somebody was keeping dogs back there, his daddy wouldn't have heard them barking because he's almost deaf. I phoned the neighbor back, and he said nobody had asked him about the shed. I asked if he had ever heard dogs barking, and he said yes, but people keep dogs and he never thought much about it."

"Good work."

She frowns. "This whole thing doesn't add up. You've got dogs stolen for who knows what reason. You've got the two dead dogs, which by all accounts were vicious enough to be killers. You've got one man dead, mauled by dogs."

"And there's the money Wilkins had on him—money that somebody wanted bad enough to attack Margaret Wilkins to get."

"And you've got the puppies from Dusty's litter that never showed up." She nods toward Dusty. He's nestled onto my lap but seems to sense that he's drawn attention. He raises his head, sighs, and flops back down and closes his eyes.

"That reminds me. I haven't tried to contact the man Cal and Pete were supposed to call when they had enough dogs. I'll do that first thing tomorrow." I get up and set Dusty on the floor. "I've been thinking about something. Suppose those dogs that were stolen had nothing to do with this business with Wilkins. Maybe it was just those boys wanting to make some money. What would we have then?"

She ponders it, her dark eyes brooding. "It's entirely possible that they're unrelated. I don't really see any connection."

I yawn, and she gets ups and grabs her purse. "By the way, there were a bunch of messages on the phone that didn't get erased. I left one for you that was interesting."

I punch the message machine. A man's voice, muffled, says, "Go check on Margaret Wilkins."

I frown. "That's it?"

216

"That's all there was. But notice what time it was."

I punch it again and look at the screen on the phone. It says the message came in at 1:45 on Monday.

"What time did we find Margaret Wilkins?" I ask.

"I looked it up in my notebook. It was a little past two o'clock."

"That means we left right before this call came in."

Maria gives me a thumbs-up. "Whoever attacked her called to have us check on her so she wouldn't lie there without being found."

"Well, well, well," I say. "A thoughtful attacker."

"Whoever wants that money didn't want to go far enough to seriously hurt or kill Margaret. But I still don't see where it all fits together."

I sigh. "It's getting dark. Go on home and we'll tackle this in the morning."

CHAPTER 25

Even though it's dark, it's immediately clear what Dooley called me about right after Maria left. A group of men are standing around, looking at a boat that has apparently run into the dock. When I get up close, I see that it's the fancy boat that Wilkins won in the poker game. Nearby, on the boat ramp, half-submerged in the water, sits a boat trailer with no vehicle attached to it.

"What happened?"

"As you might figure," Dooley says, "it's complicated. Arlo here," he inclines his head toward a skinny fifty-year-old man in jeans and a ratty jacket, "was coming in from fishing and he sees this trailer backing up and hears a big boat motor. I'll let him tell you."

I shake hands with Arlo, whom I recognize from somewhere around town. A yeasty smell of beer rises off him. "Like Dooley says, I was just coming in when I saw a pickup with that trailer backing up into the water." He points to the abandoned boat trailer. "I didn't think too much about it. Boats come and go, and I figured it was somebody hauling their rig out of the water. None of my business." He clears his throat and spits. "But I look up and see this boat headed toward the ramp. Seemed like it was going a little fast, so I start hollering and waving my arms. And I can see that the person behind the wheel is a young man. So I'm thinking, 'who would let a kid drive a fine-looking boat like that?'" He starts laughing.

"Goddammit," Dooley snarls.

Arlo laughs harder and slaps the side of leg.

"What's so all-fired funny, Arlo?" Dooley asks.

"I'm sorry, Dooley. I know it's not funny. You've got a mess here. But you had to see it." He gets out a handkerchief and wipes his eyes.

"Go on, tell me the rest," I say.

"I could see the guy trying to get the trailer into the water didn't have any idea what he was doing. The trailer was slewing around this way and that." He waves his hand to indicate the movement of the trailer.

Dooley shakes his head. "How exactly did the boat get where it is?"

He's referring to the fact that the bow of the boat has crunched into the dock. That appears to be the only thing keeping it from drifting away.

"Well, sir, the guy with the trailer is still trying to get it in place when all of a sudden the boat kind of roars and gives a lurch. If you was to ask me, I'd say the driver thought he was powering it down, but instead he moved the stick forward and revved the engine. The boat came barreling up toward the dock and *bang!*" He slaps his hands together.

"The guy in the truck gets out and he's hollering, and I go over to see if the boat driver is okay. He turns off the motor—at least he had that much sense—and comes staggering out onto the deck of the boat and scrambles onto the dock. And he runs over to the truck and says to his buddy, 'Let's get the hell out of here.' Well, sir, his buddy didn't need to be told twice. They ditched the trailer and beat it out of here like scalded cats."

He starts laughing again.

"If that doesn't beat everything." Dooley says. He's taken his hat off and his rubbing the top of his head.

"Wait a minute," I say. "How did the guy in the truck get the trailer unhitched so fast?"

"Oh, yeah, I forgot that part. The damn fool just lifted the tongue up and it came right off, which means the trailer was setting down on top of the hitch without anything holding it on!"

"Who the hell would do something so stupid?" Dooley howls. I notice his son has his head bowed so that Dooley can't see him laughing. His shoulders are shaking.

"Did you recognize either of them?" I ask Arlo.

"No. They was young boys. Maybe in their twenties."

"You didn't happen to get a license number?"

He snickers. "Now how was I supposed to do that? I was laughing too hard. Damn fools. Besides, it was getting dark."

"What kind of truck was it?"

He screws up his face and coughs a couple of times. "Black pickup. Older model. I don't know exactly what kind."

"Would you recognize the boys if you saw them again?"

"I doubt it. Best I can tell you is that one of them was light-haired; the other one, darker. The dark one didn't have an ounce of fat on him, and the lighter one—the guy driving the boat—had a little more meat on him." The description brings to mind two boys I'm familiar with.

I go back to my squad car and put out a call to the highway patrol to be on the lookout for the truck, describing the vehicle and the boys. Dooley has followed me to the car, and when I'm finished, he says, "Can I get this boat off my dock? You going to look for fingerprints or anything like that?"

"I might want fingerprints. Is it safe, being left like that at the dock?"

"Safe enough. I'll tie some lines to hold it in place and to keep the dock from being damaged any further." He sighs. "Just what I need before Christmas. Major dock repairs. If you catch those boys, I'll take it out of their hide."

"I'll get somebody out here in the morning to look it over in case the boys left something incriminating. We'll take a look at the trailer, too."

"I'd like to know who had the gall to try to steal this boat right off the dock like this," Dooley says.

"I wonder how many people knew Wilkins had that boat," I say.

Dooley folds his arms across his chest. In the dim light from my car's overhead light, I can't see his expression.

Suddenly the radio crackles to life, someone calling me.

"This is Craddock."

"This is the DPS, highway patrol. Those boys you called about?"

"Yeah."

"They got stopped halfway between Jarrett Creek and Bobtail. What do you want us to do with 'em?"

"Hang tight. I'll be there in ten minutes."

I'm on the road before I remember I was supposed to see Ellen tonight. I call her and give an abbreviated version of the events of the last half hour.

Before long, I see a bunch of red-and-white lights flashing on the side of the road. I slow down and pull up behind the patrol cars, and sure enough there's a black pickup with two young men in handcuffs standing next to it. I was hoping I would recognize them, and I do, although they are using a different, newer-looking truck.

I reach in the glove box and get my badge and pin it on, then go over and introduce myself to the patrolmen. "Thank you for holding these boys until I could get here," I say.

"They had this truck up to over a hundred miles an hour. You'd think the devil was chasing them."

"As it happens, I have an interest in these two. Tuck them in the squad car, and I'll tell you the story."

They shove the two guys into the back seat of one of the cars, and the four officers gather around me. They are highly entertained by the story and are only too happy to bring the men out for me to question. Two more hangdog faces you'd never see. Even in the poor light from the cars, you can see that Cal is flushed red. Pete has lost his swagger and now has a hopeless look.

"There are lots of things I could ask you boys," I say. "Like, what kind of harebrained scheme led you to try to steal a boat . . ."

"We weren't stealing it!" Cal says. "The, uh, the owner asked us to take it out of the water and bring it to him."

"And who might that be?"

"I don't have to tell you that," Cal says.

"Actually, you do, but we'll figure that out once we get you to the police station. Let me ask you, though. What made you think you knew how to hitch up a trailer to a pickup, drive the trailer into the water, get the boat onto the trailer, and drive it somewhere?"

Neither of them can give me a good answer, so I tell the troopers to return them to the squad car and we'll take them to the police station.

One of the troopers is grinning when he walks over to me. "I bet you don't know who that is, do you?"

"Who what is?"

"The red-headed one."

"Cal Madigan? I know that I had both of them in my custody this morning for stealing dogs and made the mistake of letting them out to create more problems for themselves—and the rest of us."

"His stepdaddy is going to pitch a fit when he finds out you've arrested them."

"Who is his stepdaddy?"

"Jerry Bodine."

"Well, I'll be damned." I walk over to the patrol car and poke my head inside. "You're Jerry Bodine's stepson?"

"Damn right. And that's his boat."

"Is this his pickup, too?"

"No, it's mine."

"So, Pete, that's your truck with the flames on the side?"

"Yeah, what of it?"

I turn back to the trooper. "I think we can get this sorted out. You guys mind waiting until I make a phone call?"

"What's going to happen to my truck?" Cal asks. His voice is indignant. He thinks I'm going to be lenient because his stepdaddy is a bigshot.

"You should have thought of that earlier," I say. He's used to having things his way. But if I've put it all together right, there's more to it than these two boys stealing dogs and boats. Now that I know who they are, I suspect it's more than coincidence that their descriptions matched the one Margaret Wilkins gave of the two men who attacked her. I just don't know why.

"It'll be safe here," the trooper says. "We'll lock it up."

When I get back to the patrol car, Dusty whimpers, so I let him out to do his business.

"What are you doing with that puppy?" One of the troopers asks.

"Long story." I'll be glad when he's a dog and can blend into the background.

I had considered calling Maria to come and get Dusty before I left the marina, but I decided that if he's going to be my dog, he's going to have to get used to the unexpected.

While the troopers wait, I call Jerry Bodine and am surprised when he answers at his office phone.

"Mr. Bodine, it's Chief Craddock. Mind if I come over and have a word with you?"

There's an overlong pause. "I was on my way out the door. Can it wait?"

"It can't, but I can come to your house if you'd prefer."

"That's not a great idea. I'll wait for you."

When I walk into Bodine's office, I can see he's all set to be in charge. "What's this all about?" he says, standing up. "I don't have time . . ." And that's when the troopers come in behind me with the two boys.

Bodine's face freezes, and then he drops back into his chair with a heavy groan. "Don't tell me they screwed up."

"Sorry to be the bearer of bad news," I say, "but things didn't go as planned."

"Cal, what the hell is wrong with you?" Bodine snarls. "Can't you do anything right?"

The boy has gone pale. "It wasn't my fault," he says.

"To be fair," I say to Jerry Bodine, "the wrong was on your side when you decided to steal that boat. The fact that your stepson couldn't get the job done is irrelevant."

"I didn't steal the boat. I figured with Wilkins dead, I had a right to take it back."

I can't believe what I'm hearing. "On what grounds?"

"Wilkins cheated. He didn't win that boat fair and square." His face is getting red.

"Last time we talked, you told me you didn't see any sign of cheating."

"I didn't. But I know that's what happened. He was too damn lucky for it to be real."

"The time to have had that discussion was when he cheated, not after he's been murdered."

"I don't care. I'm going to fight to get that boat back," he says, slamming his fist down.

"That's between you and Wilkins's estate," I say.

"Well, you're right about one thing. This is my doing, so you can turn the boys over to me."

"I'm afraid that's not going to happen for several reasons. Number one, the DPS officers here clocked them driving at over a hundred, which is reckless driving."

"He was driving!" Cal says, throwing his pal under the bus.

"Dude!" If the two boys weren't in cuffs, Cal's buddy would be pummeling him.

"Doesn't matter who was driving," I say. "You've both been drinking. I smell alcohol on you, though we may able to overlook that because of the other trouble you're in."

Jerry Bodine butts in. "What other trouble?"

I describe the damage to the dock. "And I expect there's damage to the boat as well. Your stepson was driving the boat."

"Jerry . . ." Cal whines. He's scared now. But his stepdaddy is in no mood.

"Get them out of here," he yells at the troopers, "before I kill them myself."

After they leave, Bodine looks at me and says, "Aren't you satisfied? What more do you want?"

I sit down and take my time answering. "I want to know how bad you wanted that boat back."

"I don't know what you mean."

"Bad enough to have Lewis Wilkins killed?"

"You're not pinning that on me. I did not kill Lewis Wilkins."

"Did you want it bad enough to have his wife roughed up?"

He's so angry that his face is crimson. "What do you mean, roughed up? What happened?"

I tell him. "The two men who attacked her had hoods on so she couldn't identify them. But the way she described them, they have a physical resemblance to your stepson and his friend." I'm stretching the facts, wondering if it leads anywhere.

He gets up. "Oh no. I promise you I had nothing to do with that, and neither did my stepson. All I wanted was that boat. You don't know what kind of trouble I've been in ever since I lost it. I told you I didn't have any idea my wife would pitch such a fit about that ridiculous boat. I've got half a mind to go buy another one and tell her it's her daddy's boat just to shut her up."

"Well, that's up to you." I stand up and move close to him and look him in the eye. "But if I get the slightest hint that you had anything to do with that business with Margaret, I'll haul you in so fast that your wife won't even remember she had a husband."

"That goddam boat is going to be the death of me," he says.

On the way home, I stop at a hamburger place in Bobtail. Dusty is interested in the burger, and I feed a few pieces of meat to him. He seems to think that's about the best thing he ever ate.

A RECKONING IN THE BACK COUNTRY

It's after ten when I get home, and I'm weary, but I'm too wound up to sleep. I sit at the kitchen table with a beer and a piece of paper in front of me to set down what I know and what I don't know about the murder of Lewis Wilkins. The "don't know" side is a lot longer than the "do know" side.

CHAPTER 26

Bill Odum is back at work the next morning. He seems like a stranger after all that has happened the last few days without him.

"Looks like you and that dog are a team," he says, when Dusty waddles in behind me.

"Yep. Named him Dusty."

"It'll be nice to have a dog around here," he says, reaching down to scratch him behind the ears. "Can you bring me up to date on what's been going on while I was laid up?"

I give him a summary because I don't have patience to relate details. After my consideration of the case late last night, a couple of things are nagging at me, and I'm eager to tackle them. "Anything going on here this morning?" I ask.

"I had to round up Jenks Jenkins," Odum says. "His daughter called early this morning. He had walked across the railroad tracks and was headed out of town. Something's got to be done. She can't keep an eye on him all the time, and she's worn out."

"Let me talk to Loretta," I say. "She and the church ladies were going to try to find a solution. Can you hold down the fort for a while? I've got a couple of things I want to clear up."

I go over to see Dooley's son to ask him about the conversation he and his sister Annabelle had with the Wilkins kids the night of Thanksgiving. I don't really suspect either of them of having a hand in their daddy's death, but it doesn't hurt to hear what they said to friends that they might not have said to me.

According to Bobby, Daniel and Emily were upset not so much about the fact that their daddy was killed, but the way he was killed. The only new information he gives me is that Daniel has been staying with Emily in Houston. That strikes me as odd, because they didn't seem to get along that well. Even so, nothing Bobby says makes me think I am wrong in my assessment that they had nothing to do with their daddy's murder. There's only one loose end, and to tie up that one, I'll need to go to see Emily.

Back in the office, I make two phone calls. One is to the person who originally owned the cane corsos that we found dead.

"This is Hollister," the man answers.

I identify myself and tell him that I got his number as the owner of two dogs that were registered to him. "Do you have a minute to talk?"

"About what? I haven't owned those dogs in a few years."

"Did you sell them?"

"Yes. They were quite valuable. But they made me nervous. I couldn't handle them." He speaks in clipped voice, as if I've taken him away from something important.

"Do you happen to have a record of who they went to?"

"I did at one time. I think the guy who bought them was here in Houston. Why are you asking these questions?"

"The dogs were found dead. They were shot."

"Jesus! Where did you say you are? Jarrett Creek? I don't even know where that is."

"Thirty miles west of Bryan."

"Well, it's a shame somebody killed them. They were beautiful dogs. But like I said, they haven't been in my possession for a long time. What were the dogs doing there?"

"That's what we'd like to know."

"Must have been something around there that's worth guarding. They were trained guard dogs."

"Guard dogs. Okay."

"I'm a little surprised that a chief of police is calling me about this. Is there more to it?"

"Before the dogs were shot, they were used to kill a man."

There's a moment of silence. "I hope you don't think they are still my responsibility."

"No, I'm just trying to track where they went after you owned them."

"It could have been an accident. They were potentially dangerous dogs. Maybe somebody was careless with them and after they killed somebody, whoever owned them thought they ought to be put down."

"This was not carelessness. I need to find out who you sold them to. If you can get me that information, I'd appreciate it."

After concluding the call with Hollister, I admit that it's high time I called the number of the man Cal and Pete were going to sell the dogs to. They'd said they were to ask for Rich.

"Beebee's Pet Shop," a woman's voice answers, bored, when I call.

"May I speak with Rich?"

A pause. "Who's calling?"

"He doesn't know me. I was given this number."

"Name?"

"Samuel Craddock."

"Just a minute, I'll see if he's around."

I'm not surprised when she says he's out.

"You know when he'll be back?"

"I sure don't. Anything else I can help you with?" Her sugary tone tells me all I need to know. Rich is only available to certain people.

"Can I ask where you're located?"

"It's on our website."

"I mean what city?"

Click. I don't know what good she thought it would do to hang up on me. I look on the website and find out that Beebee's Pet Shop is in Houston.

Twenty minutes later, Mr. Hollister calls back about the cane corsos. "I sold the dogs to a security firm in north Houston." He has the name and number.

CHAPTER 27

A few of the dogs we rescued belonged to people who live out in the country and can't get to the vet's office for one reason or another, so Maria volunteered to deliver the dogs. When she stops by midmorning, I tell her I'm off for Houston. She offers to keep Dusty while I drive down there.

"Let me tell you what happened last night after you left." I describe the boat incident. "You're going to like this part," I say. "Guess who the two boys were who were trying to steal the boat?"

Her eyes narrow. "Not the guys who stole those dogs."

"One and the same. And it gets better. Turns out Cal Madigan, the red-headed one, is Jerry Bodine's stepson."

"You're kidding!"

"Nope. Bodine hired them to retrieve the boat. He told me he thought the boat was still his because he thinks Wilkins cheated at cards and that's how he won."

"That's what I get for going home on time. I missed all the action. You think he killed Wilkins so he could get the boat back?"

"That was my first thought, but it seems a little extreme. Why wouldn't he just threaten to expose Wilkins as a card cheat unless he gave back the boat?"

"No clue."

"I may be gone overnight," I say.

"That's okay. My landlady doesn't have to know Dusty is at my place. What are you going to be doing in Houston?"

I tell her about the security firm that bought the dogs.

"Why don't you call them instead of driving all that way?"

"I've got a couple of other stops." I tell her everything I have to do in Houston.

"You're right. You may have to spend the night. I think I'm going to have a better time than you today. In fact, I'm enjoying myself." She's got two more dogs to deliver, so it does sound like she got the better deal.

I don't like to drive in Houston. Seems like overnight the freeways exploded and now getting anywhere involves a dizzying choice of roads that didn't exist even a year ago and that somebody decided didn't need signage. The new, brilliant idea for getting people from one spot to another is "flyovers," freeways that rise suddenly high into the air only to dip down beyond where you wanted to go. Even mapping out where I wanted to go in advance leaves me with sweaty hands and a feeling that I've entered the future by the back door.

My first stop is to see Emily Wilkins. I figured it was best to surprise her at work. I wish I had time to take a look around the Contemporary Arts Museum and see what's new, but I'm cutting the day short as it is.

Since I donated a major work a few years ago, I'm a life member of the museum and am always greeted like I'm somebody special. It works to my advantage today, since it means the woman I talk to at the desk sends me right upstairs to Emily's office. "Don't let her know I'm here," I say, putting a twinkle in my eye. "I want to surprise her."

"Absolutely," the woman gushes.

When I knock on the door, Emily calls out for me to come in. The smile she had ready fades when she sees who it is. She stands up. "Hello, Mr. Craddock. What brings you here?"

"I need to ask you a few questions."

"Why didn't you ask them when I was in Jarrett Creek?"

"You weren't around a lot during Thanksgiving, and coming to you seemed like a good chance for me to stop by the museum. I haven't been for a while."

"Well, sit down." She indicates the chair across the desk from her, and when we're seated says, "What do you want to ask me?" Her manner is softer here in her own surroundings, not so much the spoiled brat.

"Were you aware that your daddy was doing some big-time gambling?"

"Daniel told me after you talked to him."

"But you didn't know before that?"

She shakes her head. "I shouldn't have been surprised, I suppose."

"Why is that?"

She sighs. "He changed a lot in the last couple of years. He became different from the way he was when I was a child. Harder to connect with."

"Did you ever talk to him about that?"

"Oh, goodness no. He wasn't a man you could have that kind of conversation with. He was fine as long as you didn't get into the personal. Then he closed down."

"Did you think your mamma knew he was gambling?"

She shrugs. "I doubt it. He shut her down the same way he did Daniel and me."

"Why didn't you tell your mamma that you and your husband were separated?"

She eyes me with a calculating look. "I'm trying to figure out where this is going. Why is that important?"

"Your daddy was brutally murdered. Somebody hated him or wanted revenge bad enough to commit an ugly crime. That makes everything important until I figure out what isn't."

"In answer to your question, I didn't tell my mother that Nelson and I were separated because I didn't want to get into an argument with her. I had planned to tell her when I visited at Thanksgiving. The opportunity didn't present itself."

"How long have you been separated?"

"Two months."

"Why did you split up?"

"Oh, for heaven's sake! How could that possibly be of any interest in investigating my father's death?"

"I don't know your husband at all, but I have to consider the possibility that since he knew you were furious with your father, maybe he killed him in some misguided attempt to win you back." I kept thinking about how Ellen Forester's husband became enraged and violent when she left him. Maybe Emily's husband went off the deep end the same way.

She sinks back into her chair and laughs. "If you knew Nelson, you'd know how ridiculous that is."

"I don't know Nelson, and that's why I'm asking you questions. At some point, I may need to talk to him."

Her smile is bitter. "Well, you'll have to go quite a distance to do that. The reason we split up is that he wanted to relocate to Atlanta. I told him I wouldn't go. He moved there six weeks ago, and as far as I know he hasn't been back."

Her phone rings, and she excuses herself to take the call. She listens for several seconds, during which her face takes on more color. "Thank you for telling me," she says and hangs up. "Well, well," she says. "It seems I am to offer to take you to lunch. Why didn't you tell me you were a donor?"

"It didn't seem relevant. And I appreciate the thought, but lunch won't be necessary. I do have one more question, though. You and your brother both told me the two of you weren't close. But he's staying with you?"

"We may not be close, but he's still my brother. He needed help getting back on his feet, and it happened that I now have plenty of space for him to stay."

"Back on his feet from what?"

"Last year, Daniel had an automobile accident. Before that he had a small business—a printing business. It took him a long time to recover from the accident, and he couldn't sustain the business. He asked our folks for help, and Daddy told him he didn't have any money. Daniel believed him, but I suspected that he had some squirreled away and that he was too selfish to help."

Beebee's Pet Shop is a small store with cages crammed in close to one another. It seems to sell all kinds of animals—not just puppies and kittens, but rabbits and some loud birds. There's even a section at the back labeled "Reptiles." It smells like it hasn't been cleaned in a while.

"Is Rich here?" I ask the sullen woman at the cash register.

"Rich who?"

"You don't have anybody named Rich who works here?"

She smirks and looks off as if trying to recall. She's messing with me. "I don't believe so. Can I do something for you? You in the market for a pet?"

"What would someone say if I came in here and told you I was wanting to buy some dogs for medical research?"

She smirks. "I'd say you've come to the wrong place. I don't care for that kind of business. We only sell animals that are intended for pets."

Maybe it's because I've been spending time with my pup, or maybe it's an instinct I have that this is a terrible place, but I have a childish urge to run through the shop and open all the doors and let the puppies and kittens out. There's nothing I can do about a place like this. I figure that somewhere in the back now, or sometime soon, Rich is waiting to haul dogs off to medical centers to sell and make a quick buck, not caring how terrible it will be for them.

All I can do is give a weak warning. "Tell Rich that if I ever get wind that he's selling dogs, I'll move heaven and earth to see that he goes to jail."

"Good luck with that," she says serenely.

Midtown Security is not in mid-town Houston. It's halfway to Conroe, in an industrial park that has all the soul of a concrete bunker. I'm early for my 4:30 appointment, so I drive around looking for any place that might serve coffee. Outside one of the buildings is a sign pointing to Kaffe Korner, which turns out to be better than its name would indicate. I'm able to buy a good cup of coffee and a piece of pecan pie that the girl behind the counter assures me was made this morning.

Twenty minutes later, I'm shown into the office of a Mr. Hibbard, who has a black eye and a bruise on his jawline. As bulked up as he is, I'm surprised anybody got the better of him.

"'Scuse my appearance," he says when I introduce myself. "I know this is going to sound like a complete fabrication, but I stumbled over my own doorstep in the dark last night and almost killed myself. That's what I get for being lazy and not replacing a light bulb."

"It does look like the light bulb won," I say.

He chuckles. "That it did. Now what can I do for you? You said you were calling to look at some dogs? We have a whole variety we can get for you."

"I'm sorry if I gave the wrong impression. I'm investigating a matter, and I need some information about two dogs you purchased a couple of years ago."

He nods. "Let's see what I can do. We keep real good records. We have to in this business. Tell me what you're after."

I tell him the details of the bill of sale that Hollister told me about.

"That helps. Let me look in my files."

He's got three full-sized file cabinets in the office, side by side, and he goes to the middle one and thumbs through a bunch of folders. "Here we go. Two cane corsos purchased from Craig Hollister two years ago. They have a good record. What kind of information do you need?"

"Do you still own the dogs?"

"We might. We sometimes rent out our guard dogs. And sometimes we sell them." He flips the page and reads. "From the look of it, we leased these dogs right away, and they've been at the same place ever since."

"I guess they must have been satisfactory," I say.

"We're always gratified when a dog goes to the right place. I expect you want to know where that is. And I wish I could give you that information, but it's confidential. The only way I can turn it over is with a search warrant."

There's some advantage to living in a small town where everybody knows you. The judge had signed my request earlier without even looking at it.

"You've dotted all the i's and crossed the t's. That's good. Let me make a copy of this." He looks down at it. "Oh. Lookie here. The judge is in the same town where the dogs went. Place called Bobtail."

CHAPTER 28

I'm awake too early. I didn't have the heart to spend the night in Houston last night, so I drove home, stopping on the way for dinner in the midway town of Belleville and arriving home at ten o'clock. Zelda stalked out to meet me, looking worried. She is already tuned in to having the puppy in the house, and I suspect she wanted to know what I'd done with him. I was tempted to call Maria and go get Dusty, but it seemed silly. The rest of the evening Zelda was as restless as I was and kept getting up to look for Dusty. At least I assume that's what she was doing. Who really knows what a cat thinks? I sat in front of the TV and drank a beer, and tried to push out of my mind what I knew I'd have to confront this morning.

I call Maria and tell her I'm back in town, but I need to check on something if she can keep Dusty a little longer. She's got the late-afternoon shift. "You want me to come along?" she asks. "I can bring Dusty."

"No need. I'm following a hunch, and it may not lead anywhere. I'll tell you about it when I get back."

On the way to Bobtail, I stop by the marina to see Dooley. He's standing out on the damaged dock. Even seeing him from the back, it's obvious from the way his legs are planted wide and his arms are crossed tight across his chest that he's not in the best frame of mind. He's with a couple of men, and they're all focused on where a big chunk of the dock is missing. I call out and when he sees me, he waves me over.

"I see you managed to get the boat pulled out," I say. I called him yesterday morning and told him we caught the boys who were responsible for the damage, so he could do whatever he wanted to with the boat.

"We got it back in the slip. I'd like to have a few words with the boys that did this. There's going to be hell to pay."

"I don't think you have to worry too much about that. One of the boys was your friend Jerry Bodine's stepson."

He jerks his baseball cap off and flings it down onto the dock. "That stupid kid. He has caused Jerry nothing but trouble. I don't know why Jerry puts up with him. I guess when he got married the kid was part of the package." He picks his hat back up and says, "Hold on a minute while I talk to these guys. They're fixing to start repairs on the dock."

In five minutes he comes back. "At least I know who to dun for the repairs on this place."

"You think he's good for it?"

He shoves his hands in his back pockets and gazes out over the lake. It's a gray day and the lake looks like it could be a hundred feet deep and full of dangerous creatures. "He'll make good on it. Although if I was him, I'd take it out of his stepson's hide."

"Since he was trying to take the boat back on Bodine's say-so, I don't think Bodine has much of a beef."

"What do you mean?"

"Jerry Bodine told, or hired, his stepson to take the boat out of the water and haul it to his place. He claims that he's the rightful owner since he thinks Lewis Wilkins won the boat by cheating."

Dooley's jaw drops. "Well, I'll be damned. He never said a word. And why the hell would he think that kid could even get that boat out of the water and onto a trailer? That's a delicate operation."

"I suspect Bodine doesn't know any more about boats than his stepson does. Maybe he figured it was easy to do. Or, there could be another explanation."

"What?"

"How long ago did Jerry's father-in-law die?"

"I don't know. Nine months ago? Probably longer. Seems like the older I get, the more things speed up. I think something happened a year ago, and I find out it was three years." He turns to look at me. "Why do you ask?"

"Bodine sold the business to the employees before he died. Did Bodine and his wife inherit anything?"

"He never said. He seems to be comfortable. By that I mean rich. This is a funny line of questioning. What do you want to know for?"

"I'm curious whether Bodine is as rich as he makes out."

"He always seemed to have money for the poker games." I see a light go on. "Wait a minute. Now that you ask, Connie told me something, although it may only be gossip. She told me she heard that Bodine's wife was mad when her daddy didn't leave her much. She said it left them hurting financially."

"Wonder why he didn't leave them the business? Did he and Jerry get along?"

"As far as I know, they did. Maybe he thought he'd done enough for them when he was alive. I thought it was odd that he sold the business to his employees. You'd think he'd want to set his family up when he died."

"He did leave the boat to them. How much you think that boat is worth?"

"More than you might think. Two hundred, three hundred thousand. That's why it was such a big deal that Bodine put it up on that bet."

There's no sign of anybody working at the lawnmower warehouse. The gate is closed up tight. It seems odd to me. It's Friday, mid-afternoon.

I want to talk to an employee and was hoping not to run into Jerry Bodine before I get a chance to do that. I drive down to city hall to look up the address of the manufacturing side of the operation. It's on the southeast side of town. I arrive to see a sprawling bunch of buildings and a busy scene. This is more like it. If I were Bodine, I would have my office here on the pulse of things, instead of at the warehouse.

I park my car and wander onto the site where trucks are being unloaded. I pause and watch a stocky, middle-aged man with a clipboard check off whatever items are coming in. The way he's ordering people around, I expect he's a boss of some kind. When the truck is closed up, I go over and introduce myself and ask if he can spare a minute.

"I sure can, Chief. But whatever it is, I didn't do it." He laughs at his joke.

"That's what they all say."

"Come on inside. It's cold out here." He peers off to the north. "Looks like we're going to get more weather coming in."

His office is right inside the building. He introduces himself as G.T. Roberts, foreman of the manufacturing site. "Call me G.T. Let me get us some coffee."

He comes back with real mugs, not disposable cups, steaming with coffee. He sits down and gestures for me to sit. I'm struck by how different his office is from Bodine's. This is a real working office, with a computer and invoices and charts.

"Okay, what do you need to know?"

"I understand Chuck Flynn sold this business to the employees. How long ago was that?"

He looks at the ceiling. "Two years."

"How's that working out?"

"We're doing okay. It was rocky for a while. Chuck had good business sense, and he left it in good shape, but . . . well, it takes time for new people to settle in."

"I understand he kept his son-in-law on as the manager."

"Yep." I can't read anything from his face.

"And he's still here in that capacity?"

240

He nods, but his expression has turned wary.

"Is he a good manager?"

"He, uh, he does okay. Last summer we came to a mutual agreement with him that he would only be manager of the warehouse operation, not the whole shebang. I mean, he was fine, the board just thought maybe some new blood was needed."

"And I assume that meant a salary cut."

"I'm not at liberty to talk about that."

"Assuming it did, I imagine that didn't go over so well."

His face has gotten red, and he shrugs. "I'm wondering if maybe it's not better for you to talk to the chairman of our board."

"Who is the chairman?"

"The way Chuck set it up, we have a banker who oversees everything. That will continue for a couple of more years, and then we'll be on our own. I can give you his name."

"That's not necessary. I appreciate what you've told me. None of it will leave this room. But it's helpful."

"I'm glad to hear it." Relief is in his voice.

"I do have one more question. It doesn't have to do with Bodine. Did you ever have guard dogs on either of the sites?"

"Funny you ask that. Chuck got it in his head a while before he died that we ought to have the warehouse protected. It had been broken into a couple of times, and he decided to get some guard dogs from a security firm."

"You still have them?"

"As far as I know. But I don't get over to the warehouse."

"Could you do me a favor and call over there and ask somebody?"

His uncomfortable look returns. "There's nobody there today."

"Why is that?"

"It's an internal matter."

"Meaning?"

"I really think it's better for you to talk to the head of the board."

"It'd save me a lot of trouble if you told me what's going on. I'm not going to blab to anybody."

"It's not a big deal." He drums his fingers on his desk, deciding. Then he says, "We've had a sort of work slowdown."

"You mean like a strike?"

He flinches. "Don't say that word. That's not exactly what I meant." He leans forward across his desk. "Listen. The people at the warehouse aren't happy with Mr. Bodine, all right? We're trying to figure out the best way to ease him out of there."

"I see. I imagine with his wife being Chuck's daughter, it's delicate."

"You got that right. Some people want him to be cut off entirely, but I'm of a mind that a nice severance could work to move him along, and that it's the right thing to do."

I get him to call one of the men from the warehouse who is not at work today and ask about the guard dogs. When he hangs up, he says, "Those dogs disappeared a couple of weeks ago."

So Bodine's company leased the dogs that killed Lewis Wilkins, which connects the dogs to Bodine. And according to Dooley's wife, the Bodines are having money trouble. Not only that, Bodine thought Wilkins won his expensive boat by cheating. For the first time I admit that it's a real possibility that Bodine had Wilkins killed in order to get the boat back. But if he wanted the boat back that badly, why didn't he simply tell Wilkins he was going to expose him as a cheat if he didn't return it? Why kill him?

Bodine's stepson is a possible link to all this. I'm still not convinced he and his friend Pete didn't attack Margaret. I just don't know why. Maybe a talk with him will shake something loose. I thank G.T. for his time and then head over to the Bobtail PD.

The duty officer at the jailhouse tells me I'm just in time; that Jerry Bodine is coming down soon to bail out his stepson. My first thought is, why did it take him so long? I'm glad I got here before he did.

Cal doesn't look like he missed any sleep or any meals, unlike his buddy, who practically flings himself at the bars when he sees me.

"I've got to get out of here," Pete says. "If I don't show up for work before long, I'm out of a job."

"What is it you do?"

"I work at the warehouse."

"Jerry Bodine's warehouse?"

He nods.

"What do you do there?"

"I'm on the loading dock. Why do you care?"

"How come petty criminals worry about everything but their own behavior?"

"I'm not a petty criminal. I was along for the ride. Tell him, Cal."

Calvin sneers. "You were going to make as much money as I was."

I raise my eyebrows at the friend. He's backing the wrong horse, and I expect he knows it.

"Pete, have you called somebody to put up bail?"

"I called my daddy. He told me to go whistle for it."

"Maybe spending time in here will give you a chance to reconsider your choice of friends and activities."

"Dammit." He bangs the flat of his hand against the bar.

I get an officer to bring Cal to a room where I can talk to him in private.

"You want me to cuff him to the chair?" the officer asks.

"I'll be all right. You don't plan to attack me, do you Cal?"

"No. That would be stupid."

"You haven't exactly shown me your brilliant side so far."

He sighs and slumps down into a chair. "Can I at least get a Dr. Pepper?"

The officer says he'll get one.

"Cal, your driver's license says you're twenty-eight. Did you go to college?"

"I went to the JC for a year. College wasn't my thing, so I decided to go to work." Translation: he could have gotten a college education

243

on his folk's dime, and instead he was too lazy to do the work and most likely flunked out.

"Where do you work?"

"I'm at the warehouse, too. Jerry thinks it's a good idea for me to learn the business from the ground up."

"Now, Cal, as I understand it, your stepdaddy wanted you to take that boat out of the water. Where were you going to take it?"

"I was supposed to take it to his house, and he was going to have a broker come and make an offer for it." So much for Jerry's claim that he was getting the boat back for his wife.

"You've done other jobs for Jerry, haven't you?"

"Sometimes."

"What was the latest?"

He squirms around. "I don't remember. I guess hauling some stuff."

"Did Jerry have you do a job transporting some dogs?"

"Dogs?" He has a way of screwing up his face when he's lying that makes him look nearsighted. "The only dogs I had anything to do with are those dogs you made me give up. And Jerry didn't know anything about that."

"You sure it wasn't Jerry who had you stealing those dogs? I'm thinking if he was paying you boys fifty dollars a dog and getting five hundred apiece for them, he'd turn a tidy profit for no outlay."

"I told you, we were supposed to call a guy. Wait. What do you mean five hundred?"

"That's how much a lab pays for a dog. You didn't know that?"

"Hell no. That guy was cheating me."

"You sure it wasn't Jerry screwing you out of the money? I hear he's having financial problems."

"No, I gave you the phone number of the guy. It wasn't Jerry."

"But Jerry did pay you to transport a couple of big dogs, didn't he?"

"No, I never had anything to do with those dogs."

The officer comes back in with a Pepsi. "We didn't have Dr. Pepper."

Cal frowns and opens his mouth to protest, but thinks better of it and pops the top.

"You said you didn't have anything to do with *those* dogs. You mean those two guard dogs?" I ask.

"I don't know what you're talking about," he says. "What guard dogs?"

"The ones that were at the warehouse. Did Jerry handle them? I understand they're pretty hard to handle. Did you notice that?"

"Damn right they were."

"Where did you see them?"

He looks to the corners of the room. "Just at the warehouse."

He's not ready to admit that he transported the dogs, so I change tactics. "Did Jerry ever have you follow somebody in your pickup?"

He has just taken a swallow of Pepsi, and he chokes on it. It takes some coughing to clear his throat. "Went down the wrong pipe," he says, when he can talk again.

"Who did you follow?"

"He didn't say who it was."

"Did he say why?"

"He said the guy had something of his, and he wanted to know where he went so he could get it back. So me and Pete followed him."

"What kind of car was the man driving?"

"It was a white SUV. A Chevy."

"You followed him out to a road between Cotton Hill and Burton, right?"

"I guess."

"He parked, and then what happened?"

He shrugs. "I don't know. I called Jerry and told him where we were, and he said to come on home."

"This man you followed. Did you ever see the guy again?"

"No." His voice is low.

"When was this?"

"Not long ago. Just before Thanksgiving."

"But Jerry didn't get back what he wanted, so he sent you out to shake up Margaret Wilkins."

He denies it, but I don't press him. I've heard enough for now.

On the way to my car, I see Jerry Bodine walking over from the courthouse with some papers in his hand.

"Imagine seeing you here," he says.

"I came to find out what your stepson had to say about his adventure last night."

"He filling your head full of stories? He's got plenty of 'em and I've heard 'em all."

"He's pretty subdued. I think he learned a lesson."

"And what lesson might that be?"

"Either to be careful who he works for, or to be careful to do the job right."

Bodine fixes me with a look. I don't think he can figure out whether I'm friend or foe, which is exactly what I'd like to leave him with. His chuckle doesn't go with his sour expression. "Well, I wish I had that boat back in my hands, but I guess I have to let it go."

"Your wife will have to be content without the boat," I say. "But you've got some dock repairs to pay for after last night's fiasco. Dooley is none too happy."

"Oh, Dooley will be okay. He knows I'm good for it."

CHAPTER 29

On my way home, I stop to pick up Dusty, calling Maria to let her know I'm on my way. She's out on the landing outside her apartment with him. He does his little yodel when he sees me.

"What have you been up to today?" She's holding Dusty close to her, as if she doesn't want to let him go.

"Nosing around. It looks like Jerry Bodine has money problems."

"What kind of money problems?"

"Apparently Jerry's wife didn't get the inheritance she was expecting, and instead of Jerry inheriting the family business, his father-in-law sold it to the employees. Jerry Bodine was manager of the business after that, but now the employees are trying to ease him out."

"Interesting. Do you think that has something to do with Wilkins being killed?"

"I do, but I'm not sure of the details." I hadn't planned to hang around and discuss this with Maria, but before I know it, I'm laying out the facts. I tell her I discovered that Bodine's father-in-law leased the guard dogs that we found dead. "They were used to guard the warehouse until they disappeared a couple of weeks ago."

She arches an eyebrow. "That's an awfully big coincidence."

"That's what I thought, too. Along with Bodine's money problems, that starts to form a picture."

"Let's go inside and talk. It's too cold out here." She's wearing a sweat suit, but she hates cold weather. It's at least sixty degrees, and she thinks that's cold.

I've only been in her apartment a couple of times. If Maria is buttoned up in public, she lets her personality out here. Color is everywhere—a bright blue sofa with splashy, blue-patterned cushions, and walls hung with posters from Mexican music festivals. I notice a dog toy for Dusty on the floor.

She takes Dusty back from me and sits on the sofa with him in her lap. "You've got a connection between Bodine and the dogs, and Bodine needed money, so what does that have to do with Wilkins?"

"Wilkins was into gambling. Maybe they played other high-stakes games and Wilkins ended up owing Bodine money. That could explain why he had that money on him that I found in the SUV. He was intending to pay Bodine back."

"But if he owed Bodine money, why didn't he just give the boat back?"

"Beats me. Maybe it was pride. Or maybe Bodine told him he had to have cash. We know Wilkins sold property for cash."

Maria's eyes are gleaming. She loves a good puzzle. "When Bodine threatened him with the dogs, though, I wonder why he didn't simply tell Bodine where the money was?" Dusty has turned over onto his back and is gnawing at Maria's hand.

"Maybe Wilkins didn't think Bodine was serious, and by the time the dogs attacked, it was too late."

Maria shivers. "What a horrible thought."

"There's one other possibility that would be a better explanation. Bodine's stepson said he followed Wilkins out to where we found the SUV and that he called Bodine to tell him where Wilkins was. Suppose he's lying? Suppose he and his pal took Wilkins out of the SUV and never asked about the money?"

"Right!" Maria says. She's excited now. "Bodine might not have even told them what he wanted with Wilkins, because he didn't want them to know how much money was involved."

"Exactly." I get up. "Only problem with all this brilliant guesswork is proving it."

248

I find Dooley watching the two carpenters tear out planks so they can repair the dock.

"Ain't I lucky," he says. "Getting a visit twice in one day."

"You may not feel so lucky when you hear what I have to say."

He gives me a startled look, puzzled by the steel in my voice. "Sure thing. Let's go inside and have a cup." In the café, he asks me if I want a sandwich. I'm hungry. It's past my lunchtime, but I don't feel like sharing a meal at the moment.

"Cup of coffee will do me."

He sits down with two cups. For the first time, he looks nervous. "You sound serious."

"You haven't been square with me."

He goes still. "What do you mean?"

"You said you didn't arrange any more poker games after the one when the boat changed hands, but you knew there were other high-stakes games, didn't you?"

He picks up his coffee and takes a meditative sip. "I didn't want to tell tales. Some people like to keep it quiet that they do a little gambling. You understand."

I nod. Playing poker for money is technically illegal, but the only games likely to cause problems with the law are ones with high stakes.

"The only reason I told you about the one game was to explain how Lewis came by that boat."

"Did you personally attend any more games where Jerry Bodine and Lewis Wilkins were both there?"

"No. I got asked a couple of times, but I didn't like the sound of it. They were pushing up the stakes too high for my blood."

"I need to know the names of the other men who played in those games."

His expression is grim. "I don't want to rat on anybody. I don't see the point."

I sit back and study him. He's a jovial guy, and I'm sorry I have to push, but that's the way it is sometimes. A lawman doesn't always have the advantage of being a nice guy. "Here's the way it works. You can either give me the names and I can have a friendly, off-the-record chat with them, or I can find out where the games are held—and I'm pretty sure I know where that is—and take a pack of law officers out there and bust up a game, arrest people, and cause a big stink. It's your choice."

He pulls his lower lip. "Craddock, I never figured you for an S.O.B."

"I don't need to be one unless people don't cooperate when I'm investigating a murder."

"The hell you say?! You telling me one of these fellas had something to do with Lewis getting killed? That's crazy."

"Dooley, sometimes we have to follow a lead wherever it goes. And if that means I'm an S.O.B., then that's the way it is."

He lets out a long sigh and runs a hand over his head. "I don't mean to be uncooperative with you," he says. Then he gives me the names and phone numbers of the two men he told me about earlier, the two who were there the night the boat changed hands.

"Dooley, I expect you to keep this whole thing quiet. And that means don't talk to anybody about it until I say you can."

"Why would I tell anybody?"

"Just don't."

Dusty seems glad to be back in his own house, or maybe it's just me glad to have him back. Zelda walks in and sits at the edge of the room and glares at both of us, but she's bluffing.

I heat up some enchiladas, but I could as easily be eating cardboard.

My mind is chasing my suspicions and not finding a solution for how to find out whether they are true.

I'm almost done when Loretta comes to the door. She's bundled up in a winter coat and has gloves on. Before she's even inside she says, "I came by to tell you we solved the situation with Jenks's wandering."

"That was fast."

"I don't mind saying I feel pretty smart. It was easy, once we realized we were looking at it the wrong way."

"What do you mean?"

"We were thinking somebody had to be with him all the time, and we didn't take into account that Jenks sleeps at night. Lois said he's a good sleeper. And for a couple of hours every afternoon he watches TV. So that cut the number of hours we'd need to have somebody with him. So we figure we can hire somebody for part of the day and have shifts the rest of the time."

She tells me the details of their plan, but I'm barely listening, because her words have triggered something.

Suddenly she stops. "Why are you grinning at me like that?"

"Just glad you figured out that you were going about it the wrong way."

"Well." She cocks her head at a proud angle. "If I do say so, when my circle gets together, we manage to come up with solutions." She claps her hands. "I wanted you to know. I don't have time to stay."

Sometimes you get stuck in a way of thinking. You keep adding A and B and no matter how you twist it, you end up with D. It's not the D that's the problem; it's the A or the B. In this case, like Loretta and the church ladies, I've been thinking the wrong way around. I tried to twist circumstances to fit what happened to Lewis Wilkins. Because of the lawsuit against him, I kept working on the assumption that it was Wilkins who was in debt. But suppose it was Bodine who owed Wilkins money? A lot of money. Suppose Bodine paid him off but decided to steal the money back, and ended up killing Wilkins. Looking at it that way makes sense. But just because it makes sense doesn't make it true. What I need is a clear motive—and proof of exactly what happened.

The two men who were at the poker game with Bodine and Dooley when the boat changed hands are Lonnie Casper and Roger Olivera. According to Dooley Phillips, Olivera never went to high-stakes games, but Lonnie Casper did. I don't make an appointment with Casper. I show up at his house around suppertime. He's an attorney and lives in a grand house in the only exclusive part of Bobtail.

He's got a pronounced drawl and prissy, drawn-up mouth like he's tasted something unpleasant. He takes me into a home office with Oriental rugs and a grand desk piled high with folders. When we are seated, he takes pains to remind me that he's a defense attorney. Before I approached him, I asked Jenny Sandstone if she had worked with him, and she said he was "competent, but not necessarily someone you'd beg to be on your side."

"I know you're an attorney. You don't have anything to be worried about. I'm here to ask a couple of questions that will help me with an investigation."

With a little judicious pressure, I get him to confirm the fact that the game where Bodine lost the boat wasn't the last high-stakes game, by a long-shot. And that Bodine had heavy losses in almost every game.

"I don't want to talk out of place here," Casper says, pursing his lips, "but I thought Bodine was awful reckless. I know he's well-to-do, but he's going to burn through his wife's inheritance if he doesn't hold up on the gambling."

I've been puzzling over why Wilkins was out on the road to Burton, and I have a hunch. "Where do they hold these high-stakes games?"

"I'd rather not say."

"Then let me suggest something to you, and you can tell me if I'm right. Is it someplace out on the road between Cotton Hill and Burton?"

He doesn't answer right away. He's drumming his fingers on the desk. "It might have been."

I take that as a yes. Now I know why Wilkins was out on the road to Burton. If my theory is right, Bodine paid him off, and he was on his way to throw that money into a big game. That's why he had the money with him. And Bodine knew it.

"One more thing. Were you supposed to have a game that included Lewis Wilkins the week before Thanksgiving?"

He snorts. "Yeah. For what it was worth."

"What do you mean?"

"Bodine called and said that a game was set up for Sunday. He said Wilkins was going to be there. Then he called back and told me it was going to be Monday night instead. He said the fella from Houston couldn't get here until Monday. At the game I was aggravated because Wilkins never showed up. Of course then we found out what happened and . . ." He clears his throat. "I guess we know why."

CHAPTER 30

Dusty whimpers to go with me when I head down to see the cows the next morning, but I'm so wound up that I worry that I won't keep an eye on him, so I leave him inside. I haven't put him in his box for a couple of days, but when I do, he jumps right out. Seems impossible that he has grown so much. "You better behave," I say when I leave. "I'll be back soon."

While I feed the cows, I think about how my original thinking led me astray. Because Wilkins was mauled to death by dogs, and there were rumors of dogfighting in the area, it seemed reasonable to think that he was killed over dogfighting debts. The clues have told a different tale.

Now I'm convinced that Bodine killed Wilkins. The trick will be tying him to the murder, but I intend to do just that. I'll double down on forensic details. I'll dig into Bodine's financial status. If necessary, I'll call in a team to process the shed where we found the cane corsos. And I'll make sure the medical examiner goes over Wilkins's clothing, if they haven't already done so. Bodine was desperate, and desperate people make mistakes.

Maria is supposed to be on duty this afternoon, but I ask her to come in early. I want to hash out the details with her regarding what went on yesterday. I've begun to depend on her good instincts.

While I wait for her, I dig out the notes Maria took on the phone call she made about the place where Cal and Pete kept the stolen dogs, and find the phone number.

"You talked to my deputy recently about a shed on your daddy's property where some dogs were kept?"

254

He sighs. "Yes. What now? Seems like my daddy had a few problems I wasn't aware of."

"Did your daddy play poker?"

Silence stretches out. "No. But my Uncle Lonnie did."

"Would that be Lonnie Casper?"

"Yes. He's my daddy's brother-in-law." I might have figured.

Maria comes in, carrying a package. "Got you a present. Or rather I guess it's for Dusty."

I tear it open and find a collar and a leash. "This is too big for him."

"It won't be for long. Look how fast he's growing. And before long he's going to be getting into everything. Until you have him trained, you need to keep him on a leash."

For a couple of minutes we watch Dusty explore and gnaw on whatever comes into his range. The leg of the metal desk doesn't appeal to him, but the wooden chair next to my desk is to his taste. I scoop him up and take him into the jail so he'll stay out of trouble. When he immediately starts yipping, I bring him back and put the collar on him. At its smallest, it's still too big, but when I put the leash on, he's so busy tugging it that he doesn't realize he could duck out of it.

I tell her I went to see Lonnie Casper last night. "I think I have an idea how Bodine got Wilkins on the road between Burton and Cotton Hill that night."

"How did you figure it out?"

"Something Casper told me. He said Bodine told him there was supposed to be a game Sunday night and it was changed to Monday, but I bet Wilkins still showed up out there on Sunday. At first I thought maybe Bodine had just neglected to call Wilkins and tell him about that change. Then it occurred to me that maybe Bodine set up the whole thing. He needed Wilkins to be alone so there would be no potential witnesses."

"I don't quite follow you."

"I'm thinking that Bodine called everybody but Wilkins and told them the game had to be changed to Monday. Bodine had his stepson and his friend Pete follow Wilkins Sunday night, abduct him from his SUV, and take him to wherever Bodine was waiting with the dogs."

"That still doesn't explain why Wilkins had the money with him."

"Remember the passport?"

"Yes."

"Wilkins was greedy. I think the only reason he was still in town was because of that game. He thought he might win one more big pot, and then he planned to disappear."

Maria groans. "Of course! That makes total sense. And if Wilkins hadn't been so greedy, he would have been long gone." She sits back up. "Why did Bodine come up with such a horrible way to kill Wilkins?"

"The dogs were handy. It's possible he didn't intend to kill Wilkins, just scare him."

"Your reasoning sounds good, but it's all circumstantial. It's going to be hard to get the district attorney to authorize an arrest."

"You got any suggestions?" I ask.

"It wouldn't hurt to talk to Bodine, see what shakes out."

"Not without a plan."

She gives me a rare wicked smile. "Surely we can think of something."

If you judged by the outside of Bodine's house, you'd think he didn't have a trace of money problems. The house is grand, and in the same part of Bobtail where Lonnie Casper lives. His place is on a slight ridge in the gated community. Trees hide most of the homes from the road, so until you reach the gate, you don't even know it's there.

We get in with our badges. I tell the man at the gate not to give any advance warning. We don't expect to get Bodine to confess. This first trip is to get him worried, and surprise is part of the plan.

A sleek woman wearing a jogging suit and with her long red hair pulled back in a ponytail answers the door.

"Mrs. Bodine?"

"Yes. How did you get by the guard at the gate? They should have called." Her attitude reminds me of her son Cal's.

"I wouldn't know." I introduce myself and Maria. "Is your husband home? We'd like to have a word with him."

She lifts an eyebrow, and I swear she's wondering why riffraff like us would have any business with her husband. "Wait here." She leaves us standing in the foyer.

"Low-class," Maria mutters when she's out of earshot.

I give her a look. Now is not the time for her to get on the high horse that she keeps handy.

"Hello, Craddock. I'm surprised to see you here."

Bodine advances with his hand held out. He's wearing jeans and a sweatshirt, and there's sawdust on his sleeves. I introduce him to Maria.

"Couple of things have come up I'd like to ask you about," I say.

"That sounds serious. Why don't we go in the family room? I'm all dirty and my wife would kill me if I track up the living room." He leads us down the hall to an expansive room off the kitchen. "Can I get you all something to drink?"

"No thank you, we're fine. Does your stepson happen to be around?"

"Calvin? He doesn't live here. And I don't see a lot of him. Why?"

"After we have our chat, I'm going to have a talk with him, too."

Bodine licks his lower lip. "Well sure. I don't know whether he'll be home. Here, sit down."

He points us to comfortable armchairs that probably cost more than all my living room furniture put together. I prefer to spend my money on art rather than on showy furniture. I sneak a peek at what's on these walls, and I recognize an indifferent eye for art when I see it. These paintings would be right at home in a cheap office.

"I'm afraid I have some bad news for you," I say.

"Really? What happened? Is something wrong at the warehouse?"

"You know Lewis Wilkins was set on by dogs."

"Terrible."

"That poor woman, having to see her husband like that," Maria chimes in.

He frowns at her. "I'm sure it was an awful thing," he says.

"As it happens, we know what dogs were responsible," I say.

"Well, that's good." His wary eyes don't agree.

"The thing is, it was an unusual kind of dog."

"Unusual how?"

"It was a dog that's known to be vicious, and is frequently used as a trained guard dog."

"Guard dog?" His face has paled.

"The thing is, we found the dogs."

"You what?" For the first time, he seems truly alarmed. He practically screeched the question.

I'm surprised at his reaction. Maria and I exchange glances, and she is as puzzled as I am. Suddenly I know where I made my mistake. If he sicced those dogs on Wilkins and then killed them, he wouldn't have left them out in that shed. He would have made sure they were taken away and never found. So why didn't he?

"We found their bodies, anyway. Somebody had killed them. We also found out where the dogs came from."

Bodine clears his throat. "All right. I'm still not sure where this is leading."

He has recovered his composure, but I'm trying to figure out what surprised him. "You see, the dogs were fitted with a chip that has the name and address of the owner."

"Oh." He's clutching the arms of his chair.

"I did a little poking around, and it turns out that the original owner couldn't handle the dogs, so he sold them to a security firm. And it turns out that the security firm leased the dogs to your father-in-law, Chuck Flynn."

"Oh, for heaven's sake. You mean it was those guard dogs from the warehouse that killed poor Wilkins?"

"I'm afraid so."

He produces a big sigh. "That's terrible. I have to say, I feel responsible."

"Really? Why is that?"

"A couple of weeks back, someone left a gate open and those dogs got loose, and we never found them. They must have made their way through the backwoods to that area where Wilkins lived, and then attacked him." This is completely different from what he said the first time we talked about the dogs.

It would be quite a coincidence for the dogs to make the fifteen-mile trip and end up in the woods behind Lewis Wilkins's house. "That's one explanation, except for one or two little issues. Tell me, exactly when did the dogs go missing?"

"I don't remember the date."

"Did you report them missing?"

"No, I figured they were long gone."

"That's a problem. You know, they're registered as lethal weapons, and according to the contract they were supposed to be kept under your control all the time."

A tic has developed under Bodine's left eye. "You trying to tell me the law would make a big deal out of that?"

"Yes, they would."

"Unless you have reason to believe the dogs were stolen," Maria says in her most innocent voice. "Then you're off the hook."

"Maria, I'm not sure that's true," I say. "If he had reported them stolen, then of course he'd be off the hook, but he didn't."

Bodine is chewing his lower lip. He sees a lifeline. "I didn't report it, but I think I told somebody that I thought they might be stolen. I'm pretty sure I told my assistant manager that. He'd remember it. And he should have been the one to report it. And I'll bet whoever stole them, shot them."

He doesn't seem to have noticed that he changed his story to fit what he thinks we want to hear. "Okay, then Monday if you don't mind I'll come in and talk to him."

Maria looks startled and Bodine is relieved.

When we get to the squad car, Maria explodes. "What is wrong with you? Why did you let him get off so easy?"

"Now hold on. Two things. You noticed how surprised he was that we found the dogs?"

"Yes."

"Think about it. If you had sicced a couple of dogs on somebody and they killed him, and then you killed the dogs, would you leave the dogs' carcasses lying around to lead back to you?"

"No, I guess I wouldn't."

"No, you wouldn't." I tell her what I suspect Bodine did instead.

She nods. "What's the other thing?"

"When he went along with your suggestion that somebody stole the dogs, he said the thief must have shot them. Only I didn't tell him how the dogs were killed."

"Why didn't we arrest him then?"

"We could make the case that he killed the dogs, but we still don't have a case that he set them on Wilkins."

It's a quiet afternoon at the Bobtail Police Department. The duty officer is fine with me taking a look at the pickup that got hauled in a couple of nights ago when its owner was brought in. We go over to the yard where it was towed.

"Lazy kid said he was going to come in this morning to pay the fines," the owner of the yard says. "But I haven't seen him yet."

"Makes our job easier," I say.

Maria and I realized that the boys used Pete's pickup to steal the other dogs, and we speculated that because they were being paid by Bodine, they used Cal's pickup to do the job of transporting the guard dogs. We peer into the bed of Cal's pickup, and the evidence is right there.

"There's no question there were dogs in here," Maria says. There's dried mud all over the bed. "Look at the claw marks."

"Won't be hard to match," I say. "Big claws, big dogs. And there's dog hair."

"Could be a different dog," she says. But we know it's not.

We get a careful impression of the claw marks and samples of the hair and take the evidence over to the vet's office. On my request, Doc England has kept the dogs in cold storage. He compares the hair and claws. "Same."

"You sure?"

He shrugs. "Only DNA testing can make a positive ID, but it's the same type of hair, same color, same texture. And you can't miss those claws. Unless there are other cane corsos around here, which I seriously doubt, these are the same dogs."

Now the only decision Maria and I have to make is whether to tackle Jerry Bodine or his son. "The son is a lot more likely to screw up," I say.

Maria is sitting next to me in the squad car. She turns to me, her eyes narrowed. "Sic 'em."

CHAPTER 31

Cal Madigan turns out to be hard to find. He doesn't answer his cell phone, and the house he lives in, a place in the suburbs that I suspect Jerry pays for, is deserted. In a neighborhood with small, neatly kept houses, his is the one with the overgrown yard.

Maria and I decide to find out if his buddy Pete knows where he is. We get his address from the Bobtail PD and go over to have a chat with him. He lives in an apartment building. We would ring his doorbell, but the door is open and there's loud rock music coming from inside. "Anybody home?" I holler.

"Gabe?" A familiar voice calls out before Cal Madigan rounds the corner.

"Oh." He looks panicky. "Just a minute. I'll get Pete."

"That's okay," I say. "It's you I'm looking for."

"What do you need me for?" If he's hoping to project innocence, this kid does not have a great acting career ahead of him.

"I have a few follow-up questions for you. Shall we come in, or would you prefer to answer questions down at the Bobtail PD? I'm sure they'll accommodate us."

"Um, I guess you can come inside."

Pete's place is neater than I thought it would be. It's cheaply furnished but looks like a grown-up lives there and not somebody wishing he was still in high school. Pete walks into the room and looks startled.

"Nice place," I say. "I hope you don't mind if we talk to your friend Cal."

"I guess that's okay."

"We need some privacy."

He shrugs and leaves the room.

Cal plops down on the couch, and Maria and I sit in opposing chairs so that Cal can't see both of us at once.

"Let me ask you something," I say. "Do you ever lend your truck to anybody?"

He frowns. "I helped somebody move last summer, and he borrowed the truck for a while. Why?"

"Anybody recently? Like right before Thanksgiving?"

"No."

"Here's my problem," I say. "It appears to me that you didn't tell me the truth when I talked to you at the jail."

"I told you everything I know."

"I asked you if you transported those dogs, and you said you didn't. You were lying. Where did you take them?"

"What dogs?"

"You know what dogs," Maria says. "Don't act like you're stupid."

He glares at her. "Don't call me stupid."

"I didn't say you were stupid," she says with exaggerated patience, "I said you were trying to act like you were. We know you transported those two guard dogs. Where did you take them?"

He seethes silently and then comes out with the only smart thing he's uttered since I first laid eyes on him. "I need to call Jerry."

"You could call him," I say. "But I think you'd be better off just answering the question. Where did you take those dogs?"

He swallows. "If I can't call my stepdaddy, I'm not going to tell you anything."

"Right. Let's give him a call, then."

Cal takes out his cell phone and punches in some numbers, but then he stops. "I need to talk to him privately."

"Tell you what. Why don't I call him?" I ask.

Cal sighs and punches the call button on his phone. We hear only Cal's side of the conversation, but it doesn't take a genius to figure out that Jerry Bodine is not happy. When Cal hangs up, he says, "Jerry's coming, but it could take a few minutes."

"That's all right. We have plenty of time." I wait a minute or two, while Cal fidgets, and then I say, "Let me tell you what I think happened. I think Jerry Bodine told you to get those dogs and meet him somewhere."

"Wrong."

"Where did he say to meet him? Was it out in that area where we found Wilkins's body?"

"I don't know anything about where his body was found."

"Was it at night?" Maria says. "Had to be. You couldn't risk somebody seeing you."

"I told you, that didn't happen."

I lean back and lace my hands behind my head. "When you got there with the dogs, Jerry had Lewis Wilkins tied up, and he turned those dogs on Wilkins; and then they killed him."

He's breathing heavily, and sweat has formed on his brow.

"You know that bringing the dogs there makes you guilty of second-degree murder, right?" I say.

"Oh, no, no, no. I took the dogs there. That's all I did. Then I left. I don't know what happened after that."

Bingo. We've got him. And he knows it. His face loses color.

"Where did he tell you to take them?"

"I . . . I don't remember the exact place. And I'm not saying anything else until Jerry gets here."

"How can you not remember? It wasn't that long ago," Maria says.

"Well, I just . . ."

"Well, if you can't remember where it was," I say, "you can at least remember if you turned the dogs loose, or did you put them in a pen or in a shed?"

He stares at me, face getting paler by the second.

"Did you handle the dogs by yourself, or did you have your buddy with you? I can call him in here to ask him."

The apartment door swings open, and Jerry Bodine strides into the room like he owns it. "What the hell is going on here?"

"Just a friendly talk," I say.

Cal says, "He's asking me about . . ."

"Don't say another word," Bodine says. "I've called a lawyer for you."

"A lawyer?" I say. I smile at Cal. "Why would your stepdaddy think you need a lawyer?"

Cal's eyes widen. "Jerry, what the hell?"

"I told you, don't say a word."

"He's already said a good bit," I say. "He tells me he transported those two guard dogs of yours and met you with them."

"I did not!" Cal yells.

"Him and his friend Pete."

Cal's eyes light up. "That's right, it was Pete. Jerry was paying him, not me . . ."

"You goddam liar!" Pete bursts into the room. "You aren't going to pin this on me. I only went along to help you. Those dogs scared the crap out of me."

Cal leaps up. "You better keep your mouth shut. You were in it as much as I was."

"That's not true. It was Jerry who . . ."

"Shut up!" Cal yells. He lunges for Pete.

I jump up, but Maria is faster. Maria unsnaps her weapon and yanks it out of the holster. She's not big, but she has the ability to make herself look commanding.

"Now hold on," Bodine snarls.

Cal holds his arm out as if to ward off Maria. "You can't . . ."

"I can!" She takes one hand off the weapon and points to Cal and then to a chair across the room, "Over there!" I'm by his side now, and I grab his arm, steer him away, and shove him down into the chair.

Bodine steps toward Pete, his fists clenched. "Both of you shut up. Can you manage that for ten minutes?"

"I want him out of my place," Pete says, glaring at Cal. "He showed up here and said he needed to hang out for a while. I should have told him no."

Cal snorts and looks daggers at his friend.

I look down at him. "So you came here to hide out?"

"He's lying."

Bodine's phone pings, and he looks at it. "Lawyer's on his way."

At that we all settle in to wait. Ten minutes later, there's a knock on the door. Bodine yanks it open, and who walks in but Bodine's poker buddy, Lonnie Casper.

"Hello, Lonnie," I say.

Maria darts a glance at me.

"Let me introduce you to Lonnie Casper, Maria. Mr. Casper, this is my deputy, Maria Trevino."

Casper smirks. "I'm afraid this little chat is over. Mr. Bodine has hired me to represent his stepson, and you no longer have the right to question him."

"Shame about that," I say. "Cal, stand up."

He gets to his feet, looking confused.

I pull out my handcuffs. "Hold out your hands, please."

He throws a desperate look at Bodine. "Jerry."

"Now wait just a minute," Bodine says. "What are you doing?"

"I'm arresting Cal for the murder of Lewis Wilkins." I spiel out the *Miranda* warning. All of this drama is having its effect. Cal looks terrified.

"Casper, can he do that?" Bodine asks.

"I'm afraid so. Not that he has any grounds to, but he can arrest anybody he wants to. Don't worry, we'll . . ."

"I didn't kill anybody," Cal says, his voice shaking. "It was those dogs that did it. At least I heard that's what happened."

"But you transported the dogs, which is all the evidence I need. Sorry, Pete, but you're in this, too. Both of you are going to jail."

"No way," Pete says. "Not me."

"I'm going to make the case that the two of you kidnapped Lewis Wilkins out of his SUV, took him back to where you had the dogs tied up, and set the dogs on him."

"This is ridiculous," Bodine says. "A wild accusation."

Casper clears his throat. "We'll get this sorted out. But for right now, you boys need to go with Chief Craddock."

"Hell no!" Pete says. "I'm not taking the blame for this. We took the dogs where Bodine told us to. That's all."

"Shut up!" Cal screams.

Pete says, "You and Jerry can rot in jail. It had nothing to do with me."

"No such thing happened," Bodine says. "I don't know what you were up to, Pete, but it had nothing to do with *me*."

Maria says to Pete, "Were you there when the dogs went after Wilkins?"

"No. He told us to leave. We didn't know what he was going to do."

"The kid's lying," Bodine says.

I tune Bodine out. "And later Jerry told you to go back and get rid of the dogs' bodies, is that right?" I ask.

Maria chimes in. "Except instead of taking them off somewhere, you hauled them farther back into the thicket. You found a shed there and left them."

"That's right," Pete says. "We just thought Jerry had shot the dogs. We didn't know the dogs killed somebody. Not until we heard later."

"Oh, for heaven's sake," Bodine says to Casper. "Can't you stop this?"

"Jerry, I'm not representing Cal's friend."

"What does it take? A deposit?"

"Just your request that I represent him."

"Done. Now you boys are both under Mr. Casper's care."

"I don't want it," Pete says. "I didn't do anything."

"Well, until we can clear up exactly what happened, you two are going back to jail," I say. "Maria, how about if you call the Bobtail PD and ask them to come get these boys?"

Maria reads Pete his rights. "Do I need to handcuff you?"

He shakes his head, and she makes the call to the Bobtail PD. It's no time before a squad car arrives.

"I guess that's that," Bodine says. He gives me a hard look and turns to Casper. "You're on this, right?"

He shrugs.

"We've got a lot of evidence to connect your stepson with the murder," I say. "But I would like to ask you a few questions to clear up what Pete was talking about. Why don't we sit and discuss it?"

"Hold on a minute." He looks around Pete's apartment as if getting his bearings. "This whole thing has taken me completely by surprise."

"I understand. I'm giving you a chance to set me straight."

"I don't think I have to answer any questions. Isn't that right, Casper?"

"What makes you think that?" I ask.

"I've retained Mr. Casper to represent those boys, and since I'm paying the bill, I'm his client."

I catch Maria's eye. A smile is playing on her lips. She knows the law on this matter as well as I do. It's important that officers understand the laws on interrogation so that they don't slip up and ruin their case. "I wish that was true," I say, shaking my head as if I truly regret it. "But I believe Lonnie can set you straight."

"Lonnie?" Bodine says. His eyes have the look of a rabbit searching for a place to run.

"Uh, I believe what Craddock is referring to is a ruling that there is an exception to the attorney-client privilege. True?" He nods to me.

"That's the one. Bottom line," I say, turning to Jerry, "somebody paying another person's attorney fees can't hide behind privilege."

"That's not exactly the way I would put it," Casper says, pursing his lips. "But close enough."

"So let's get to it," I say.

"I don't have anything to hide," Bodine blusters. "Ask away." He eases onto the sofa. Casper looks like he'd rather be anywhere else.

"Mr. Casper, you don't have to stay here if you don't want to," I say.

He shoots a calculating look at Bodine. He knows that Bodine doesn't have the money to pay him. This is all on a buddy basis, and that's wearing thin. He glances down at his watch. "I'm sorry, Bodine. I'm supposed to be in court. Remember, you don't have to answer questions if you don't want to. And you can call another lawyer."

"That's probably not necessary," I say. "We're just going to get a timeline straight."

Casper meets my eyes. He knows that's not true. But he also heard Pete's claim, and he knows that his pal Bodine might very well have murdered Lewis Wilkins. If he was Bodine's lawyer, he might dig in his heels. But that opportunity doesn't exist anymore now that the attorney-client exception has been called up.

Casper scoots out the door, and I turn a friendly smile in Bodine's direction.

"Can I get you a glass of water?" Maria asks.

"I'd appreciate that," Bodine says. He turns to me, "I told you Cal had some tall tales to tell."

"It isn't just Cal, it's also his friend Pete. You heard him tell me they delivered those two guard dogs to you, and that they don't know what happened after that. But they also said they followed Wilkins. I'm betting they delivered Wilkins to you, too. So how about if you tell me exactly what happened."

"Pete can't be trusted. His hide is on the line. Of course he's going to lie."

Maria comes back with the water, and he gulps down half a glass.

"The problem is," I say, "I believe him."

Bodine leans forward, forearms on his legs, and speaks as if in confidence. "You know he and Cal get up to a lot of mischief. There's no telling what they did with those dogs."

"I think what happened is that you lost a lot of money to Wilkins in those high-stakes poker games. He demanded the money, and you paid him off. But it was money you didn't have, so you decided you had to get it back."

"I don't know where you got that idea." He sits back, watching me like I'm a rattlesnake.

"Here's what I think you did. You told your high-stakes buddies, including Lewis Wilkins, that there was going to be a poker game on Sunday night. But then you called the other men and told them the game had been changed to Monday night." I continue spelling out the way I think it happened.

"That's ridiculous! That is the craziest story I ever heard."

"Well, the problem is, one of the guys you play cards with told me you had switched the game from Sunday to Monday." I don't mention that the guy who told me was Lonnie Casper.

"That doesn't mean a thing." His reply is fast, and he's breathing in gasps.

"I suppose there's another possibility. It's possible you were too much of a coward to take care of Wilkins yourself, so you sent your stepson and his friend to do it."

"No." He gets up and takes a few steps toward the door before he turns back to us. "Casper said I don't have to answer questions, and I don't have to listen to idle speculation."

I stand up, too. "You heard it for yourself. The boys admitted that they transported the dogs, but they said they delivered them to you. Are you saying that's not true?"

"You can't prove a thing," he says, marching for the door.

"We can prove one thing. We have solid evidence connecting your stepson and his friend Pete to the dogs. And we have their word about what they did."

He has his hand on the doorknob and stands frozen.

"Do I need to remind you? Pete also said you wanted them to haul the dead dogs away. But all they did was take them to a shed farther into the back country. That's where we found them."

He's shaking his head.

"And one more thing. When I talked to you earlier and mentioned that the dogs had been killed, you slipped up."

"Slipped up how?" His voice is a croak.

"I didn't say how they had been killed, but you said they had been shot."

"It—it's the only thing th-that made sense." He's stuttering.

"So somewhere between the boys bringing the dogs to you and the dogs being shot, Wilkins was killed. You going to let them take the blame for that? I imagine your wife wouldn't be thrilled to find out you were pointing the finger at her son."

He lowers his head. I see all the fire go out of him. "No, I don't suppose she would be." He turns back around to face me.

"We didn't find the gun used to kill those dogs, and I suspect you still have it in your possession. You never thought it would come back to you, right? If you have it, a ballistics test will point right to you. I'll have a team out there with a search warrant within the hour. And if we don't find it, I'll be charging your stepson with the murder."

He staggers over to a chair and sinks into it, putting his head in his hands. "Wilkins was a cheat. He cheated me out of everything. He deserved what he got."

Once he says that, there's no turning back. He comes clean and admits that he owed Wilkins the two hundred thousand, and after he paid off the debt, he decided to steal it back.

"I'm still curious how those boys came into the equation. You knew on Sunday Wilkins was going to be carrying that two hundred thousand you paid him. You had your stepson follow him to the canceled poker game. The boys admitted that. Did you have them bring him to you, or did they meet you somewhere?"

"This has nothing to do with them."

"At Bobtail PD, Cal told me they followed Wilkins and then called you to tell you where he was—but that didn't make sense. It would have taken you a while to get there, and by then Wilkins would have been in the house where the game was usually held. So I expect they delivered him to you."

He looks up. His face has aged ten years in ten minutes. "Listen, Craddock, this is all on me. Let's make a deal to leave those boys out of it."

"I think we can make a deal in exchange for your confession."

I see that Maria is ready to protest. I give her my "don't touch this" stare, and she stays quiet.

I give him his *Miranda* warning and then he lays it out.

"I didn't like making the deal any more than you did," I say to Maria when we're at the jail in Bobtail, waiting for Bodine to be processed. "But you know as well as I do that there were too many holes in the case. We needed that confession."

"I just hated to see that kid weasel out of his part in it."

"He isn't weaseling out of anything. He and Pete attacked Margaret. And even if we can't pin that on them, he'll trip up before long. That's the kind of kid he is. Bottom line, we needed to nail Bodine for murder; that was the important part."

It's dark when Maria and I arrive at the Wilkins lake house to tell Margaret we made an arrest.

When she opens the door, Margaret looks diminished, as if the death of her husband has shrunk her mentally and physically.

"I have some good news for you," I say.

She invites us into the living room, which smells stale, the way it would if a house had not been occupied for a long time.

I tell her about finding out that the dogs that killed her husband were guard dogs leased by Jerry Bodine's father-in-law, and that following that led to Bodine's arrest. I explain his motivation for the murder.

"That poor man," she says.

Maria and I exchange looks. "You mean your husband?"

She looks at me, and rage animates her face. "Him? No. I'm sorry for Bodine—the man who got suckered into Lewis's nasty little world."

"What do you mean?" Maria says.

"Haven't you figured it out by now?" She sighs. "Of course not, why would you?" Her expression changes, the flare of rage dying out. "Lewis was a liar and a cheat."

She gets up and paces to the fireplace, where cold, dead ashes add to the bleak atmosphere in the room. "When I married Lewis, things seemed great. He made good money and we enjoyed our lives. There was just one thing." She shakes her finger in the air. "We couldn't keep friends. After they got to know Lewis, people weren't so keen on him. I found out that medical staff he worked with said Lewis cut corners in the operating room, and they had to clean up the messes he left. Doctors protect each other, you know. But they don't have to like it."

Maria and I shoot uneasy glances at each other. Margaret has been sitting on this, and she's finally letting it out. She stalks over to the window, rubbing her arms as if they're itchy.

"He liked to play poker with the guys. First it was doctors, and then when they wouldn't play with him anymore, he'd find games somehow. Surprise, surprise, he won a lot more than he lost. He probably lost just enough to keep people happy so they'd continue to play. But eventually he couldn't keep himself from cheating, and no one would play with him. And then he had that lawsuit, and it gave him permission to become his true self. He cheated every chance he got."

"Did your kids know this? Did you tell them?"

She shakes her head. She has stopped moving and is standing over us. "I didn't have to tell them. It's funny how kids seem to sense when somebody is not trustworthy. When they were children, they adored him. But as teenagers, they got his number. You know what really twists me? My daughter blames me. She never said anything, but I know she does. God knows why."

She runs out of steam and lowers herself into a chair.

"Why didn't you leave him?" I ask.

She chuckles. "Right. It would have made sense, wouldn't it? But I didn't know what to do. I had never held a job, had no skills. When things went to pieces, I thought about moving here and telling him he couldn't come to this house. But I hate this place." She bites her lip. "Wait. That's not fair. Everyone is nice, and if I moved here I'd probably learn to like it. . . . I think I hated it because I was trapped here with Lewis."

"You'll figure out something," Maria says. Ever the practical one. "There's the money he left, and the boat."

"All of it gotten by cheating." She moans. "God, I'd give anything if I could give it back. But that would be stupid, wouldn't it? It would leave me destitute. I feel as if I'm caught in a web of fishhooks. They hurt going in, and they tear flesh when they're pulled out."

I get up, and Maria follows my lead. "Tell your kids," I say. "Tell them everything. Ask their advice. You'll work it out."

She shrugs. "Maybe."

CHAPTER 32

I'm writing out the full report on the resolution of the murder of Lewis Wilkins the next morning, when the phone rings.

"Is this Chief Craddock?" A cautious female voice.

"It is. Who am I speaking with?"

"I'm Vera Macom, out in Cotton Hill."

"What can I do for you, Vera?"

"Well, sir, I heard you was asking around about some pups."

I sit up, alert. "Yes, ma'am, you know something about that?"

"My husband was out hunting squirrel right before Thanksgiving, and he come upon this dead bitch and she had some puppies with her, so he brought them home for me to take care of. We didn't steal them or nothing."

"I know you didn't, and I appreciate the call." I tell her about finding Dusty.

"Oh my, he missed one. I'm glad you found him. We have four of them and I guess if you want them back, we'll have to give them up. I was thinking I'd give one to my son, and the fellow on the next farm over said he wouldn't mind having one."

"Oh, no," I say firmly. "I'm just glad they're all right. And I thank you for letting me know. I wondered."

I hang up and call Doc England and Hershel, out at the lake, to let them know the resolution. I know Maria will be happy when she comes in.

I had hoped that a few days away from Wendy would give me perspective, but when she called last night, I knew that was a joke. I told her that I had made an arrest in the case.

"Should I come home early so you can tell me all about it?"

I said I'd like that. She was quiet for a second. "But you need to tell me if you've settled things with Ellen."

"No, not yet. By the time you get back I will."

"Two more days. That's all the time I've giving you." Her voice was mock severe.

For whatever reason, Ellen and I have never talked a lot about our relationship. When I first met her, she was skittish because she had just left her brute of a husband. Also, it'd not been that long since my wife died. We drifted into an easy companionship. I have enjoyed her company, and we have had some laughs. But I've had a taste of something more. I have no idea where things will go with Wendy. Maybe I'm burning my bridges, but I've made my decision.

My first impulse was to take Ellen out to dinner so I could tell her what was on my mind. But she said she wanted to cook tonight, so I agreed to come over.

From the minute she greets me at the door, I'm tense, and she seems to catch the mood from me. Thank goodness I've brought Dusty, and that gives us something to focus on. I give Frazier a lot of attention. He's a good dog, and I don't want him to feel left out because of the puppy. Or abandoned when I don't come around as much.

Ellen and I grab for glasses of wine and smile at each other. Is it my imagination that her smile is as strained as mine feels? Has someone told her I'm seeing Wendy? "Let's sit in the living room," she says. "Dinner is ready, but let's have a glass of wine first."

"That sounds good."

"I'll bet you're glad that case is over," she says, when we're settled, sitting so we face each other.

"I am, but I wish I had never gotten involved. I should have left it to the highway patrol."

"Why do you say that? You did a good job. You're just tired."

"I am tired, but a case like this leaves me with a bad feeling. Grubby. Honestly, no one connected with this case comes out looking innocent. Everybody had something to hide or an ax to grind."

She stares at me. I've never talked to her much about the bad part of my job.

"I apologize. I'm letting off steam. I shouldn't burden you with this."

"I'm surprised, that's all. What do you mean no one looks innocent?"

I consider. "Jerry Bodine is obviously guilty. But even though Lewis Wilkins may not have deserved the death he got, he did deserve some kind of comeuppance. Wilkins disappointed everyone who knew him. He was a coward and a cheat. But his family and friends also aren't innocent. They let him get away with it." I go get Dusty and sit down with him.

Ellen seems stunned.

Dusty has flipped over on his back so I can stroke his stomach. "I'll be glad for things to get back to normal, that's all."

"What about the widow, Margaret? What's she going to do?"

"She's got some decisions to make." She has no good choice. But I don't admire her. She has kept herself dependent. I'm sitting here in a room with a woman who took her own future in her hands. That, I admire.

Ellen is watching me, her head cocked. "You don't seem satisfied."

I sigh. "The bad guy is in jail. What more should I want?"

She stands up. "I need to stir something on the stove." I follow her into the kitchen, bringing our wine glasses, and watch her stir a pot. "I'm glad your case is over, for more than one reason," she says, her back to me.

"Oh?"

She turns around to face me, chin raised as if she's defiant. "I've been wanting to talk to you about something."

Uh-oh, am I too late? It sounds like she did hear about Wendy from someone, probably Jenny. Should I jump in now and explain?

"Okay, I'm ready to talk," I say.

I realize she's blinking back tears, and I feel awful. She didn't deserve this. "Listen," I say, "I . . ."

"No, wait. Hear me out. This has been on my mind. I should have told you a long time ago. I think it's why we're stuck in our relationship. Let's sit down." We take a seat at the little kitchen table that's barely big enough for the two of us. She takes a sip of wine. I can tell she's stalling. I want to say something, but I'm curious about what she has been holding back. Finally she gives a tremulous smile. "You're such a good guy. I didn't want to tell you. I didn't want to be judged badly."

This isn't going the way I thought it would. I have no idea what she's talking about. "Why would I judge you?"

She takes a deep breath and a tear slips down her cheek. "I let you think that Seth and I split up because I left him for being cruel to me. That was a lie."

"Ellen, you don't have to . . ."

"Yes, I do have to. It's about Seth."

Is she going back to him, as I suspected?

"I let you think that Seth was violent with me because he was a little bit crazy. But that wasn't true. The reason Seth was so furious was that he found out I had been having an affair. For a long time."

To hide my utter amazement, I take a sip of wine. I should say something, but what? Do I tell her it's okay? Do I confess that I'm having my own fling? Do I ask who she had an affair with and what happened? "Well."

"You have every right to be angry. I lied to you. I let you think I was the wronged party." She swallows. "You probably have a lot of questions, and I'm ready to answer them."

"I, uh, I need to think about it. How did Seth find out?" I'm feeling trapped, squeezed in at her small table.

"He suspected something was going on, and he hired a detective. When he confronted me, he was so hurt and angry I actually thought he might kill me."

I remember going to see Seth early on, after Ellen came to town, to warn him not to bring his violence here to Jarrett Creek. When I confronted him, he said disparaging things about Ellen's reputation. At the time I thought it was sour grapes. "Do you still see the man you had an affair with?"

"I saw him last weekend." She holds her hand up. "Not to renew our relationship. We just wanted to talk. He's gone back to his wife, and he said he felt bad because I got divorced. I told him that it wasn't his fault."

I nod but don't say anything, because I find that I'm put out. All this time, I thought I was protecting Ellen from an irrationally angry ex-husband. He went overboard with his anger, sure, but he wasn't irrational.

"I understand if you don't want to see me anymore," she says. "It was unfair."

I stand up, relieved to have some room. "I need some time to digest it," I say. "It's something I never expected. Do you wish you were still with this guy?"

She looks up at me, hesitating. "I want to be completely honest with you now. Sometimes I think about him."

It washes over me that what I want right now is to leave. I want to go somewhere and have a steak by myself and think about nothing. I'll have to tell Ellen about Wendy in the next day or so, but not tonight. I'll tell her she has nothing to apologize for and that I value her friendship and that I didn't mean to make her feel wrong. But not tonight.

"You know, it's been a hard week," I say. "I think I'd like to be alone this evening. It's not just what you told me, but the mood I'm in." I go into the living room, pick up Dusty and give Frazier a pat, and then go back to the kitchen. Ellen is still sitting in the same place.

"I'm glad you told me, but for tonight, I'm going to bow out."

She gets up and sees me to the door, and I lean down and give her a peck on the cheek.

The weather has cleared, and it's warmed up to a fine, crisp evening. I stand next to my truck and look at the stars, thinking that nothing has quite gone like I thought it would these past couple of weeks. Instead of closure, Margaret Wilkins seemed to see bitter recrimination ahead. And my intention to tell Ellen that our situation has changed got short-circuited in the oddest possible way.

Dusty yips and I ruffle his ears. I did get one good thing out of the Wilkins case. I got a nice little dog. We get in the cab and he sits on the seat, looking expectant. I see the fine dog he'll become, alert and ready for action.

I say, "Dusty, what do you say we go to dinner? We'll go over to Bobtail and get a steak, and then we'll come on back home."

He doesn't say anything, which I take as a yes.

ACKNOWLEDGMENTS

During the course of a writer's career, there are many unsung heroes who help in the learning process. I've been in writers' groups, attended writing courses and conferences, and had beta readers, and they helped me become a better writer. My current writers' group— Staci, Laird, Robert, and Brad (newbie!)—read diligently and seriously. Their comments and suggestions make my work stronger. I depend on them, and I am grateful to them for their help.

I also want to thank the members of writers' groups; the teachers; the readers; and my fellow writers whose comments and suggestions might have been incomprehensible to me at the time, but which later came back to speak to me. I recall a beta reader who asked about a motivation I had thought was clear, and by questioning she taught me about deep motives. Another pointed out that descriptions come alive when you choose the right things to highlight rather than trying to describe everything in a scene. Examples are myriad.

Thanks to all of you who took me more seriously than I took myself, gently pushing me to embrace the positive act of writing rather than just putting words on paper.

ABOUT THE AUTHOR

Terry Shames is the author of *A Killing at Cotton Hill*, *The Last Death of Jack Harbin*, *Dead Broke in Jarrett Creek*, *A Deadly Affair at Bobtail Ridge*, *The Necessary Murder of Nonie Blake*, and *An Unsettling Crime for Samuel Craddock*, the first six Samuel Craddock mysteries. She is the coeditor of *Fire in the Hills*, a book of stories, poems, and photographs about the 1991 Oakland Hills Fire. She grew up in Texas and continues to be fascinated by the convoluted loyalties and betrayals of the small town where her grandfather was the mayor. Terry is a member of the Mystery Writers of America and Sisters in Crime.